Doggie Day Care Murder

Center Point
Large Print

**This Large Print Book carries the
Seal of Approval of N.A.V.H.**

A Melanie Travis Mystery

Doggie Day Care Murder

Laurien Berenson

CENTER POINT PUBLISHING
THORNDIKE, MAINE

This Center Point Large Print edition
is published in the year 2008 by
arrangement with Kensington Publishing Corp.

The text of this Large Print edition is unabridged. In other
aspects, this book may vary from the original edition.
Printed in the United States of America.
Set in 16-point Times New Roman type.

ISBN: 978-1-60285-280-8

Library of Congress Cataloging-in-Publication Data

Berenson, Laurien.
  Doggie day care murder / Laurien Berenson.
     p. cm.
  ISBN 978-1-60285-280-8 (library binding : alk. paper)
  1. Travis, Melanie (Fictitious character)—Fiction. 2. Women private investigators—Fiction.
3. Dogs—Fiction. 4. Large type books. I. Title.

  PS3552.E6963D65 2008
  813'.54—dc22

2008017473

Heartfelt thanks are due to two people without whom these books would never have existed: my wonderful agent, Meg Ruley, whose support and enthusiasm is always an inspiration; and my editor, John Scognamiglio, whose expertise and guidance are invaluable and make my job easier in so many ways.

1

A baby changes everything. Don't ever let anyone tell you that it doesn't.

Once upon a time when I was younger and more foolish, I thought that new puppies and new babies had a lot in common. I must have been deluded, or maybe just oversimplifying. Because now it's clear to me that I was insanely wrong.

For one thing, when a puppy doesn't sleep through the night, nobody has to get up and feed him and rock him back to sleep. For another, puppies are happy to entertain themselves for a while if you need your hands free to do something else. But perhaps the biggest difference is that new puppies, wonderful as they are, don't turn your whole world upside down in that mystical, magical way that somehow simultaneously reconnects you to the cosmos and to that vast well of human experience, while at the same time making you feel that if your heart expands any more it might possibly explode.

Trust me, it takes a baby to wreak that kind of havoc.

Having been through this once before, you'd think I might have remembered how it went. But that was nine years ago when I was in my early twenties. I was young enough then to bounce back from almost anything—stretch marks, ten hours of labor, or the aggravation of a mostly absent husband.

In the intervening years, my life had changed dramatically. Now I had friends and relatives I could depend on, a terrific son in fourth grade, and a second marriage that was eons better than my first. In short, when my second son was born on a wintry March night, my world was complete.

The doctor placed him in my arms while my husband, Sam, dashed out of the delivery room. He returned moments later with my son, Davey. The two of them stood on either side of the bed, and Davey stared at the new arrival in awe. Or maybe consternation.

"I didn't think he'd be so red," he said.

"Don't worry," said a nurse, passing by, "that goes away."

Busy cleaning up, she took time to lean in for a closer look. Snuggled tight in his receiving blanket, the infant's face was the only part of him that was visible. His eyes were closed, his expres-sion peaceful. Oblivious to all the activity around him, he was enjoying a brief post-delivery nap.

"He's a cute one," she said. "What's his name?"

Davey, Sam, and I looked at each other. We'd been working on this for months. Boys' names, girls' names, unisex names, we'd had them all. But right at that moment, in the magnitude of him actually *being* there, my mind was utterly blank.

"Kevin," said Sam.

"Kevin," Davey echoed. "He's my little brother."

"And aren't you the lucky one?" asked the nurse. "You be sure to take good care of him now."

Davey reached up and placed his hand on the tiny sleeping form. He looked like he was taking a vow. "I will," he said firmly.

Now, three months later, Kevin was no longer a newborn. He was a member of the family, his presence so entrenched in our lives and our hearts that it was hard to remember what life had been like without him.

With everything going so well, I knew I shouldn't complain. But there was just one thing I desperately needed. Six hours of blissful, uninterrupted sleep. Did that seem like too much to ask?

"I have a problem," said Alice Brickman. She was standing in my kitchen doorway and looked like a woman with a lot on her mind.

"Welcome to the club," I replied. "My hormones are bouncing around like a Ping-Pong ball, Kevin's decided he prefers bottles to breast-feeding, and just about every piece of clothing I own has spit-up on it. Have a seat and let's compare notes."

Sam and Davey were off running errands. Kevin had just been fed. A couple of our Standard Poodles had gone along on the car ride; the other three were snoozing contentedly at my feet. Alice's timing was perfect, which is no small feat in a home that has a new baby.

But then, right from the start Alice and I had been

on the same wavelength. We'd met at a play group right after the birth of our first children and been best friends for nearly a decade. I'd married Sam the previous year and moved to a different Stamford, Connecticut, neighborhood. Before that, Alice and I had lived right down the road from one another.

The shared experience of motherhood is a powerful bonding tool. Through car pools, PTA meetings, and soccer games, we'd compared notes, juggled juice boxes, and covered one another's backs.

Davey and Alice's son, Joey, had finished fourth grade together the previous week. Alice also had a seven-year-old daughter named Carly, who was a budding ballerina. Her husband, Joe, was a partner in a prestigious law firm in Greenwich.

Alice was every bit as comfortable in my house as she would have been in her own. And since my dogs were equally comfortable with her, none of them had bothered to get up for her arrival. Three big, black Standard Poodles were asleep on the kitchen floor. Alice navigated her way through the recumbent canine bodies and headed directly for the playpen in the corner.

Kevin was lying on his back, kicking his feet in the air and eying a spinning, pinwheel-colored mobile I'd just fastened above him. Alice leaned down over the side bar, inhaled his baby smell, and sighed deeply.

"Aren't babies the best?" she said.

I'd been on my way to the refrigerator. Alice and I always seem to talk better when our mouths are full. Now I stopped and turned.

"You're not," I said.

"Not what?"

"Pregnant."

"Oh that." She laughed. "No way. I'll amend my earlier statement. *Other* people's babies are the best."

I opened the fridge and pulled out a couple of diet sodas.

"Believe me," I grumbled, "there are times when I feel the same way."

"And then you get over it," Alice said practically.

No whining allowed around here.

I nodded in agreement and handed her a drink. We both found seats at the kitchen table. Kevin gurgled, and cooed, and looked cuter than anybody had a right to as he tried valiantly to insert his toes into his mouth. At moments like that, it was hard to remember why I was feeling grumpy.

Alice popped the top on the soda can, tipped back her head, and took a long swallow. "When did you start drinking diet?"

"Guess."

"How much baby weight do you have left?"

After Carly was born, Alice had struggled with the last ten pounds for years. Finally, she'd given up the struggle and simply resigned herself to buying clothes in a larger size. By any standards, except those promoted by celebrities and fashion magazines, she wasn't plump, just pleasantly rounded.

But still, I noticed, she hadn't given up drinking diet soda. For every woman who accepts herself as she is, there's another who's angling to raise the bar ever higher. Sisterhood, indeed.

"Five pounds," I said. "But it's not the weight, it's the shape. None of my clothes fit the way they used to."

Alice stared at me over the top of her soda can and lifted a brow, a small gesture every bit as telling as the words it replaced.

"I know, but this didn't happen last time."

"Right. And how old were you when you had Davey, seventeen?"

"Twenty-five," I corrected primly.

"Same thing," Alice sniffed.

She was five years older than me. As if *that* made a huge difference.

"And now you're thirty-five," she said. "Things change."

"So I've noticed. I thought gravity wasn't supposed to start having its way with me until I turned forty."

"Good luck with that."

Alice got up, walked over to the pantry, and had a look around.

"Oreos on the left," I said.

She grabbed the bag and brought them back to the table. This wasn't going to help anyone's diet.

We each fished one out, twisted them open, and ate the cream filling first.

"Have we talked about your problems long enough?" she asked. "I don't want to seem insensitive here, but I haven't got all day."

Newly fortified by sugar, I was good to go.

"Your turn," I said. "Have at it."

"This part isn't a problem, exactly, it's an announcement."

I sat up straight and paid attention. In my experience, announcements don't always augur well.

"I'm done with being a stay-at-home mom," said Alice. "I'm going back to work."

This was momentous. And very exciting, as news went. In this one particular aspect of our lives, Alice and I had always been opposites.

I'd been a working mother, and a single mother, for most of Davey's life. Alice, meanwhile, had a husband who went to work and supported the family, which gave her the luxury of staying home to take care of the kids.

Now it looked as though our roles were reversing. At the end of the previous semester, when my pregnancy had reached the six-month mark, I'd taken a leave of absence from my job at a private school in Greenwich. While I'd be staying home for the near future, Alice was gearing up to rejoin the workforce.

"Congratulations," I said, tipping my cookie in salute.

"Not so fast." Alice laughed. "It's been years since anyone offered to pay me for what I can do. Let's see if I can make this thing work first."

"What kind of job are you looking for?"

"That's the good part." Her laughter faded. "At least I hope it is. I already have a job."

"Wow, that was fast. Am I totally out of the loop or did that happen overnight?"

"Kind of the latter," Alice admitted. "I'm going to work for Joe's law firm."

"Plummer, Wilkes, and Hornby?" I said, even though we both knew the name. I was buying time and thinking fast, wondering what she'd be doing there. Finally, I gave up and just asked.

"You know, the usual paralegal stuff."

That brought me up short. I even put down my cookie.

"What usual paralegal stuff? When did you become a paralegal?"

"Right out of college. That's what I did before I met Joe."

Utterly amazing, I thought. "How can I have known you for ten years and not known that?"

Alice shrugged. "With the kids around all the time, I guess it never came up. But now Joey and Carly are both in school full time for most of the year. And even their summers are filled with activities. Joey will be at soccer camp for eight weeks."

I nodded. Davey was doing the same thing.

"And Carly's doing a ballet program over at the Silvermine Guild. So I've been thinking about this for a while. Neither one of them needs me to be home all the time anymore. Which makes me feel kind of superfluous—like all I do is sit at home and wait for the people who are out doing interesting things to come back. So enough of that. It's time for me to see what else I can be besides just a mother."

Just a mother. The phrase made us both wince, but neither of us bothered to comment on it. I knew what she meant.

"Congratulations," I said again, applauding the decision as much as its execution.

"Yeah, well, it'll be interesting to see how this all shakes out. The good thing was that I got a job without having to apply to a million places, go through some huge interview process, and then justify what I've been doing for the ten years that are missing on my résumé. The bad news is, I'll be working for Joe."

I liked Joe. He was a good father and a nice guy. But even so, I could see how all that togetherness might strain things around the house.

"What does Joe think of the idea?" I asked.

"He's the one who came up with it. At first he wasn't crazy about the notion of me going back to work, but eventually I managed to convince him that the kids wouldn't miss me when they weren't even around to know that I was gone. Oh yeah, and that I'd still make sure that the dry cleaner put the right amount of starch in his shirts."

She paused, rolled her eyes, and grabbed another Oreo. "Then he thought of this. I think somehow it made the whole thing seem more palatable to him, like maybe he thought he could keep an eye on me or something. Plus, as he said, think of all the gas money we'll save!"

Alice and I laughed together. I could just hear Joe saying that. He was the kind of guy who liked to keep his eye on the bottom line.

"So give it a try," I said. "If it works, great. If it doesn't, quit and go somewhere else."

"That's what I'm thinking," Alice agreed. "Flexibility's a good thing. There's just one problem with the plan. In fact, that's why I'm here."

Sad to say, that's the story of my life. People always seem to bring their problems to me.

"I need to find something to do with Berkley. If I'm going to be gone all day, I can't just leave him sitting home by himself."

Berkley was the Brickmans' eighteen-month-old Golden Retriever. Though he'd been purchased as a pet for Joey and Carly, predictably the bulk of his care had fallen to Alice. He was a beautiful, smart, rambunctious, teenage dog; and as long as he had company, he mostly managed to stay out of trouble. Bored and left to his own devices, however, I could see how he might be tempted to entertain himself by tearing the place apart.

"That's where you come in," said Alice.

I opened my mouth, but she hurried on before I could speak.

"Don't worry, with a new baby and all, I wouldn't dream of asking you to look after him. So I found a place in town that offers doggie day care."

Now, she paused. Like it was my turn to say something. For a moment, I couldn't think what that should be.

"*Doggie* day care?" I managed finally.

Despite the subject matter, none of my Poodles even looked up. Though they understand most things I say, the Poodles possessed far too much dignity to ever think of themselves as doggies.

"Don't make fun," said Alice. "Apparently it's a very successful facility. And hard to get into. There's a waiting list."

"A waiting list," I echoed faintly. It was all I could do to keep a straight face.

"The place is called Pine Ridge Canine Care Center. And you know I'm hopeless when it comes to things like this. I wouldn't have the slightest idea what to look for. But you know all that important dog-type stuff. So I was wondering if you could go and check it out for me. You know, see if it's the kind of place where Berkley would be happy."

She'd played the flattery card, and no surprise, it was working. Besides, while I was delighted that I have the chance to stay at home and take care of Kevin, Alice wasn't the only one who'd spent some time recently looking around the house and wondering what to do next. A job like this sounded like it would be right up my alley.

"Sure," I said. "I can do that. No problem."

You'd think I'd know better than to make predictions like that.

2

Sam and Davey arrived home right after Alice left. I walked out to the garage and helped them carry in several bags of groceries.

The five Poodles—reunited after a mere two-hour separation—behaved as though they were greeting long-lost relatives from the Old Country. They barked, and jumped, and chased each other around our legs.

For Sam and me, getting married had involved merging not only the human element of our lives, but also the canine. Davey and I had had two Standard Poodles: Faith and Eve, who were a mother and daughter pair. Sam had added three Standard Poodles of his own. His two bitches were named Raven and Casey. The third was a young dog named Tar.

In the beginning, the newly blended canine household had existed in a state of wary détente. Now however, more than a year later, the Poodles were all the best of friends. They played and functioned like a tight-knit team, and I imagine I wasn't the only one who realized that they outnumbered us.

"How's my boy doing?" asked Sam.

He juggled two bags of groceries to one side and swooped in to give me a quick kiss. If the honeymoon was over, neither one of us had noticed yet.

"Yeah," Davey echoed. "How's my boy?"

No longer the youngest member of the family, Davey was feeling very grown-up. His actions, however, were often at odds with his words. Now he came spilling out the side door of the SUV. Mid-descent, he tripped over a passing Poodle, dropped the half-eaten apple he was holding in his hand, yet still somehow managed to land on his feet.

"We were gone forever," he said, without missing a beat. "Did Kevin miss me?"

"Every minute," I replied. "He's awake in the kitchen and waiting for you to come and play with him."

Davey whooped with delight and raced into the house. Predictably, he didn't bother to take a bag of groceries with him.

"He really loves having a little brother," said Sam.

"I know," I agreed happily. "I'm only sorry he had to wait so long."

Sam cocked a brow. "And whose fault was that?"

We both knew the answer. I was the one who had

dragged my feet. My first marriage had ended in divorce, and the second time around I'd wanted everything to be perfect before I made another commitment that would dramatically change both Davey's and my lives.

So I'd waffled, and procrastinated, and made excuses. And along the way I'd learned that perfection was an unattainable goal in anybody's life. I'd also learned that Sam was right. Just like he'd been telling me all along, he and I were meant to be together for the long haul.

"Have you ever noticed?" I asked. "Mothers always get the blame."

"I can't imagine why," Sam said, deadpan.

I scooped up the last bag and we headed into the kitchen. Davey was leaning down over the side of the playpen, dangling his fingers just above Kevin's reach. The baby batted the air with his hands and laughed at the game.

Tar, who'd followed Davey inside, was sitting on the floor beside the enclosure. His nose was pressed up against the mesh, and he cocked his head to one side as he watched the two boys play together.

Most Poodles are smarter than the average second-grader. Unfortunately, Tar, beautiful and kindhearted as he was, was utterly lacking in that department. It was clear he'd been baffled by Kevin's sudden appearance in our lives, and nothing that had happened in the intervening months had made the situation any clearer to him.

While Eve had quickly appointed herself Kevin's canine guardian—coming to fetch me at the first sound of the baby's cries and picking up toys that had fallen beyond his reach—Tar was still somewhat wary of the tiny interloper. A small, chubby hand waved in his direction could send the big, black Poodle skidding back across the room in frantic retreat.

"He hasn't grown any," said Davey.

"You were only gone a couple of hours."

"No, I meant since yesterday. I heard you tell Bertie on the phone that he looks bigger every day."

Bertie was my sister-in-law, married to my brother, Frank. She was also a new mother herself. Her daughter, Maggie, had turned a year old right before Christmas.

"That's a figure of speech," said Sam. "It only seems like he's growing that fast because none of his clothes fit for more than a week."

"The same used to be true of you," I told Davey. "It seemed like I was always buying new sneakers."

"Speaking of which, we stopped at the sporting goods store and Sam-Dad got me new cleats and shin guards for soccer camp."

"Great." Cross one more item off the to-do list.

Idly I wondered if anyone actually ever got to the end of their lists. If they did, they probably weren't mothers.

"Anything interesting happen while we were gone?" asked Sam.

I paused from unpacking the groceries. "Actually, yes. Alice stopped by."

Davey looked up. "Did she bring Joey?"

"No, she came by herself."

"Everything all right?" asked Sam.

"I think so. She's getting a job."

"Hard thing to do after so much time off."

"Yes, although that part is already accomplished. She's going to be working at Joe's law firm."

"Paralegal work?" asked Sam.

I stopped and stared. "Am I the only one who didn't know about that?"

"Apparently so," he said with a wink. "Maybe you don't ask the right questions."

It looked that way.

"Anyway, she's thinking about putting Berkley in doggie day care."

"You're kidding."

"Would I joke about something like that?"

"Doggie day care? Like in that song, *git along little doggie?*"

"I think those doggies were cows," I pointed out.

"That's stupid," Davey said from his spot on the floor. "Nobody would put a cow in day care."

Sam was chuckling as I went on to explain. "The place is called Pine Ridge, and it's right here in Stamford. Have you ever heard of it?"

"No, but that doesn't mean anything. Day care for dogs isn't something I've given much thought to. In fact, none is probably closer to the mark."

"Me too," I agreed. "But after lunch, I'm going to go have a look. Alice asked me to check the place out. She wants to know if Berkley would be happy there."

"Give Berkley a soft bed and a rawhide bone, and he'd be happy anywhere," said Davey.

Wisdom from the mouths of babes.

"Good," I said. "Then that should make my job easy."

Pine Ridge Canine Care Center was located just off of Long Ridge Road. The area had once been entirely residential, but the northward expansion of Stamford's business district, combined with a change in zoning and rising land values, had caused most home owners to sell out. The street was now mostly commercial in nature. I passed a gas station and a little strip mall before coming to a tall white gate that marked the entrance to PRCCC.

It looked a little pretentious to me, but what did I know? In my world, doggie day care was a foreign concept. Obviously the facility was meant to cater to an upscale clientele. But hopefully most dog owners would realize that the frills and embellishments that they found appealing wouldn't mean a thing to their canine companions.

I turned in the driveway and drove a hundred yards to a white clapboard building. There was a sign reading OFFICE out front, and I parked nearby in the shade. As I got out of my car, I was still trying to reserve judgment.

Chimes jingled in the air as I pushed open the office door. The reception area was a spacious room, decorated to look bright, cheerful, and welcoming. Eyelet curtains hung on the windows. A grouping of wicker furniture with plump, flower-sprigged cushions formed a waiting area. Poster-sized pictures of happy-looking dogs covered the walls.

The room smelled of air freshener, and I found the scent cloyingly sweet. I could only imagine what the dogs, with their much more sensitive noses, thought of it.

A teenage girl was sitting behind a high white counter opposite the door. Her neatly pressed white polo shirt looked at odds with her long, spiky bangs and the ring pierced through her eyebrow. She was thumbing through a magazine but looked up with a perky smile as I entered. "Dropping off?" she asked brightly.

"No, I—"

"Picking up?"

"No." This time I kept it short. No use trying to talk if she was going to interrupt.

I glanced down at the open page she'd been reading and saw that it appeared to be part of a gun catalog. Interesting choice.

She folded the magazine closed and tucked it away in a desk drawer. "May I help you?"

"I'd like some information about your facility.

And maybe a tour of the premises."

"Do you have an appointment?"

"Do I need one?"

"We prefer that our customers call in advance. We don't want people just showing up whenever they feel like it."

Well, that was a red flag, wasn't it? If I was going to leave a dog or a child in someone's care, I'd certainly like to know what was going on when they weren't expecting to see me.

"I'm not a customer yet," I said. "I'm shopping for day care for my dog, and before I make any decisions about which facility I'm going to entrust him to, I need to investigate all the possibilities."

"Well, then, that's easy." The girl smiled again. "Pine Ridge Canine Care Center is the only full-care, fully accredited, doggie day care center in all of Stamford. We offer nothing but the best. All our people are screened for knowledge and compatibility, and we have a nutritionist and a certified play therapist on staff—"

"Certified by whom?" I asked.

It seemed like a reasonable question. If play therapy was something one could genuinely get certified in, I figured a lot of mothers were due advanced degrees.

"Pardon me?"

She stopped. Blinked. I'd interrupted her spiel. Now she wasn't sure how to get started again.

She reached across the counter. There was a

stack of glossy pamphlets in a clear plastic stand, right next to a bowl containing dog biscuits.

"Let me give you a brochure. I'm sure it will answer any questions you might have."

"That's a start," I said. "But I'd also like to see some dogs."

She was blinking again. Maybe it was a nervous tic.

For the second time, I'd baffled her, and it hadn't even been that hard to accomplish. The teacher in me was shaking her head ruefully.

She handed me the brochure, and said, "What?"

"You know, four legs, one tail, wet nose? Woof?"

"Yes, but—"

"Reading about your facility won't do me nearly as much good as walking around and seeing what it looks like and how it runs. I need to know that Berkley will be happy here. So that's what I'd like to see . . . you know, happy dogs? Unless, of course, you don't have any of those here. Which would be a problem for both of us, I would think."

I was aiming for mild sarcasm, but the comment went right over her head. I hoped for the teenager's sake that this was a summer job and she'd be going back to school in the fall.

"You can't just go walking around by yourself," she said. "It's not allowed."

"No problem." I leaned down on the counter. Close to her, like we were friends. "You can come with me."

"No, I can't. I have to stay here and do my job."

"Reading magazines?"

"Greeting customers." She shot me a dirty look. "Real ones."

"I might become a real customer, how do you know I won't? All I need is more information to help me make the decision."

"We're not set up to do that," she said stubbornly.

"Seems like a funny way to run a business. How do you get new clients?"

"We do advertising." The girl seemed relieved to be asked a question she could answer. "And we have great word of mouth."

"And then what?"

"What do you mean?"

"People must want to come and visit. Surely they'd like to see where their dogs are going to be staying while they're gone."

"You'd be surprised," she said. "Most people aren't that curious."

"And the ones that are?"

"They call in advance and make an appointment with Steve or Candy."

The teen sounded triumphant. As if clearly the entire problem we were having had been my fault for not knowing the correct procedure and calling ahead.

Duly noted, but I was already there now. And a lone teenager guarding the front desk wasn't enough of a deterrent to keep me from accomplishing what I'd come to do.

"Who are Steve and Candy?" I asked.

"Steve and Candy Pine. They're the owners. If you had read the brochure or seen the advertising, you'd know that."

"Or presumably if I'd heard the word of mouth."

She stared at me blankly.

Right. I'd forgotten. Sarcasm didn't work.

At least she wasn't blinking.

"How about this?" I said. "Are the Pines here?"

"Of course. They're always here. This is their business."

"Could one of them give me a tour?"

She glanced down at a calendar on the desk. As if she really needed to check. "You don't have an appointment."

"I'm pretty sure we've established that. But just for the heck of it, let's try calling them and asking, okay?"

"I guess I could do that."

She picked up the phone reluctantly, then turned her back and shielded her mouth for the duration of a brief phone call, as if she was afraid I might listen in.

Which, of course, I would have.

"Why don't you take a seat," she said at the end. "Steve will be right in."

"Thank you." I gave her a perky smile of my own. "Now, was that so hard?"

Apparently so, judging by the look I got in return.

So far, I hadn't made any friends at Pine Ridge Canine Care Center. I could only hope things went better with the owner.

3

Steve Pine was cute. Like seriously cute.

Okay, I know. I'm married and a new mother. I'm not supposed to be noticing things like that. But right now, I'm taking no responsibility for my wayward hormones.

So let me tell you again in case you missed it the first time. This guy was a doll.

He came striding through a door in the back wall of the room, his walk easy and confident, his smile self-assured. His eyes were so blue that I wondered for a moment if the color could possibly be real. Steve wore his dark hair long, and a narrow leather strip gathered it into a ponytail at his nape.

Like the receptionist, he was dressed in a crisp white polo shirt and creased khakis. The outfit looked better on him.

He didn't spare the teenager a glance as he crossed the reception area. Instead, those blue eyes found mine and held them, never wavering as he drew near. This was a man who knew how to focus.

I think the temperature in the room rose ten degrees in the time it took him to reach me. I was tempted to lift a hand and fan my face like an old-fashioned Southern belle.

Thankfully, before I could move he held out his hand, and said, "I'm Steve Pine. Nice to meet you. I hope you haven't been waiting long."

"Not at all."

I was so dazzled, the words didn't even feel like a lie. I gave myself a mental kick.

"I'm Melanie Travis," I replied. "And it's a pleasure to meet you too."

Steve nodded as though he were confirming my response. Which he probably was. No doubt women often felt that making his acquaintance was a pleasure.

"I hear you're looking for a daytime situation for your dog."

"For a friend's dog, actually. She has a Golden Retriever named Berkley, and she's about to start working again for the first time in years. Naturally, she doesn't want to leave him alone all day."

"That's why we're here," Steve replied heartily. "It's our job to allay dog owners' fears about their pets' quality of life. We want every single one of our clients to know that their dogs are in the best possible hands."

Well, at least he wasn't lacking in enthusiasm. This guy would have made a great professional cheerleader. Or maybe a team mascot.

"I'm sure you must have questions for me," Steve said. "Go ahead and fire away."

"What I'd really like is to take a tour of your facilities, if that's possible. Then maybe we can talk along the way?"

"Perfect!" Steve agreed.

He turned to the teen. She was now sitting behind the desk, hands neatly folded on the counter and looking rather angelic. I've worked with kids for too many years to trust a pose like that, but her easy acquiesence didn't seem to bother Steve.

"Madison, you have everything under control here?"

"I do."

"Excellent. Then we're on our way."

We exited through the door in the back of the room, which led to a short hallway with offices opening up on either side.

"This is where Candy and I do the drudge work," said Steve. "Accounting, working out the schedules, ordering supplies. Nothing interesting to see here, but it's the quickest way to get back to the compound."

"Compound?" I repeated, peering into each of the rooms as we passed by. "How much land do you have here?"

Both offices looked more functional than luxurious. One had masses of paperwork scattered across every flat surface, an empty dog crate sitting in one corner, and a dead plant hanging by the window. The other office was much smaller and held only a desk whose top was pristine and a comfy-looking chair by the back wall that was covered in pet hair.

"We have three acres, which is terrific," Steve said. "Especially since the price of real estate around here keeps going up and up. We were lucky to buy in when we did."

"How long ago was that?"

Steve passed through a door at the end of the hall and I followed. We exited the clapboard building and went down two steps to a gravel path that branched out in several directions. Steve paused and looked out over the facility with pride.

"Two years. I can't believe we've accomplished as much as we have in such a short amount of time. There was definitely a huge, untapped market for the services we provide to the community. We like to think of ourselves as a full-care facility. Anything your dog needs or wants, we'll find a way to make it happen."

In front of us was another building, this one much larger than the one we'd just left. Off to the right were a number of fenced paddocks, most containing a variety of durable outdoor toys. I saw everything from big, bright rubber balls to open canvas tunnels.

Several of the pens were occupied. In one, a Dalmatian was chasing an Irish Setter carrying a large, hemp-colored chew toy in his mouth. In another, two Vizslas and a Scottish Deerhound were resting side by side in the shade. Their heads were up, their gazes intent, and I realized that the three of them were watching a man who was working in an adjoining paddock, making repairs to a wooden climbing set.

He, too, was wearing the Pine Ridge uniform. In his case, however, the polo shirt he wore was grimy and untucked, and the spread of his stomach strained the seams of his rumpled khakis. As I watched, the man paused in what he was doing, pulled a kerchief out of a back pocket, and ran it up over his balding head. Noticing us standing across the way, he lifted his hand in a desultory wave.

Steve returned the gesture with a brief wave of his own before turning back to me. "That's Larry. He does maintenance for us. Of course, it's vitally important to us that all our equipment be kept in perfect working order."

"Of course," I echoed under my breath. While I appreciated Steve's enthusiasm, the nonstop hyperbole of his sales pitch was beginning to wear a little thin.

"These are the outdoor play areas," he explained, as though I couldn't have figured that out for myself. "We have indoor playrooms as well, but weather permitting we like all of the dogs that are physically able to spend at least part of the day outside. Many go out in groups of two or three, according to their owners' preference, and of course they're always supervised."

"What do you mean physically able?" I asked.

"Unfortunately, some of the dogs that come here are with us because they require special care and it's impossible for their owners to be there for them during the day. Some have chronic illnesses and require medicine, others are simply geriatric. Nathan, for example, who's one of our regulars. He's everyone's favorite."

Steve started walking again. He was heading toward the second building and I hurried to catch up.

"Nathan?" I said.

"An eighteen-year-old Wirehaired Dachshund. Still spry for his age and as endearing as he can possibly be. He's been here with us from the very beginning. All the staff have grown so attached to him, he feels like a member of the family."

"That's a great age," I said.

"Nathan's a great dog. And of course his owner is wonderful too. She wants nothing but the best for him. This business . . ." Steve paused for a moment before continuing, "Well, it *is* a business, but let's just say it doesn't always feel that way. We become very fond of the dogs that come and stay with us. They're such a part of our everyday lives, how could we possibly help it? We've formed our own little community here. Everyone works in harmony with everyone else. It makes for a peaceful, low-stress environment, both for the dogs and for everyone else, and that's just the way we like it."

"It sounds wonderful," I said honestly.

Steve was quite the salesman, but that wasn't the reason that my impression of Pine Ridge was growing increasingly favorable. More important than what he had to say was the fact that all the dogs I'd seen thus far had appeared contented and well cared for. It wasn't hard to imagine that Berkley would be happy here.

"Let's go into the Dog House," Steve said, heading toward the bigger building. "I'll show you the rest of the accommodations."

I stopped myself just short of laughing.

"I know, I know." He caught my eye and smiled. "The name does sound a little silly. But we didn't want to call it a kennel. That word seemed to convey such negative connotations about confinement and isolation. Which is the opposite of what we're aiming for."

As we approached the entrance, I realized there was a square, cut-out seam in the door's lower panel. The Dog House had its own doggie door. Its presence seemed superfluous under the circumstances. Considering the amount of supervision I'd seen, it was hard to imagine that dogs might be allowed to come and go at will.

"Use that much?" I asked as Steve drew the door open.

"Not at all, unfortunately. As you can probably

guess, its function is strictly decorative. Just another small attempt on our part to make the dogs feel more at home while they're here. Indeed, we like to think that our facility is more like a doggie spa than what you might picture as your typical boarding situation."

If the term spa implied that the accommodations would be luxurious, then Steve's description wasn't far off the mark. Inside, the building didn't even remotely resemble any kennel I'd ever seen.

Instead of pens, the dogs were housed in individual rooms that were large enough for several compatible dogs to share comfortably. Most contained furniture, usually low chairs and couches that were easily accessible from the floor. Television sets were mounted on the walls.

Peeking in through the viewing windows as we walked past, I saw a Maltese watching *Animal Planet* and an Afghan who seemed fascinated by the flashing lights and screaming contestants on a game show.

"Who controls the remote?" I asked.

I'd been joking, but Steve took the question seriously.

"There are foot pedals on the floor beneath the screens," he informed me. "It doesn't take most dogs long to learn that if they step on them, they can change the channel. There's also an on/off switch if they would prefer quiet."

Speaking of quiet, in a building that housed such a

multitude of dogs, it was somewhat surprising not to hear any barking. Either the walls of the individual compartments were soundproof, or else the occupants were too content to stand around making noise.

Score another point in Pine Ridge's favor.

"How many dogs do you have here on a usual day?" I asked.

"As you can imagine, it varies. The number is usually somewhere between twenty-five and thirty. Most of our business is made up of regulars, dogs whose owners live in the area and work full-time jobs, so we see those clients every weekday. But we also get the occasional drop-in. People are supposed to make reservations in advance, but if they show up and we have space available, we try to be accommodating."

Steve and I were standing in a wide, brightly lit aisleway situated between two long rows of rooms: individual compartments on one side and multidog playrooms on the other. Abruptly, a door toward the end of the hall burst open and a woman came hurrying out.

She was small and dainty, and wearing the outfit I'd come to expect: a pristine white polo shirt and pressed khakis. Frizzy blond curls bobbed around her head like a halo. Her face was tipped downward; she was studying something written on a clipboard she held in her hand.

"Good news," she said without looking up. "I

finally got Bingo Johnson squared away, and I've just placed a second call to the Abernathys. When do you want me to—"

"Candy."

Steve's voice was low, his tone moderate. It stopped the woman in her tracks.

"Oh, hello," she said, finally lifting her eyes and taking in the two of us. "I didn't realize you were busy."

"Obviously not. This is Melanie Travis. She's taking a tour to see if she would like to become a client." Steve lifted a hand to motion me forward. "Melanie, meet my sister, Candy."

Steve and Candy Pine, the receptionist had said. I'd just assumed the owners were husband and wife. Really, you'd think I'd know better.

Candy's handshake was firm and brisk. My fingers throbbed a bit when she released them. Maybe she was compensating for her small size.

"So what have you already seen and how do you like the place so far?" she asked.

Steve shot her a look. "You don't have to answer that if you don't want to," he said quickly. "My sister can be very direct. Some people find that off-putting."

"I don't mind," I said. "I think your place looks terrific."

Candy smirked at her brother. I didn't have to be a relative to know she was saying, *I told you so*.

"We're always happy to meet new people and

new dogs," she said. "Tell me about yours."

The surest way to make friends among the crowd I ran around with was to ask exactly that. Of course in this case, Candy wasn't asking about my Poodles. Alice's Berkley was the dog she was interested in.

"He's an eighteen-month-old Golden Retriever named Berkley. Beautiful, smart, very well-meaning. Great with kids, but he needs his exercise. I'm glad to see that you have outdoor paddocks. He loves to run around outside."

"Most of them do," Candy said with a quick nod. "We want happy dogs here, and happy dogs are ones that aren't bored. We think happy dogs lead to happy owners."

Good lord, I thought. Another cheerleader. Between the two of them, Steve and Candy generated enough intensity to power a hot-air balloon.

"I should mention," I said, "that Berkley isn't actually my dog. He belongs to a friend, Alice Brickman. She's the one who's looking for a day care situation for him. But she's not particularly knowledgeable about dogs and she was afraid she wouldn't know what to look for, so she asked me to come and see what I thought."

"So that makes you, what . . ." Candy said with a smile, "a surrogate dog owner?"

"Not at all." I laughed at the idea. "I have my own dogs as well. Five Standard Poodles. You know, the big ones?"

"I love Standard Poodles! They're the best. Do you put them in those crazy clips? The ones that make them look like they belong in the circus?"

"Sometimes," I admitted. "When they're showing, they have to be trimmed that way. But once they retire, I just keep them in a regular sporting trim."

"You have to meet Bailey," said Candy. "She's going to love you."

"Our in-house groomer," Steve explained. "Bailey's in charge of keeping all our dogs' ears clean and nails trimmed. And of course, if a client wants a full bath and trim for their dog, she can do that too. But I'm afraid she never gets to work on anything quite as exotic as your Poodles."

Candy grabbed my hand and pulled me down the hallway. "Come on. The grooming room is down here. Bailey's going to be thrilled to meet a real Poodle expert."

"I'll leave you now," said Steve, lingering behind. "Once Candy has you in her clutches—"

"Surely you meant capable hands, didn't you?" she threw back over her shoulder. Our headlong progress didn't slow down in the slightest. "Don't worry, if Melanie has any more questions, I'm sure I'll be able to answer them for her. Go on back and lock yourself in your office and do whatever it is you do when I'm out here working."

It didn't take an expert, or a relative, to discern the edge in that comment.

"I'm doing accounts payable this morning,"

Steve said mildly. "I'd be happy to trade jobs if you like."

"Me, do the books? Not on a bet. I'd be comatose inside of fifteen minutes. Here we are."

Candy stopped in front of a glass-paneled door. Sadly, when we paused, I had to catch my breath. What can I say? I used to be more fit before I had a baby.

"Nice meeting you, Melanie." Steve turned and headed back toward the door.

"Likewise," I called after him.

"You'll like Bailey," Candy said, as she pushed open the door. "She seems all shy and quiet at first, but once you get to know her, she never shuts up. Plus, she absolutely loves dogs. The two of you are bound to get along splendidly."

Shy and quiet was an understatement, I thought, ten minutes later, as I walked back around to the front of the compound where my car was parked. Bailey had barely said more than a dozen words the entire time we'd been together. Of course, Candy's constant stream of happy chatter had left few opportunities for either of us to get a word in.

Thanks to Candy's volubility, I now knew that

Pine Ridge offered a host of extra services such as pick-up and drop-off for busy clients, scheduled disc-dog playtime, and classes in clicker training. Not only that, but plans for a custom line of canine couture were in the works. It was all a little much to take in.

While Candy had been talking, Bailey had been grooming a chocolate Labrador Retriever. I'm using the term loosely, because in actuality the part of the process we were watching involved her lifting the dog's heavy lips and brushing his large white teeth.

True to his breed, the Lab was placid and good-natured. He also had all his teeth and a correct bite, I noted absently. Apparently, he loved the taste of the toothpaste Bailey was using because he kept swabbing his long pink tongue around the long-handled brush and trying to pull it out of her fingers.

The attempts made Bailey giggle, and the giggling made the Lab's heavy tail thump up and down on the rubber-coated tabletop. The two of them looked as though they were sharing a joke they'd enjoyed together before.

"You have a nice hand on a dog," I said to Bailey when Candy stepped across the room to check on an Afghan Hound that was sitting in a crate under a blow-dryer.

"Thank you. I love my job."

Bailey's round face creased in a happy smile. She was older than Madison, perhaps in her early twenties, and had the pale complexion and bland features of a German milkmaid. She hummed softly under her breath as she worked.

"Candy said you show your dogs," she said, her tone tinged with awe. "I'd love to be able to do that someday."

"It's a great hobby. My husband and I have Standard Poodles. Lots of people who show them also groom professionally. I'd be happy to—"

"Right, then," Candy said, swooping back in to join us. "I'm so glad you two had a chance to get to know one another. But now I'm afraid we really have to let Bailey get back to work. She's busy, busy, busy all the time, and that's just the way we like it, isn't it, Bailey?"

The groomer nodded.

"Don't forget you have Mrs. Parker's Cockers to do this afternoon," Candy continued, checking the list on her clipboard. "Six P.M. pick-up, right?"

We were out of the grooming room and on our way before Bailey had time to reply.

"So—have you seen everything you wanted to see?" Candy asked as she escorted me out of the Dog House. "Do you have any more questions I can answer before you go?"

"No, I think I'm good." I took a last look around. "This really is a nice setup you have here."

"We think so. Steve and I work very hard to make sure everything runs smoothly. And of course, our prices are very reasonable for the array of services we offer. You won't find another facility like Pine Ridge in all of Fairfield County. I'm sure your friend, Alice, will be very pleased with what we can do for her and Berkley."

My initial skepticism had disappeared, and I had to agree. The facility really *was* nice. I'd be passing along a favorable recommendation to Alice, along with the advice that she try not to get suckered into buying Berkley any designer clothes.

I followed the path around the front building and had just reached the parking lot when a gold Lexus came flying up the driveway. The driver overshot a parking space and braked abruptly when the car rolled onto the grass. The car was still rocking when a scrappy-looking older man shoved the door open and climbed out.

He glared in my direction. At least that was how I read his body language. Dark, mirrored sunglasses covered his eyes.

"Do you work here?" he asked.

"No."

"Then who does?"

Rudeness irritates me. Especially unnecessary rudeness. I thought about ignoring him, but decided I'd probably get rid of him faster by just answering the question.

I waved a hand toward the office door. "There's a receptionist right inside. I'm sure she can help you."

I suspected fireworks would be forthcoming, but I didn't wait around to find out. Sometimes it was nice just to mind my own business for a change.

Back on the road, I pulled out my cell phone and called home. Predictably, Sam had everything under control. He and Davey were outside, shooting hoops. Kevin was nearby, napping in his baby seat in the shade.

When I'd met Sam five years earlier, he was a freelance software designer. In the intervening time, he'd unexpectedly regained the rights to a video game that he'd designed while in business school. The game had since gone on to sell millions of copies to ardent teenage fans.

Sam still worked, but now he chose his own projects and adjusted his schedule to suit himself. When I'd arranged to take time off after Kevin was born, Sam had decided to do the same. Having waited until his late thirties to become a father, he was eager to enjoy every aspect of the experience. And having been forced to raise Davey as a single mother, I knew enough to appreciate his input and his involvement for the blessing that it was.

Since I wasn't needed at home, I got on the Merritt Parkway and headed down to Greenwich instead. Margaret Turnbull, my Aunt Peg, has a house on five acres in the "back country" north of the parkway. At one time, she and my Uncle Max had kept a whole kennel full of Standard Poodles on the property, and their Cedar Crest line had been known nationwide for the beauty, health, and tremendous temperament of its dogs.

When Max died, however, Aunt Peg scaled back the scope of her breeding and showing operation. She still had half a dozen Poodles, but the kennel building behind the house now sat empty. The dogs shared her home like the members of the family they were, and Aunt Peg delighted in their companionship.

It was because of my aunt that I'd initially gotten involved with Poodles, as she was the breeder of Davey's and my first dog, Faith. Aunt Peg had given us the Poodle puppy partly as a present, partly as a reward for some help I'd contributed, and partly as a bond to cement our future relationship.

Then—because no good deed on Aunt Peg's part comes without strings attached—she had announced that Faith was going to be shown to her championship. To aid in that quest, my aunt had taken me in hand and shepherded me through the exhibiting process using a teaching technique that had felt like equal parts inspiration and dire threats.

Aunt Peg doesn't suffer fools or foolishness, and woe to any relative of hers who can't keep up. She had taught me more about dogs in five years than most people have the opportunity to learn in a lifetime, and I would always be grateful for her guidance and her support.

"I was just thinking about you," Aunt Peg said ten minutes later, as I got out of my car.

I hadn't bothered to call ahead, but as I parked beside the garage, Aunt Peg already had her front door open. Her Poodles serve as a canine alarm system, and visitors are announced long before they're able to reach the porch and ring the doorbell.

Big, black Poodles eddying around legs, Aunt Peg came down the steps from the wide porch and approached the Volvo. "Where is everyone?" she asked, peering in the back of the station wagon.

"Everyone who?" I asked innocently.

Of course I knew what she meant, but sometimes I just can't resist baiting her. And besides, what was I, chopped liver?

"My nephews, your husband. Kevin, Davey, Sam?" Aunt Peg frowned and had another look, as if that might turn up someone she'd previously missed. "Faith? Eve? My goodness, I don't even see a dog in there. The very *least* you could have done is bring Tar for a visit."

Yet again, I'd failed to live up to my aunt's expectations. Unfortunately, that was nothing new.

"I brought myself for a visit," I said.

"Well, I guess you'll have to do."

"I could leave."

"Oh pish," said Peg. "Now you're just being pathetic. Of course I'm happy to see you. I was just hoping I might have the opportunity to see my new nephew as well. Babies are like puppies, they seem

47

to change from minute to minute. And you know me, I hate to miss a thing."

That was certainly true. But what Aunt Peg neglected to mention was that she'd been at our house at least once a week since Kevin was born and had had dinner with us just two nights previously. So by my estimation, she wasn't missing much.

Aunt Peg's Poodles offered me a brief and genial greeting, then chased each other away for a romp around the front yard. Racing in large, looping circles, they checked the area for new smells, looked for previously abandoned toys, and had a run at a hapless squirrel.

Of the six Standard Poodles in residence, only one was currently being shown, a young male named Custer. He had competed in puppy classes, wearing the puppy trim, before he was a year old. Now, fourteen months of age and nominally an adult, he was taking some time off from the show ring to grow the copious neck and topknot hair that would be required to balance his new continental clip.

Automatically, Aunt Peg kept an eye on her Poodles as they played, making sure that none of the older dogs dared to pull on Custer's oh-so-precious neck hair. Which, of course, they didn't. They were Poodles, after all. They knew the drill.

"I've just made a pitcher of iced tea," said Aunt Peg. "Let's go inside and have something cold to drink. I'm sure you must have lots to tell me."

I considered for a moment, then said, "Not really."

Nevertheless, I followed her up the steps and into the house. Second in line, I held the door until all the Poodles had followed us inside.

"That's all right then, because I have lots to tell you."

No surprise there.

Aunt Peg led the way to the kitchen. I got out glasses while she opened the refrigerator to get the tea. And the butter.

I lifted a brow.

"Blueberry scones. The bakery had a batch freshly made."

Visiting Aunt Peg was never good for my waistline. Six feet tall and with the vigor of the Energizer Bunny himself, she never had to worry about her weight. The only time I'd been able to match her, sweet for sweet, had been in the latter weeks of my pregnancy.

And of course, I was paying for that now.

Which didn't stop me from taking a scone. I did sigh as I selected one, however. It made me feel a little better.

"So tell me about your day," she said. "Where have you been?"

Aunt Peg was temporizing, which wasn't a good sign. Usually she can't wait to tell me what's on her mind. Rather than calling her on it, I decided to play along.

"This might be interesting to you," I said. "I've

just come from visiting Pine Ridge Canine Care Center."

Aunt Peg looked up. "Is somebody sick?"

"No, it's not that kind of place. Pine Ridge is a doggie day care center."

"Oh." The single, clipped syllable conveyed her disdain. "For people who want to own dogs but can't be bothered to put in the time to take care of them themselves."

"Or for mothers who are going back to work and trying to do the right thing by their pets."

"Not you, I hope."

Aunt Peg vetted potential puppy owners with incredible care and attention to detail. The day a Cedar Crest bred Poodle ended up in day care, she would raise holy hell.

"No, I was checking the place out for my friend Alice. Now that her kids are older and in school, she's decided to get a job."

"Berkley," said Aunt Peg.

She was probably picturing the Golden Retriever in her mind. I doubted if she could tell you how many children Alice had, or what their names were. She was also probably somewhat hazy as to what Alice looked like.

But Berkley Aunt Peg knew immediately. It was just the way her brain worked.

"And—what did you think?"

"It's a nice place. Nicer than I expected, actually. I was prepared to be pretty wary of the whole idea."

"I should hope you would be."

Aunt Peg reached for her second scone and buttered it. The older Poodles were stretched out around us on the floor, most of them asleep. Only Custer was sitting up and keeping a hopeful eye on Aunt Peg.

I could have told him he was wasting his time; my aunt wouldn't dream of feeding dogs from her plate. No doubt he'd learn that for himself soon enough. In the meantime, Davey's frequent visits and his habit of slipping forbidden handouts under the table kept the young dog just spoiled enough.

"I trust you asked all the right questions."

I gulped. By her standards, possibly not. Conversation with Aunt Peg always had a way of making me feel like I was on the hot seat.

"I took a tour," I said brightly, "and checked out the accommodations. I saw outdoor paddocks and indoor playrooms, and I met the groomer. The dogs have televisions in their rooms and couches to lie on while they watch."

"That's the dumbest thing I ever heard."

"They looked very comfortable."

"Dogs don't need television to make them happy. They need people, and games, and someone who cares about them."

"Pine Ridge seemed to be doing a good job with those things too."

Aunt Peg narrowed her gaze. "Did you ask which vet they have on call in case of emergencies?"

Missed that one. And it was a good thought.

"Um . . . no."

"How about which food they feed and why they chose that particular brand? Hopefully the deciding factor wasn't that someone offered them a bulk discount."

Oops. Strike two.

"Don't worry," Aunt Peg said briskly. "New mothers are allowed to be distracted. I'm sure you'll do better on your second visit."

"Second visit?"

"You did intend to go back, didn't you? Otherwise how will you know whether or not you simply caught them on a good day? Believe me, Berkley will thank you for it."

Not Alice, Berkley. Did you catch that?

"Now then," said Aunt Peg. "Let's get to my news. I've had a positively brilliant idea. And you hardly have to do anything at all."

"Me?" I put down my scone. "How did I get involved?"

As if I even needed to ask. Aunt Peg had a plan, which meant that everyone in the vicinity should strap themselves in because, like it or not, we were all along for the ride.

5

"Junior showmanship," she announced.

"What about it?" I asked.

Junior showmanship is a dog show competition for child handlers. There are three age categories and both Novice and Open divisions are offered. Exhibitors can show any breed of dog they want in the classes, and they're judged on their presentation and handling skills, rather than the quality of the dog itself.

Once he turned nine, Davey had become eligible for the youngest division. But although he'd spent much of his life accompanying us to dog shows, he'd never shown any desire to enter the ring himself.

"Davey and I have been talking about it," said Aunt Peg.

"You have?"

There was no point in trying not to sound surprised. Aunt Peg had pulled something off behind my back and we both knew it. The satisfaction on her face was easy to read.

"Well, more than talking, actually. I've been giving him a few lessons."

"Handling lessons?"

"Do try to keep up, Melanie. That is what we're talking about, isn't it?"

I stared at her suspiciously. Davey enjoyed playing soccer and basketball. He'd tried a little acting and he liked to write short stories. He had plenty going on in his life without being coerced into adding another activity that suited Aunt Peg's interests more than his own.

"Whose idea was this?" I asked.

"Davey's, of course."

I sat and waited.

"And perhaps a little of mine."

Now we were getting closer to the truth.

"Admit it, you've been very busy lately," said Aunt Peg.

"I had a baby three months ago! There's a reason I've been busy."

"Nevertheless, Davey might have been receiving a little less attention than he was used to."

I sat back in my chair, feeling deflated. That hit me where it hurt. Had I been so wrapped up in Kevin and his needs that I'd been shortchanging Davey? Was it possible that I'd been too sleep deprived to notice that my older son was feeling left out?

Motherhood. If there's a harder job, I'd like to know what it is.

I looked down at my plate and realized that while I was listening, I'd managed to eat the entire scone. With butter.

"Did Davey tell you that?" I asked.

"Not in so many words."

Drawing information out of Aunt Peg was like trying to call a hunting dog off a scent. You might as well just give up and wait until she was darn good and ready to give in.

"Davey didn't say anything. But the circumstances speak for themselves. You have a new husband and a new baby. There have been a lot of changes in Davey's life recently, along with many new things for him to adapt to."

"You're talking about changes that Davey wanted . . . changes that he likes . . ."

I heard myself protesting and stopped. Aunt Peg was making me feel guiltier by the moment. Which, knowing Aunt Peg, was probably her intention.

"With everything else that's going on in your life right now, I thought it might do him good to have a special project to work on by himself. Something that was all about him and nobody else."

"But junior showmanship?" I asked dubiously.

"Think about it," said Aunt Peg. "It's what I know. It's not as if I was going to teach him tap dancing or origami. Showing dogs is what I'm good at."

Even so. "Does Davey want to learn to show dogs?" I asked.

"Funny that you can't answer that question for yourself," said Aunt Peg. "How is it that you've never asked him?"

"I have—" I said, then stopped and thought.

Maybe I hadn't. Maybe I'd been waiting for him to indicate an interest on his own. Kids these days, especially those who grew up in high-achieving, high-stress areas like Fairfield County, were pressured to learn, and perform, and excel in so many different ways. Whenever possible, I tried to back off from adding more expectations to Davey's already full agenda. Maybe I had been remiss.

"You've been giving him lessons?" I asked.

Aunt Peg nodded. "He's quite good for his age. Considering the length of his arms and his stride, someone his size would probably do better with a smaller dog. But the Poodles are very accommodating and they know what's expected of them, which helps. So between them they manage to make it work."

I gazed around the room. All of Aunt Peg's Standard Poodles, with the exception of Custer, had competed in the show ring long enough to earn the fifteen points required to complete their championships. They were probably just as good at teaching Davey what was expected of him as Aunt Peg was.

"And Davey's enjoying this?"

That seemed to be my role in this conversation, just asking one semi-repetitive question after another. But I wanted to make sure that I got things exactly right. For Davey's sake and my own.

"The few lessons we've had, very much so. He likes being the one holding the end of the leash—

56

and having someone he can tell what to do. And of course, the Poodles play along and let him think he's in charge."

They would.

"So now what?" I asked.

"Now we let him practice some more until we think he's ready to venture out into the real world and try his hand at a few dog shows. I imagine there will be someplace this summer where he can get his start."

"He'll need to show a Poodle in hair in order to be competitive."

All of Sam's and my dogs were cut down. Once a Poodle had stopped showing, maintaining the elaborate clip required for the ring took entirely too much time to be feasible. Although Davey would be allowed to show a Poodle that wasn't wearing the traditional continental trim, he would have a harder time winning if his dog didn't look the way the judges expected it to.

Aunt Peg smiled. "I've been having him practice with Hope, so there's no long hair to get in the way of everything else he needs to learn, but I'm sure that Custer will be happy to step in and help out when the time comes. Indeed, I suspect the two of them might have quite a bit of fun together."

"Thank you," I said.

Aunt Peg raised a brow. Just one. Don't ask me how she does it.

"For starting all this behind your back?"

"For noticing something that I should have."

"Oh my dear." Aunt Peg laughed. "You must have realized by now. I notice everything."

Wasn't that the truth?

On the way home, I called and checked in with Alice.

Most people can drive and talk on the phone at the same time; I see them doing it all the time. For me, however, the maneuver is a major challenge. Either I'm thinking about my driving or I'm thinking about the conversation I'm holding. When I try to do both, my brain short-circuits.

Which was why shortly after she picked up, I took a wrong turn. It would have been fine if I'd noticed where I was going, but of course I was so busy talking that I didn't. So instead of driving home, I drove to Alice's house.

On some convoluted level, I'm sure that made sense to my subconscious.

We'd barely gotten past the small talk before I found myself turning onto the road where the Brickmans lived. Which, as it happens, was also where Davey and I had lived until fairly recently. The small, Cape Cod house we'd shared was now the residence of Davey's father, my ex-husband, Bob.

It's kind of a long story how that came about. Just another one of those things that seems to make more sense when you're in the process than it does later when you look back and try to explain how it

all happened. But since I was already in the neighborhood, I figured I might as well stop in and see
Bob later on too.

Alice is well acquainted with most of my foibles,
and I'd already explained about the driving thing
while we were talking, so she was standing out on
the sidewalk, waiting for me, when I turned onto the
road. She had Berkley on a leash beside her. The
Golden Retriever looked thrilled at the prospect of
an unexpected, midafternoon walk.

Alice snapped her phone shut as I got out of the
Volvo. Stepping up onto the curb, I reached down
and greeted Berkley first. He was wriggling in
place with excitement; his long, feathered tail
lashed back and forth across Alice's legs.

"Berkley, sit," she said firmly.

The Golden had been to obedience school. In
fact, I seemed to recall that he'd taken the six-week
beginner course three times. But since no one had
taken the time to practice with him between ses-
sions, much of what he'd learned in class hadn't
stuck.

Now Berkley brushed his big butt briefly across
the ground before using the position as a launching
pad to spring back up in the air. I jerked back just in
time. Otherwise the dog's broad head might have
broken my nose.

"Sorry about that." Alice shortened the leash and
hauled him back to her side. "He gets a little exu-
berant around people he likes."

As far as I could tell, Berkley liked everybody. Which made exuberance his way of life. Trying to hold him still, Alice looked a little desperate. She might have outweighed Berkley, but when it came to energy level, he definitely had her beat.

"Let's walk," I proposed.

When the Golden Retriever's first step turned into a high-spirited lunge, I reached over and took the lead from Alice, giving it a little snap so that Berkley would know he'd changed handlers. His collar was made of thick, rolled leather, however, and I doubted he even felt the tug. Nevertheless, once we were moving, he was happy to accompany us. He matched his strides to ours and fell into step.

"I'm thinking I'll lie," said Alice.

"About what?"

"You know, on the application for Pine Ridge? Whatever kinds of questions they ask about your dog's behavior, I'm pretty sure I'm going to have to tell some big, fat, whopping lies." She sighed heavily. "I'm a terrible person, aren't I?"

"You've got to be kidding."

"No," Alice said sadly. "I'm pretty sure I'm terrible."

"Not about that, about the application." I slowed my steps as Berkley paused to sniff an interesting tree. "Are you serious? I know you said there was a waiting list, but it never occurred to me that dogs actually had to apply to get in."

"That's what they told me on the phone. I've been

worrying ever since that he wouldn't get accepted."

It was bad enough that getting children into the right schools and activities was a trial. Who would have guessed that dogs had to be judged worthy as well?

"Nobody said anything about that to me when I was there," I said. "And I met both the owners."

"Steve and Candy Pine, right? I saw their pictures in the brochure they sent. And of course everything seemed perfect on the web site. But how did the place look to you in person?"

Berkley, having finished lifting his leg, took off down the sidewalk like a dog on a mission. I could have corrected him, but I figured power-walking probably burned off more calories than strolling. Beside us, Alice adjusted the length of her stride to keep up.

"There's a little gray-and-white Lhasa Apso that lives right around the corner," she said. "Her owner absolutely refuses to have her spayed. So twice a year, Berkley thinks he's in love."

Luckily the Lhasa was nowhere in sight. Berkley slowed briefly, lifted his nose to sniff the air, then kept going.

"I thought Pine Ridge looked great," I said. "Much better than I was expecting. It doesn't have the feel of a boarding kennel at all. And while some of the things they offer seemed a little over the top, I have to admit that the dogs I saw there looked pretty happy."

"Good." Alice nodded. "Then it's settled. I'll download the forms from the web site and fill them out."

"Not so fast. Aunt Peg seems to think we need to make another visit. You know, so that we're sure it's the right place for him?"

Alice didn't bother to argue. She knew enough about my aunt to know that where dogs were concerned, her word was pretty much law.

"I suppose I could find some free time tomorrow," she said.

"You can fill out the application while you're there. Kill two birds with one stone."

She glanced down at Berkley dubiously. The Golden looked up at her and grinned, his long pink tongue lolling out of the side of his mouth.

"You don't suppose they're going to want to interview him, do you?"

"I can't imagine."

Well actually, once I stopped and thought about it, I could.

Davey had gone to an interview for an upscale preschool at a point in his life when his entire vocabulary consisted of about two dozen words. I had watched through a window with the other mothers as the children under consideration engaged in "organized group play" under the supervision of the school's headmistress. My son had been the only three-year-old boy in the group not wearing a suit and tie.

After that experience, I supposed I'd believe almost anything.

"Berkley will do just fine," I said. "Just look at him. He's like a big teddy bear. Who wouldn't fall in love with him?"

"You're a dog person. You have to feel that way."

"Steve and Candy are dog people too. Don't worry, he'll do fine."

"I hope you're right," said Alice. "But I'm not taking any chances. We'll leave him home tomorrow. That way, they won't even meet him until after they've already cashed the check for the first month's board."

I would have laughed except for the fact that Alice had gone through the preschool experience too. In fact, she'd done it twice. So maybe she knew what she was talking about. Instead, I reached down and scratched behind the Golden Retriever's ears.

"Berrrkleey," I crooned. "You're such a good boy. Are you hearing these terrible things she's saying about you?"

Berkley lifted his head and added a little swagger to his step. He had no idea what the words meant, he just liked the fact that we were talking about him.

Dogs really have it easy, you know?

6

By the time we'd finished circling the block, Alice and I had made a plan to meet at Pine Ridge the next morning. Then she and Berkley went home and I walked a couple doors down to see if Bob was around. His Ford Explorer was parked in the driveway, so I figured the chances were pretty good.

Earlier in the spring, Bob had had the house painted. When Davey and I had lived there, the small Cape had been yellow. Now it was gray with white shutters. Bob had found a couple of large clay flowerpots and filled them with peonies. They flanked the front steps and added a nice touch of color.

But despite the changes, walking up to this house where Davey and I had lived so happily for so long, still felt like coming home. I didn't bother to ring the doorbell. Bob never bothers to lock his door, so I just opened it up and stuck my head in.

"Hello?" I called. "Anyone home?"

This is the point where, at my house, unexpected visitors would be mobbed by a charging herd of Poodles. Until I assured them all was well, the noise would be pretty intense.

Not here. A cream-colored Siamese cat with

brown ears and a brown nose was asleep in a band of sun that fell across the couch in the living room. Bosco lifted his head briefly, glanced in my direction to assure himself that the interruption was nothing to be concerned about, then went back to sleep.

Okay, that's the part I don't get. People always talk about how curious cats are but really, not so much. No self-respecting Poodle would have let an intruder enter the house without a challenge. But as long as the sun was warm and the cushion beneath him was soft, Bosco couldn't have cared less.

It looked to me like apathy was more likely to kill that cat than curiosity.

"I'm in the kitchen," Bob yelled in reply. "Come on back."

I did, and found that the room was in a state of siege. Bob had already ripped out the cabinets and countertops that had been in place since the house was built more than half a century earlier. Now he was stripping the flower-sprigged wallpaper from the walls.

I'd been rather fond of that wallpaper, I thought, feeling a small pang. I'd put it up myself. But this was no longer my house, and my opinion of what went on here no longer mattered.

Abruptly, I found myself wondering what was behind Bob's recent flurry of redecoration. Perhaps there was a new woman in his life. I'd been so wrapped up in my own family, I might have overlooked something like that. Maybe I should do a little fishing around and find out.

"Want to help?" asked Bob.

He was standing midway up a stepladder, holding a putty knife in one hand and a long tangle of discarded wallpaper in the other. A streak of wallpaper solvent was smeared across the front of his T-shirt.

"No thanks," I said. "I'm happy to watch."

Bob began to shake his hand hard. He was trying to drop the sheet of discarded wallpaper, but it was stuck to his fingers. When the paper finally came free, it fluttered to the floor and became attached to the bottom step of the ladder. I was betting it would get stuck on Bob's shoe next.

"What's up?" he asked as he went back to trying to peel the next strip of paper away from the wall. "I saw you walk by with Alice. Just visiting? Where are the kids?"

"Home with Sam," I replied. It seemed amazing that after all the years I had spent as a single mother, my sons now had two men in their lives. "I had some running around to do and this way was easier. Feel free to stop by later, if you want. I know Davey would love to see you."

Several cane-backed chairs from a dinette set had been pushed up against a wall and partially covered by a drop cloth. I pulled one out and gingerly took a seat. When Bob started to pull things apart nothing in his path was safe, but the chair seemed to have escaped unscathed thus far.

"Maybe I'll do that. I could use a break after I get done with this. If the weather holds, it might be a nice night for a barbeque. I could bring the burgers . . ."

"Consider yourself invited," I said with a laugh. "Come around six or so. That will give you a couple of hours until Kevin goes to bed. And if there's anyone you'd like to bring with you . . ."

I let the thought dangle and waited for Bob to fill in the blank.

"Like who?" he asked innocently. His back was turned so I couldn't read the expression on his face.

"I don't know . . . a girlfriend maybe?"

Bob's hands stilled. He stared back over his shoulder at me. "What girlfriend?"

"Any one you like," I said with a grin. "What's her name?"

He shook his head and went back to work. "I don't know where you got that idea. There is no name. In fact, there is no her."

"Are you sure?"

"Trust me. I'm pretty sure I'd be the first to know."

"Too bad. I thought that was why you were redecorating."

"Nope, I'm redoing stuff because nobody's done any serious work to this house in decades."

"I would have, but I was a little short on cash," I said tartly. "There were months when just getting the mortgage paid was a stretch."

No use bringing up the fact that over the years his child-support checks had been few and far between. We'd hashed all that out and gotten past it. In fact we'd gotten past a lot of things, which was why we were able to be such good friends now.

"I'm not criticizing," said Bob. "Merely stating a fact."

A piece of uncooperative wallpaper stuck in place. He pulled out a wide taping knife and began to scrape.

"That might come off easier with a steamer," I mentioned.

"I'm saving that for my next trick. But while we're on the subject of when this was your house . . . Amber lived here when you did, right?"

Amber Fine was Bob's next door neighbor, formerly mine. For most of the time Davey and I had lived in the house, an elderly Italian woman had occupied the home next door. But shortly after Sam and I got married, Edna had gone to join her family in Seattle and Amber had moved in. I'd never had the opportunity to get to know her well.

"For a little while," I said. "Really just a couple of months. She moved into the neighborhood right before Davey and I moved out."

"Did you ever think that maybe she was just the tiniest bit . . . odd?"

"Odd?" I repeated sweetly. Truth be told, Amber and I hadn't exactly hit it off. "You mean aside from the missing husband and the half-dozen cats?"

"Thank God," Bob said on an exhale. "I thought maybe it was just me. What's up with James, anyway?"

James was Amber's husband. Or at least that was what Sam and I had been told. Personally, I'd never even seen any evidence that the man actually existed.

"How should I know? You're the one who's been living here a year. I never even met the guy."

"Me either," said Bob.

"You're kidding. All this time and James *still* hasn't shown up?"

"Not that I've seen. But what do I know, it's not like I'm keeping tabs on the place. Maybe he comes in late at night and leaves before dawn."

"Like a vampire?"

"Or a confirmed workaholic. Amber says he travels a lot on business."

"I seem to remember her telling me that too. Something about importing or maybe exporting?"

"Not that it's any of my business," said Bob. "But it just seems unusual that the guy is *never* around."

"Maybe they're divorced and she doesn't want to admit it."

"Who wouldn't admit that? Everyone's divorced these days, present company included. I was thinking along more sinister lines. Maybe Amber cut him up into little pieces and buried him in the basement."

"You've been reading Edgar Allan Poe again, haven't you?"

"Thomas Harris," said Bob. "And that guy's writing is keeping me up nights. But anyway, I was thinking you should ask her."

"What? Where her husband is?"

"Something like that. You know, just have a little chat. Woman to woman. And find out what the heck is going on over there."

Right, I thought. That would be the day.

Bob used to be an accountant and he's very precise. He showed up that evening at six on the dot, bearing not only hamburgers, but also a dozen ears of corn and a bucket of cole slaw.

"The cookout was my idea," he said. "The least I could do is bring the ingredients."

Most visitors to our house these days go directly to Kevin. A new baby is a source of fascination, a magnet for parents and wannabe parents alike. A bundle of joy that's somebody else's responsibility. What's not to like?

People ooh and aah over Kevin. They tickle his tiny feet and ask if they can hold him. They comment on how much his eyes or his nose looks like ours. They remark on how much he's grown.

But Bob's arrival was different. He walked in the front door, handed the bags he was carrying to Sam, and yelled up the stairs to Davey to see if he wanted to have a catch.

Davey had heard the doorbell ring and was already on his way down. He skidded around the newel post at the top of the staircase and came flying down the steps. At the speed he was moving, it was a wonder he didn't kill himself. Ah, the joys of being nine.

"Sure thing!" he cried.

His baseball and catcher's mitt were in the mudroom off the kitchen. Davey went dashing in that direction, then abruptly stopped.

"You probably want to hold Kevin first," he said.

"Who?" asked Bob.

"Kevin. You know . . . *the baby*."

Bob waggled his eyebrows comically. "You guys have a baby around here?"

Davey giggled. "He's my little brother."

"I'll bet he's not as much fun as you."

"That's not what most people think."

"Lucky for you, I'm not most people."

Bob's arms reached out to grab his son and pull him close. His fingers tickled Davey's sides. Davey squealed in delight and struggled to get away. When he realized Bob's hold was too strong, he gave up trying to escape and began to tickle his father back.

Bob dodged one way, then the other. He looked up and winked at me over Davey's head. "Truce!" he cried. "You're killing me here."

It was a good thing he called a halt to the tickle fight. Bob didn't realize it, but the Poodles, who'd been milling around the hallway, were about to enter the fray. I was betting they were going to take Davey's side.

"All right, let's get serious. Are you going to throw a ball with me or not? Don't tell me I have to play catch with *the baby*."

"You can't play catch with him." Davey was laughing and trying to catch his breath. "He's too little."

"That settles it then," said Bob. "He's not nearly as much fun as you are. Now go get your stuff while I see if Sam wants to join us."

"What about me?" I said as Davey went scampering toward the back of the house. "Don't I get an invitation?"

"Men play ball," Bob pronounced in a deep, manly voice. "Women cook."

"Easy to see why you're not married," said Sam. He was still holding the groceries. "You guys go ahead and play. I've got a grill to fire up."

The rest of the evening proceeded at a leisurely pace. Davey and Bob played ball while Sam and I cooked. It stayed light past eight o'clock and we ate outside on the deck.

I balanced Kevin on my lap, holding him with one hand and eating with the other. The Poodles, who knew a good opportunity when they saw it, gathered around my chair and waited for handouts to fall their way. Fortunately, my rules about feeding dogs from the table aren't nearly as strict as Aunt Peg's.

Kevin stayed up past his usual bedtime, falling asleep in my arms at nine. Bob stayed long enough to help with the cleanup. Before he left, I saw him slip Davey a baseball card for his growing collection. Davey ran upstairs to add it to the others.

It was the kind of evening where everything seems to go just right. It was comfortable, peaceful, and perfectly ordinary. The way my life had been proceeding for a while now. You don't get much luckier than that.

As we were coming from two different directions, Alice and I had agreed to meet at Pine Ridge. The facility opened at seven-thirty for early arrivals. I'd been up since before six with Kevin. Getting there in time to meet Alice at eight-thirty was no problem at all.

The previous day the office had been empty when I'd arrived in early afternoon. Mornings were a totally different story. Rush hour was in full swing.

"Goodness," Alice said as we joined the back of the line waiting to check in. "You didn't mention this place was such a madhouse."

A Springer Spaniel, an Airedale, and a Bichon Frise held the spots in front of us. All three of their owners, two men and a woman, were dressed for success. One of the men was tapping his toe while he waited. His dog, the Airedale, pounced repeatedly on the tip of the highly polished loafer as it rose and fell.

73

"Yesterday, it wasn't. I guess I wasn't here during a peak time. But this is good to know, especially if this is about the time when you plan to be dropping Berkley off. We should be sure to ask Steve how long a wait to expect on an average day."

This time we'd called and made an appointment. Alice had spoken with the co-owner the previous afternoon, and he was expecting us. Indeed, as our wait to check in with Madison stretched from five minutes to ten, I was surprised that Steve didn't come looking for us.

A staff member entered the room through the back door to collect the Bichon. His owner handed over the leash and quickly disappeared. Dog and owner parted without much visible regret on either side. I figured that either boded well for the care offered by the facility or badly for the relationship between the Bichon and its owner.

The line inched forward. Now the Airedale's owner was leaning over the counter and talking to Madison.

Realizing that his owner's attention was occupied elsewhere, the big red-and-black terrier turned around and touched noses with the Springer behind him. The spaniel's owner was talking on her cell phone and paying no attention to her charge. The Springer wagged its stumpy tail.

An invitation had been offered and reciprocated. It didn't take a dog person to know what was going to happen next.

The Airedale lowered its front end to the ground, hindquarter high, thick tail whipping back and forth. The Springer jumped up on her hind legs, waving her front paws in the air. Dark eyes twinkling with mischief, the Airedale bounced up to join her.

The terrier was big and strong. His first leap snatched the leash out of his owner's hand. His second bound took him past the Springer and he landed on Alice's feet. She lost her balance and tumbled into me as the Springer in front of us whirled around to continue the game.

The spaniel's owner gave a little cry of distress. Her cell phone went flying.

I reached down and nabbed the Airedale's leash before he could make a run for it. The Springer's owner similarly tightened her grip.

"Cookie, settle down," she said sternly as she retrieved her phone and tucked it into her purse.

"Good catch," said the Airedale's owner. The man held out his hand and I placed the leash in it. "I hope Logan didn't hurt you?"

"No, we're fine." I spoke for both of us. "Is it always this slow in here?"

"No," he replied with a small frown. He had thin lips that were topped by a perfectly manicured moustache. "This is unusual. I don't know what's going on today."

"Mr. Cavanaugh?" Madison said from behind the counter. "We're ready for Logan now."

Another one of the kennel girls had appeared. Logan was delivered into her waiting hands and led away.

Another couple minutes passed while the procedure was repeated with the Springer spaniel. By the time Alice and I reached the front of the line, we were the only ones left in the office. It was nearly eight-fifty.

"We have an appointment with Steve Pine," Alice said to Madison. She sounded as impatient as I felt.

"Time?" the teenager inquired brightly.

"Twenty minutes ago," I said. I didn't sound nearly as bright.

"Oh."

She glanced over at the clock on the wall. "I don't know what's keeping Steve. He should have been out here by now. Either he or Candy usually does the morning check-ins, but I haven't seen either of them yet today. They must be here; I saw their cars when I pulled in. Let me call around for you and see what I can find out."

That involved more waiting. Madison buzzed the offices, then the Dog House, then somebody's cell phone. And every time she spoke with someone, the conversation ended with her glancing over at us and shaking her head.

A Collie arrived for the day, followed by a Cavalier King Charles. Alice and I took seats in the waiting area. And all the while, I kept watching the door in the back wall. I was expecting Steve to come bustling through it like he'd done the day before.

So when a woman on the other side screamed, a sound so shrill and panic-stricken that it made the hairs on the back of my neck rise, I was on my feet and pushing through the door before the sound had even died.

Candy was standing in the hallway. Her face was white; her mouth, half open. Her hands were raised and clasped tightly together in front of her chest as if in prayer.

"What's the matter?" I asked.

She looked at me with stricken eyes but didn't answer.

"What?" I said again.

I was striding toward her as I spoke, and then, all at once, I saw what she'd seen.

Steve's office door had been pushed partway open. Just inside, a body was lying on the floor. Steve's face was turned upward and his eyes stared sightlessly at the ceiling. A dark pool of blood surrounded his head like a viscous halo.

Steve wouldn't be making our meeting that morning. Or any other meetings for that matter.

7

"**C**all nine-one-one," I said quickly. It's what people are supposed to do under circumstances like this. Even when they knew better than to think it would do any good.

Madison must have followed me into the corridor because she was standing behind me, staring over my shoulder. I grabbed her, turned her around, and gave her a little push.

"Go!" I said. "Call for the police and an ambulance."

"Oh God, no!" said Candy. She backed away down the hall, her head shaking frantically from side to side. "No, no, no . . ."

The door at the far end, the one that led outside, drew open. Bailey came walking in. She and Candy just about collided, though Candy didn't even seem to notice.

Now her hands were up and covering her mouth. As if they were holding in a scream.

"Bailey, stop right there!" I said.

The groomer complied, then looked at me in confusion. "What's going on?"

"There's been an accident. The police are coming. Does that door have a lock on it?"

"Yeah, sure. I guess so."

"Would you please let yourself out and lock the door behind you?"

Bailey glanced over at Candy, who was now standing with her back pressed against the wall. Her eyes were wide and unfocused. She looked like she was going into shock.

"Who put you in charge?" Bailey asked me.

"I did," I said firmly. "Now go."

She looked once more at Candy as if hoping for guidance. None was forthcoming.

"Believe me," I said, "you don't want to be here right now. I mean it. Go!"

Bailey finally complied. I saw her adjust something on the knob and heard the latch click shut behind her.

The phone in Steve's office began to ring. I ignored it.

Candy was ignoring everything. I doubt she even heard the sound.

After four rings, it stopped. Then the phone in Candy's office across the hall began to shrill. Someone was persistent. And they were going to have to wait.

"I called," said Madison. She opened the other door but didn't enter the hallway. Her eyes looked up, down, anywhere but at Steve's office. "They said someone's coming."

"Good. Make sure no one comes in here until they get here, okay?"

"What about her?" Madison was looking at someone behind me.

Alice. I'd forgotten all about her. Apparently she'd followed me into the hallway, too, and had been standing there the whole time.

"I'm going," said Alice. She, too, had her hand over her mouth. I hoped she wasn't about to throw up. "I'll wait for you out in the reception area. Unless . . ."

"What?"

"Do you need any help?"

Bless her heart. Once a mother, always a mother. Alice looked like the last thing on earth she wanted to do was get more involved in the situation than she already was. But still she had to make the offer. What a trooper. What a friend.

"I'm just standing here," I said.

That wasn't strictly true. I was also keeping an eye on Candy. The paramedics were going to be too late to help Steve, but his sister looked like she could probably benefit from their services.

"Why don't you wait out front?" I said. Alice looked like she could use some fresh air. "When the police get here, you can show them where to go."

Alice disappeared. That left me and Candy alone in the back half of the building. Well—and Steve —but I wasn't counting him.

Candy hadn't moved at all for several minutes. She was making a small mewling sound that seemed to come from deep within her throat.

Skirting the doorway to Steve's office as widely as possible, I tiptoed down the hallway to her. "Are you okay?"

Stupid question under the circumstances, but it was the first thing that came to mind.

Still mute, she shook her head.

"Is there anything I can do? Someone you want me to call?"

"Is he . . . dead?" she whispered.

I hadn't checked. After one look through the open doorway, I hadn't gone any closer. But something, presumably a bullet, had opened up Steve's cheek. And then there was the blood. Lots and lots of blood.

"Yes," I said gently. "He's dead. Do you want to sit down?"

Candy took me literally. It was as if her bones had suddenly stopped supporting her. Back still braced against the wall, she simply slid down it until she reached the floor.

I sat down beside her.

"How did this happen?" she asked.

"I don't know."

"Someone must have broken in. A robber. We don't keep a lot of money here. What did they want?"

"I don't know," I said again. It was the only thing I could think to say.

Candy lifted stricken eyes to mine. "Last night, last time I saw Steve . . ."

Saw Steve alive, she meant. Neither one of us needed to say it.

I nodded.

"He and I had a fight . . . an argument over something stupid. How terrible is that? And now I'll never have a chance to fix things. . . ."

Candy's slender body began to shake. Then she was alternately sobbing loudly and gasping for breath. I wrapped an arm around her and pulled her close. It was warm in the hallway, but her skin felt cold and clammy against mine.

Twenty-four hours earlier, we had been strangers. But right now, at least for the moment, I was the closest thing to comfort she had.

The wait for help to come seemed interminable, but Alice told me later that the first police car arrived in under ten minutes. It was followed shortly by an ambulance. Moments after that, the building was swarming with activity.

I handed Candy off to a sympathetic EMT and joined Alice out in front of the building. The people who handled this type of thing for a living had arrived. They would know what to do. Our part in the calamity had ended.

"Ma'am?" An officer came running out of the office after me. "I'm going to need to get your information. And could you wait here until the detectives arrive? They're going to want to ask you some questions."

"I don't know anything," I said.

"We still need to talk to you."

The officer took out a pad and wrote down Alice's and my names, addresses, and phone numbers. Then we went and sat in Alice's car and waited some more.

I called Sam and told him I'd been held up. There was no point in going into details over the phone. Later, after I'd put some distance between myself and everything that had happened, it would be easier to talk about.

Authorities continued to arrive. Marked and unmarked police cars pulled in next to ours, followed by a coroner's van.

"I know things like this have happened to you before." Alice watched the activity that bustled around us with huge, haunted eyes. "How do you stand it?"

"Not easily," I said quietly.

"I mean, you went right in there and took charge. Like you knew what you were doing."

I shook my head. It hadn't been that big a deal.

"Anybody could have done it. All I knew was to call for the authorities and try not to mess up the area. I learned that from watching TV."

Alice looked at me speculatively. "You talked to Steve yesterday, didn't you?"

"Yes, he was the one who gave me a tour around." I paused and swallowed heavily, remembering Steve's energy, his enthusiasm, his affection for the dogs like Nathan, the old Dachshund. What a terrible shame this was. What a loss.

"So now you're involved again."

"No, I'm not." The protest was automatic. "I'm a mother now."

"You were a mother before and that never stopped you."

"That was different."

"How?"

I didn't answer and Alice didn't push me.

"I wonder what will happen to this place now," she said instead.

The two of us gazed over at the front building where things seemed to be calming down. People were still going in and out, but they weren't moving with the same sense of urgency they'd had when they first arrived.

"Maybe Candy will continue to run it. Otherwise, an awful lot of dog owners are going to be out of luck."

"Including me," Alice said glumly.

Eventually the police remembered that we were still waiting there to speak with them. A detective came out of the building, stopped and looked around, then strode our way.

He was tall and stocky, carrying more fat than muscle on a frame that looked like it might once have belonged to an athlete. In deference to the heat of the day, he had pulled off his jacket, rolled up his shirtsleeves, and loosened the knot of his tie.

He leaned down and looked in the open car window. "I'm Detective Minton. Are you the ladies who found the body?"

"No." I replied before Alice could speak.

Over the years, I've discovered that it pays to be very precise when talking to the police. Otherwise, they have a tendency to quickly form conclusions that give them what they need rather than waiting patiently and listening for the truth.

"We're the women who came running when we heard Candy scream," I corrected. "She was the one who found her brother's body."

"You mind stepping out of the car? I have a couple of questions for you."

We complied. The detective stood for a minute and looked both of us over carefully.

It was, no doubt, a gesture designed to make us feel guilty. Maybe it was working on Alice, but I'd dealt with the police often enough that I was pretty much immune. If he was hoping that we'd fall to our knees and confess, and he could have the case wrapped up by noon, he'd come to the wrong place.

"Which one of you is Miss Travis?" he asked.

"It's Ms.," I said.

It's not that I'm a fanatic for feminism or political correctness, but calling myself Miss negated Sam's presence in my life. And Mrs. didn't exactly work either, considering that I'd kept my own name rather than taking Sam's. So the semantics of the situation were a little tricky.

And judging by the expression on Minton's face, I could see that they'd already caused us to get off on the wrong foot.

"*Ms.* Travis," he repeated. Now there was a hostile edge to his tone. "What were you and Ms. Brickman doing here this morning?"

"Alice and I had an appointment with Steve Pine."

"About?" He gaze swung back and forth between us.

"My dog, Berkley," said Alice. "He's a Golden Retriever. I got him for my kids for Christmas. Not last year, the year before."

Oh Lord, I thought, I'd forgotten about that. When Alice got nervous, she babbled. And once she got going, who knew what she might blurt out in an attempt to be helpful? I hoped she didn't babble us right into trouble.

"How nice."

The detective favored her with a smile. Like he was sure they were going to be friends. This was a variation on good cop/bad cop that I hadn't seen before, considering that there was only one of him and two of us. Nevertheless, it wasn't hard to see that I wasn't the favorite.

"And your dog, Berkley, he comes here for day care?"

"Not yet, but I was hoping he was going to be accepted. You see, I'm going back to work. For the first time in years, I'm going to be gainfully employed. Well, you know, not just a mother. It will be mostly half days in the beginning, but then full time in the fall when the kids go back to school. Carly and Jocy are their names. She's seven and he's nine. Would you like to see pictures?"

Amazingly, she got that all out without even pausing for breath.

"No, that won't be necessary. So you came here this morning to meet with Steve Pine. Did you see him?"

"No," I said. The answer seemed pretty obvious to me. "He was dead."

"And when did you find that out?"

"Right after Candy screamed."

"Where were you when that happened?"

Alice shot me a look. I don't think she liked my brief answers any more than the detective did. She decided to take over and elaborate.

"We were sitting in the reception area. And we'd been waiting, like . . . *forever*. The girl behind the desk was supposed to be locating him for us, but she kept stopping to do other things."

"Like what?"

"Check in morning arrivals," I said.

"You mean dogs?"

I left that one for Alice. Once again, it seemed to me that the answer had to be obvious.

She nodded her head. Her strawberry blond curls bobbed up and down. "There was a little white one, and a big terrier-type dog, and a Collie, and a couple of spaniels, right?" She looked to me for confirmation.

Close enough, I thought. "You got it."

"Okay, so you were waiting for Mr. Pine to come to the front office. What time was that, by the way?"

"We got here at eight-thirty," I said.

"And then what happened?"

With help from Alice, I walked Detective Minton through the rest of the morning's events. It didn't take very long. As I had told the other officer in the beginning, we didn't really know anything.

"Here's what I want to know," he said when we were finished. "According to Madison Vega, you were here yesterday."

The detective nodded in my direction.

"That's right," I said.

"You didn't think that was worth mentioning?"

"No, not particularly."

"Why not?"

"Well for one thing, Steve Pine seemed fine yesterday."

Okay, maybe that was a little rude, but *come on.* Plenty of people had been at Pine Ridge both days, including probably most of the employees and the clients. So why was my presence, in particular, considered to be suspicious?

Detective Minton was simply yanking my chain, I suspected. Just because he could.

"Melanie was here yesterday because I asked her to come," Alice said quickly. "I asked her to

88

scope out the place because she knows more about dogs than I do and I wanted to be sure that Berkley would be happy here. I mean, I know he's a Golden Retriever and all, but other than that he's really like part of the family. Joey and Carly have their own activities now so they don't care what I do during the day. But if Berkley was going to be miserable all the time I was gone, then maybe I was going to have to rethink the whole job thing, you know?"

"I see," said Minton. "I guess that explains it."

Either that, or he just wanted to find a way to put an end to the flow of words.

"One last question. Do either of you have any idea why someone would want Steve Pine dead?"

"I met him for the first time yesterday," I said. "And Alice only spoke to him on the phone. We don't have a clue."

It looked like we weren't the only ones. Detective Minton frowned at our answer and dismissed us.

Alice and I parted with a heartfelt hug. Then we got in our cars and went home.

8

Aunt Peg showed up at our house that afternoon. I swear, sometimes I think she has a police scanner hidden away somewhere. Nobody gets news faster than she does.

Sam and I were just finishing lunch. Davey, who can scarf down a peanut butter and jelly sandwich in under a minute, had already left the table. He was out on the deck, watching Kevin in his baby swing.

From what we could hear, the two of them seemed to be engaged in a conversation about cars. Davey was doing most of the talking.

While he was out of earshot, I'd been bringing Sam up to date on the morning's events. I was only about halfway through when we heard the doorbell ring, followed almost immediately by the sound of Aunt Peg letting herself in.

The Poodles jumped up and raced to the front of the house. A minute later, they were back. Their tails were up, their step jaunty, as they preceded Aunt Peg into the kitchen. They were as proud of themselves as if they'd conjured her out of thin air. Which, come to think of it, maybe they thought they had.

Aunt Peg passed out peanut butter dog biscuits, and watched in satisfaction as the crew settled down around her feet to chew on the treats. Then she pulled out a chair at the table and sat down.

"It's show time," she announced grandly.

"Don't you mean show-and-tell?" I asked.

"That goes without saying. I can hardly continue Davey's handling lessons without speaking."

"Oh," I said. "That's what you were talking about?"

Sam smirked. I kicked him under the table.

"Certainly. What else?"

When I didn't reply right away, Aunt Peg's eyes narrowed.

"Now what?" She glanced outside, saw Davey and Kevin happy together on the deck. "Sam, you're well?"

He nodded. He was enjoying this.

"Faith, Eve, Casey, Raven, Tar?"

The four female Poodles lifted their heads in turn. Tar just kept eating.

"I see present company is well accounted for." Aunt Peg relaxed slightly. "So who died?"

Talk about cutting straight to the chase.

"Why do you always assume the worst?" I asked.

"Because, my dear, around you that usually seems to be a safe assumption. Anybody I know?"

"Steve Pine," I admitted.

"Mr. Doggie Day Care?"

"The very same. Alice and I had an appointment with him this morning. We were going to ask about dog food and vets on call."

"Worthwhile questions," said Aunt Peg.

Of course they were. She was the one who'd come up with them.

"He was dead when you arrived?"

I nodded.

"Cause of death?" she asked.

"He was shot."

"Oh my."

Aunt Peg's hand dropped down beside her chair. Her fingers began to stroke the nearest Poodle. In times of stress, there's nothing like a dog to provide a soothing influence.

"The police?" she asked.

"On the scene shortly thereafter. Possibly there still."

"It sounds as though your friend Alice had better start looking for other arrangements for Berkley."

"That's all you have to say?"

She tipped her head inquiringly. "Should there be more?"

"Don't you want to know who did it?"

"Well, if you knew *that,* why didn't you say so?"

"I don't."

"Then why did you ask?"

Sam had stopped smirking. Now he was grinning.

"Who's on first?" he asked.

Aunt Peg sent him a look. "Now you're just being silly."

Then she sat up again and got down to business. "Let's recap. Steve Pine, whom you met yesterday, is dead today."

I nodded.

"You don't know who did it or presumably why."

"Right."

"Yet you seem to think that I should want to know the answers to these questions?"

Aunt Peg's voice rose slightly. Her tone was tinged with just the merest hint of incredulity. I wasn't having any of it.

"You *always* want to know the answers," I said.

"I don't even know these people. Or their dogs," she added after a slight pause. "Why should I want to get involved in their business?"

"It's what you do."

"No," Aunt Peg replied. "Unless I'm very much mistaken, it's what *you* do."

She was very much mistaken all right.

But I'm a new mom and my time's at a premium. I wasn't about to use any more of it trying to correct her. So I changed the subject instead.

"Everybody up," I said to the Poodles. "You heard the lady. It's show time."

Confirming Aunt Peg's assertion that Davey was enjoying his introduction to handling, my son was delighted to discover that he was going to have another lesson. Even better, a group lesson.

"We've been working solo for several weeks," said Aunt Peg. "Now it's time for you to learn how to manage your dog in company."

While Sam went and got several show leashes from the hooks hanging in the grooming room, I took a baggie of dried liver out of the freezer and zapped it in the microwave. As soon as the distinctive smell filled the air, the Poodles gathered around. They'd all been show dogs at one time; they knew something was up.

"I'll handle Eve." I slipped the thin nylon noose over her head and tightened it just behind her ears. "Faith, you can sit this one out."

As a consolation prize, I snuck the older Poodle a big chunk of liver. She tucked it surreptitiously inside her lip and carried it out to a shady spot in the backyard.

"I'll take Tar," said Sam.

That was a smart move on his part as it prevented Davey from choosing to handle the big male dog who would probably prove to be too strong for him.

"What about me?" he asked.

"I think Raven will suit," said Aunt Peg. The dainty black bitch had originally been Sam's, but now, of course, she was part of our blended family. Raven was a sweetheart—smart, willing, and always eager to please. "She should do quite nicely."

In no time at all, Aunt Peg had the three of us, and our dogs, lined up in front of her. Kevin, who wasn't the least bit impressed by the proceedings, had fallen asleep in his swing. Casey stayed behind on the deck to watch over him while the rest of us moved out into the spacious backyard.

At one point in her life, Peg had been the consummate exhibitor. She'd spent nearly every weekend on the road, traveling to show her Poodles. But more recently she'd turned her talents toward judging, rather than exhibiting. She was now approved to judge all the breeds in both the Non-Sporting and Toy groups.

For obvious reasons, I had never shown under Aunt Peg myself. But I had watched her judge on many occasions, and she took her duties very seriously. Peg was a fair, but demanding, taskmaster in the show ring. And any thoughts I might have entertained about her lowering her expectations for Davey's sake were rapidly dispelled.

"Sam, I want you in front," she said. "Melanie second. Davey, you'll bring up the rear for now. Keep an eye on what those in front of you are doing and try to follow suit."

"I thought I was supposed to be watching my dog," said Davey. "That's what you told me before."

He already had Raven posed four-square in a reasonably creditable stack, and the little bitch was cooperating beautifully. I made a mental note to slip her an extra treat when we were finished.

"You have two eyes, don't you?" Aunt Peg said tartly. "Do both at the same time. Nobody told you this was going to be easy."

A giggle from the end of the line signaled that Davey wasn't upset by Aunt Peg's sharp tone. At his age, I'd have probably wilted. Hell, there are still times when Peg manages to intimidate me. Not Davey; he calmly returned to working with his dog.

Aunt Peg braced her feet apart, crossed her arms over her chest, and stood and stared at us for a minute. Her eyes moved slowly down the line.

Tar had retired from the show ring only recently; Sam was free-baiting him—standing off in front and letting the dog show himself. Eve was a little rusty. I set her feet where I wanted them, then used one of my hands to support her head, the other to lift her tail. Davey maneuvered Raven into position, then checked to see what I was doing with my hands and did the same with his. Good boy.

Still maintaining her silence, Aunt Peg approached the front of the line. Sam stepped back to Tar's side, balled his leash up in his hand, and prepared to show his dog to the judge. Aunt Peg leaned down and placed her hands on the Poodle's head.

Her eyes never leaving the Poodle in front of her, she said, "Davey, what are you doing?"

"Just standing here."

"Wrong answer."

Davey thought for a moment before trying again. "I'm making Raven look good."

"Still wrong."

"No, it's not." He sounded surprised. "I'm a dog handler. That's what I'm supposed to do."

Aunt Peg straightened and stepped back. "Before when we practiced, you were by yourself. If a situation like that were to occur in the ring, you would have the judge's undivided attention. In a class of one, you would be in the ring for a relatively short amount of time and you would be expected to work your dog the entire time you were there."

"Okay." Davey reached down and gave Raven a pat. "I can do that."

"But this is an entirely different situation. Now you have competition."

My son sent a cheeky grin down the line. "I'm not scared."

"Let me approach this another way," said Aunt Peg. "Which takes longer to judge, a class with one dog in it or a class that has three dogs?"

Davey stopped and thought before answering. I could tell he suspected a trap.

"I guess the one with three dogs," he said finally.

"Correct. Now what if you had a class with six dogs in it or even ten?"

"Longer still?"

"Correct again," said Aunt Peg. "And in those larger classes, the judge won't be able to pay attention to everyone at once. Knowing that, a smart handler will give his dog a break whenever he gets the chance. If you make Raven keep posing now while I'm looking at Tar, and then still while I'm looking at Eve, the end result is that she's going to be tired and bored by the time I approach her. When it's your turn for the individual examination, you want to show the judge a dog that's fresh and eager, not one that felt that way five minutes ago."

"Okay," said Davey. "How do I do that?"

While Sam and I maintained our positions, Aunt Peg showed Davey how to let Raven fall back out of line and relax.

"Keep her attention," she instructed. "You don't want her sniffing the ground or dropping her tail. Use your squeaky toy. Let her play a bit."

"Can she sit down?"

"No!" Three voices cried in unison.

Poodles never, under any circumstances, sit down once the elaborate show ring hairdo has been banded and sprayed into place. A movement like that would pull apart the topline and totally destroy their distinctive look.

"Sheesh," said Davey. "Don't shoot me or anything. I was just asking."

The lesson continued and Aunt Peg spared no effort to put us through our paces. Davey was pleased to note that she criticized my handling technique every bit as harshly as she picked apart his own. I was not nearly as amused.

After the first go-round, Aunt Peg had Davey move to the front of the line. A short while after that, she placed him in the middle. And each time she adjusted his technique to suit his new position.

Davey worked and laughed and scrambled to keep up with her rapid-fire instructions. Even Sam and I found ourselves hustling. Aunt Peg's sharp eyes missed nothing, even when she appeared to be facing in the opposite direction. The three Poodles, remembering how much fun they'd had in the show ring, got into the spirit of the exercise and began to show themselves off as well.

Finally, half an hour later, Aunt Peg made her final cut. By that time, I was flushed and out of breath. Kevin was beginning to stir in his swing.

Aunt Peg lifted her arm dramatically. One might have thought she was anointing Best in Show at Westminster. She pointed to Sam and Tar for first place. Davey and Raven came in second. Eve and I brought up the rear.

Davey wasn't happy with the results. He pushed out his lower lip.

"I wanted to win," he said.

Aunt Peg wasn't having any of it.

"You didn't deserve to win," she told him. "At least not today. With more work on your part, that could change. In time, with practice, you might be as good a handler as Sam."

Davey shot me a sly look. He made it perfectly obvious that he had to look back over his shoulder to do so.

"I'm already better than Mom."

"Hey!" I cried. "No fair. I'm a little out of practice."

"Your technique needs working on," said Aunt Peg.

"I'm rusty."

"You've let yourself get careless. You can do better."

Like I'd never heard that from Aunt Peg before.

Up on the deck, Kevin's swing had stopped moving. The baby opened his eyes and looked around. Then he gave an experimental wail. Casey quickly sat up and pushed her warm nose into his small hand. Immediate response, canine style.

I handed Eve's leash to Sam and went to pick up the baby. Kevin's diaper needed changing, and after that he'd be ready to eat again. I was finished handling for the day.

"There's a dog show at the end of the month," Aunt Peg mentioned casually.

I'd been on my way inside the house. Now I stopped and turned around. Even Aunt Peg's most offhand comments usually have an ulterior motive.

"There's a dog show at the end of every month," I said.

You know, just to goad her. That comment about my being careless was really uncalled for. Even if it was true.

"I was thinking we might put in an entry," said Peg.

Davey's head jerked up. His gaze spun back and forth between us. Even from across the yard, his excitement was palpable. How could I ever have doubted that this was something he wanted to do?

"For me?" he asked.

"For you and Custer in the Novice Junior Class," Aunt Peg confirmed. "Think you can be ready by then?"

"I'm ready now!"

"Not quite," Sam said with a smile. "But we like your enthusiasm. And that gives us three more weeks to work on things."

"Great!" cried Davey. Then he looked back at me, holding the new baby in my arms. "But what about Kevin? He keeps you guys pretty busy."

"Are you kidding?" I asked. "Kevin's going to come with us to the dog show and watch you handle Custer in your class. Think how proud he's going to be of his older brother."

"You mean me?"

I walked back out to the yard, leaned down, and gathered Davey into a hug so that I had both my sons encircled in my arms. Davey squirmed as I knew he would; he's at that age where mothers are an embarrassment. Kevin laughed and tried to grab his brother's nose.

"Of course I mean you," I said, stepping back and disentangling the two boys. "Kevin's just a baby, he doesn't know anything yet. He's going to learn lots of things by watching you. So you're going to have to be sure to set a good example."

"I'll try," Davey said solemnly.

"I know you will. I'm counting on you." I looked over at Aunt Peg. "Go ahead and send in the entry. We'll be there with bells on."

"Aww, Mom," cried Davey. "That's not fair. Can't I just use a leash like all the other kids?"

9

"Guess what?" said Alice, two days later.

I was out in the yard, weeding our fledgling vegetable garden, when my cell phone rang. Truth be told, I'm not much of a gardener. This was my first attempt to grow something that people might actually be expected to eat.

Having a baby had ramped up my nesting instincts and this was the result. So far, however, I wasn't sure whether my weed-pulling was helping or hindering the tomatoes I was trying to grow. So frankly, I was perfectly happy to be interrupted.

I removed my gardening gloves and sat down in the grass. With luck, this might take a while.

"Candy Pine called me," Alice said. "Apparently she's been touching base with all the Pine Ridge clients after . . . you know, what happened. She wanted to assure me that business is going to proceed as usual at Pine Ridge and that I shouldn't make any other dog care arrangements for Berkley."

"So what are you going to do?"

"I don't know. It would feel really weird to go back over there."

Faith had been lying nearby, chewing on a stick, while I worked. Now that I was taking a break, she got up and came over. The Poodle lay down beside me and rested her head in my lap. I tangled my fingers in her topknot absently as I spoke.

"Then maybe you want to choose another place," I said. "It's not like you'd made a commitment to Pine Ridge. The way things turned out, you never even filled out an application."

"In theory you're right, but here's the problem. There *are* no other places. At least none that are conveniently located. Land is at such a premium in lower Fairfield County that the other similar facilities I managed to find are all pretty far away. We're talking Ridgefield or Milford."

"Well, that won't work," I said flatly. The whole point was for Alice to drop Berkley off on her way to work, not commute an extra hour out of her way.

"Tell me about it."

"So now what?"

"I guess I'm thinking that I should give Pine Ridge another try. Um . . . Mel?"

It wasn't like I couldn't guess what she was going to ask next.

"I don't want to go back there alone. I mean, who would? So how busy are you today? What would you think of going with me?"

I surveyed the yard and sighed. "Here's how busy I am. I'm gardening."

Alice snorted into the phone. I was pretty sure she was trying to cover a laugh.

"You hate plants."

"I don't hate them exactly. I just never seem to have much luck keeping them alive. I thought maybe outdoor plants were different. You know, like grass. That stuff pretty much grows itself. I figured tomatoes could do the same thing."

"And are they?" asked Alice.

"Not so far," I admitted.

"What about Kevin?"

The change of subject threw me for a moment, but I rallied.

"He's growing just fine."

"That's not what I meant." Now she was laughing. "Do you want to bring him with us?"

Notice how she'd moved us smoothly to the assumption that we both were going to Pine Ridge. As if I'd already agreed to that. Which I was pretty sure I hadn't.

What the heck, I thought. I wasn't accomplishing anything constructive in the garden. My assault on the weeds, or the tomatoes, or whatever it was I'd been pulling out of the ground could wait.

"Sam's here," I said. "I'm pretty sure he can cover for me. Why don't you come and pick me up?"

"I'll be there in ten minutes."

That was fast for Alice. She must have already had one foot out the door.

Inside the house, I found Sam holed up in his office. He was playing around with a new software design for some clients he'd had for years.

Everything else was quiet. That in itself was unusual in my experience, but it felt kind of nice. Soccer camp had started and Davey wouldn't be home until late afternoon. Kevin was upstairs napping in his crib. The baby monitor on Sam's credenza was blissfully silent.

"Think you can hold down the fort for an hour?" I asked.

Sam looked up from his computer screen. "Shouldn't be a problem. Where are you going?"

"Alice is picking me up. She still needs a place for Berkley and Pine Ridge is open for business again. She wants to go have another look."

"Sure," said Sam. "That's fine."

He sounded distracted and probably was. Otherwise, having uttered the Pine Ridge name, I might have been subjected to more questions. Sam was looking in my direction, but I was willing to bet that his thoughts were still centered on the application on the screen.

"I shouldn't be long," I said.

"Right. See you later." He was back to work before I'd even left the room.

I let myself out and walked down to the end of the driveway to wait for Alice so that the Poodles wouldn't bark at her arrival and wake up Kevin. True to her word, she appeared a few minutes later.

"I called Candy back and told her we were coming," she said as I climbed in the car.

I reached around and fastened my seatbelt. Alice was already pulling away from the curb.

"Good. Let's hope this visit works out better than last time."

Alice lifted her foot from the gas pedal. Immediately, the Honda began to slow. She took her eyes from the road and turned to look at me.

"If you think for one minute that it won't, you had better tell me now. Because if there's even a remote possibility of something else going wrong, I'm not going."

"I was kidding," I said quickly.

That wasn't strictly true, but I figured it probably made Alice feel better. At any rate, she resumed driving.

"When you were talking to Candy, what did she say about Steve?" I asked.

"Nothing."

"Nothing?"

"Not one word about the whole business. She never even mentioned his name. And it's not like I was going to bring it up."

"I wonder if the police know who killed him."

Alice spared me another look. "She probably would have said something about that."

"The newspapers haven't. I've been reading the

coverage and it hasn't even mentioned any suspects. But Candy is family. She must know more than *The Advocate* does."

"It's only been a couple of days. Maybe there's nothing to know yet."

Arriving midday, Alice and I found Pine Ridge looking much the same as it had on my first visit. There was only one other car in the front parking lot. Things appeared relatively quiet.

That illusion didn't last long, however. As we approached the door to the building, it flew open and a man came striding out. Candy filled the doorway behind him.

"Don't come back here," she said angrily. "We have nothing to say. Nobody here will talk to you."

Body blocking the doorway, hands on her hips, she watched until the man climbed into the other car. Then she turned away and noticed us for the first time. Her expression softened slightly, but she still looked annoyed.

"Sorry about that. Those damn reporters are everywhere. They're like ghouls, trolling around and searching for bad news."

Then abruptly, she stopped talking and stuck out her hand. "And they're making me so crazy that I've forgotten my manners. You must be Alice, Berkley's mom. It's nice to meet you. I'm Candy."

Considering what she'd been through recently, Candy was looking pretty good. No dark shadows or red-rimmed eyes. She smiled as she shook Alice's hand. I guessed she was working on keeping up a good front for the customers.

"Come on," she said. "Let's go inside and talk."

Madison glanced up briefly as we passed through the reception area, then went back to perusing her magazine. When Candy opened the door in the far wall that led to the offices, Alice hung back. I slowed my steps and waited for her.

"I'm sure there won't be anything to see," I said under my breath. Indeed, I could already see that the door to Steve's office was firmly shut.

"Even so . . ." Alice's voice squeaked.

Already halfway down the hall, Candy noticed for the first time that we hadn't kept up. She stopped and turned.

"I thought we'd talk in my office," she said. "Would you rather we went somewhere else?"

Even as I started to shake my head, Alice said, "Yes, please."

"No problem." Candy retraced her steps. "Let's go back outside."

With Candy leading the way, we took the path that circled the building and ended up on the back walkway that led to the outdoor paddocks. Dogs, some by themselves, others in groups, were frolicking in several of the enclosures.

The nearest paddock held Cookie, the English Springer we'd met the other day. The black and white spaniel had flopped down in the shade, panting. A red rubber ball was balanced between her front legs.

Candy glanced over at the dog and smiled. "Coming out here was a good idea. Now you can see for yourselves that everything at Pine Ridge is proceeding absolutely normally. Of course, Steve's death was a huge blow to us all, but I want you to know that the quality of our care and our customer service will remain unchanged."

The speech sounded like something Candy had repeated many times over the last couple of days. Days she should have been able to spend taking care of herself, rather than reassuring customers and tending to business.

"I know you said you had some questions for me," she said gamely. "Go ahead. Feel free to ask me anything."

I looked at Alice. She looked at me. I could tell we were both thinking the same thing. All at once, Aunt Peg's concerns about emergency vets and the quality of kibble just didn't seem that important anymore.

"I'm really sorry we took up your time," I said to Candy. "It looks like you're doing a great job. We don't have any questions. Alice just needs to fill out an application, and then we'll be on our way."

"All right. If you say so." Candy looked confused, but she recovered quickly. "We'll have to return to the front office then. Madison has the application forms at the check-in desk."

"I do need to know one thing," Alice said as we resumed our stroll. "How soon will you have an opening for Berkley? I'm going back to work and I need to be able to make plans."

"That's easy, we can take him right away. You can start whenever you're ready."

"Really? That would be great. I'd had the impression that you were full and there might be a wait involved."

"That was true before," Candy said slowly, "but now things have changed somewhat."

"You've lost clients in the last few days," I said.

A short, sharp nod betrayed her annoyance.

"For some reason, people seem to think that Steve *was* Pine Ridge. That without him, we'll be utterly unable to cope. And nothing could be further from the truth. Of course he was important here, on both a personal and a professional level. But this place has always been as much mine as it was his.

"Steve will be missed terribly in every aspect of what we do," Candy said fiercely. "But the business will go on. It has to. We've worked much too hard to lose everything we put into it now."

She turned her head away, and I got the impression that she was blinking back tears.

"Don't worry," I said gently, "you'll recover. It will take time, but eventually everything will get back to normal. Your good clients will remember what a great job you did for them and come back.

And as for the others, they're just idiots. Who needs them anyway?"

"Right." Candy's voice sounded watery. "Who needs them? You wouldn't believe some of the phone calls I've gotten. People say the most awful things. They tell me that after what happened to Steve, they wouldn't feel safe leaving their dogs in my care."

"Surely they don't blame you for what happened?" Alice said incredulously.

"Who even knows what they think anymore? These last few days have been totally surreal. My whole life has been turned upside down. As if what happened to Steve wasn't bad enough, now I have police and reporters nosing around everywhere. Everybody keeps asking questions but nobody has any answers. Those people who are worried about their dogs, how do they think *I* feel? This place is my business, my life, and now the worst thing is that I don't feel safe here anymore either."

Candy had stopped walking. Her hands were clenched into fists at her side. Her body hummed with tension.

"The only thing I can do . . . the only thing that makes my life even remotely bearable right now, is to put my head down and go back to work. I've lost my brother, but I'll be damned if I'm going to lose Pine Ridge too."

She looked so alone standing there, that without thinking I reached out and placed a comforting arm around her shoulders. I'm not big, but Candy felt tiny within the circle of my arms.

"Do you have any family you can call?" I asked. "Someone who could come and help out, or even just lend some support?"

"No, there was just me and Steve." She offered up a wan smile. "The two of us against the world. That's what we always said. So I guess there's just me now."

"And us," Alice said stoutly. She's always been a soft touch for a sad story. "Let us help you. Melanie and I will be your support team, at least until you can get back on your feet."

"Thank you. That's very kind of you, but it's really not necessary."

A tear rolled down her cheek. Candy lifted a hand and brushed it quickly away.

"Look at me," she said, "bearing up when people behave horribly and then crying the first time someone tries to be nice. I'm really sorry about all this. I don't know what's the matter with me."

"There's nothing the matter with you," I said firmly. "You're going through some terrible things right now. Of course they're taking a toll on you. There's no reason you should feel like you have to be strong. Certainly not in front of us."

Candy swallowed heavily and forced another smile. "I'm fine now. Really. Let me just run inside and get that application for you."

"Poor thing," Alice said as soon as Candy was out

of earshot. "We can't just fill out the application and walk away. We have to do something to help her."

"Candy needs customers," I said, "so you're helping her just by signing Berkley up for the program."

"There must be something more."

"Stop it," I said.

Alice was all innocence. "Stop what?"

"Trying to make me feel guilty for not getting involved in Candy's problems. It isn't working. I'm busy all the time now. I have a new baby."

"Liar. Even before Kevin arrived, you were always doing a hundred things at once. If you were so busy all the time, you wouldn't be gardening."

"I *like* gardening."

"Say that to my face."

All right, so I couldn't.

What people saw in gardening was beyond me. It was an activity built around weeds, bugs, and dirt. And in the end, if you were lucky, you ended up with tomatoes nearly as good as the ones you could buy at the market.

I knew some people felt a sense of accomplishment, growing things with their own hands. But to me, it was nothing but a source of frustration.

Alice was still standing there glaring at me when Candy returned, paper in hand.

"If you want, you can fill this out at home and

bring it back when you drop Berkley off for the first time," she said. Then she stopped and looked at the two of us. "What's the matter?"

"Melanie solves mysteries," Alice blurted out. "She does it all the time. She's really good at it."

Candy turned and stared. "You do?"

"I've been lucky a couple of times."

"She's being too modest," said Alice. "She's like Nancy Drew. Melanie finds murderers and makes them confess. I was thinking maybe you could use her help."

"Well . . . yeah." Candy exhaled softly. "You'd be willing to do that? Really?"

As if Alice had left me any choice.

"I could try," I said.

10

So we went back inside to talk.

This time, when Alice started looking squeamish as we headed toward the offices, I gave her a hard look and told her to get over it. This whole getting involved thing was her idea. Under the circumstances, the least she could do was buck up.

"Get over what?" Candy asked as she led the way into her office which was across the hall from Steve's.

"That." Alice nodded toward the closed door. "Sorry, but it just kind of gives me the creeps."

"Me too," Candy said with a grimace. "I locked Steve's office as soon as the police left and I haven't been in there since. They gave me the name of a cleaning service I'm supposed to call, but I haven't even been able to make myself do that. I know it's childish of me, but for now I'm just ignoring the whole thing."

"You should take all the time you need," I said. "I'm sure it's hard enough just being back at work this soon after what happened."

"It's not like I had a choice." Candy motioned us inside her office and shut the door.

The room was small; with the three of us in there, it felt crowded. A plump chair sat in one corner. It was occupied by a fawn colored Welsh Corgi with white feet and a white stripe down the middle of its face. The dog was snoozing contentedly on the cushion, but he opened his eyes at our arrival, hopped down off the chair, and trotted around the desk to say hello to Candy.

She stooped down to greet the Corgi, scratching behind his ears and cupping his wedge-shaped face in her hands. "This is Winston," she said. "He's my best friend."

"Cute," said Alice. "How old is he?"

"Four. I've had him since he was about eight months old. His breeder had sold him to a family that didn't know the first thing about how to raise a puppy and they messed him up pretty good. By the time he was seven months old, they'd decided he was incorrigible."

She snorted her disdain. "Can you believe that? Idiots. They dropped him off at the pound. Luckily a friend of Steve's was working there at the time. He called us and said we had to come and see this guy. We went right over, and the rest is history."

While she was talking, Winston had flopped over on his back on the rug. As Candy rubbed his stomach, the Corgi's back arched from side to side and his stumpy legs pumped joyously in the air.

"It looks like things turned out just right all the way around," I said.

Giving the dog a final pat, Candy stood up and opened a small closet. She pulled out a couple of folding chairs and handed one to each of us.

"Sorry, things are a little cramped in here. I'm not really set up for visitors. Mostly when we entertained clients we used Steve's office . . ."

"This will be fine," I said quickly.

Alice and I unfolded our chairs and sat down. Candy took a seat behind the desk. Winston hopped up and settled down on her lap.

"I hope you were serious about wanting to help," she said. "Because I'm going to take you up on your offer. I gotta tell you, the police don't seem to have accomplished much yet, and that's making me more than a little nervous."

"It would make me nervous, too, knowing that

there's a killer running around loose." Alice gave a little shudder.

"That's just the half of it." Candy's fingers fiddled absently with an eraser on her desk. "The first thing the police do is look at the people who are closest to the victim. I guess those are the ones who are easiest to make into suspects. It didn't take me long to figure out that puts me right on the firing line."

"There's a reason for that," I said practically. "The police want to know who gets the money. Steve was not only your brother. He was your partner. Did you inherit his share in the business?"

"Yes, just as he would have inherited mine if I had been the one to die first. We both wrote our wills up at the same time, and both of us were looking to protect Pine Ridge."

"What about insurance?"

Candy started to shake her head, then paused. "Well, sure, the business is covered. I mean, it has to be. But Steve didn't have any life insurance and neither do I. At our ages, neither one of us thought it was necessary."

I supposed Candy was finding out just how costly that mistake had been. Still, as far as the authorities were concerned, that would score a point in her favor.

"How was your relationship with your brother?" I asked. "Good?"

"Yes, of course." The answer was quick. And automatic.

"I'm not the police," I said. "Try to remember that I'm on your side."

"Even so," Candy replied, "there isn't that much else to say. We had the usual brother-sister squabbles, both when we were growing up and now. Working together, there were times we were at each other's throats—usually with good reason. Steve and I can both be pretty opinionated. And neither of us *ever* wanted to admit when we were wrong."

"You sound like me and my brother," I said. "Except that in our case, I'm always right and he's always wrong."

The three of us laughed together.

"So you get where I'm coming from," said Candy. "Steve and I made a good team. Work-wise, we compensated for each other's faults."

"Meaning?"

"Steve was meticulous about facts and figures, so he was the one who did the books. I have no aptitude for math and zero desire to sit inside on a nice afternoon poring over stupid numbers. On the other hand, put Steve out in the real world and he was an organizational nightmare. He'd think nothing of scheduling Bailey to groom a Sheltie and a Miniature Poodle in the same time slot, and then he couldn't figure out why she'd get pissed at him.

"Plus, his idea of being on time was to roll in somewhere an hour late. That was the kind of thing that drove me crazy, but Steve always figured it didn't matter what time he got started on something as long as he was willing to make up the time at the other end. That's why I always opened the place in the mornings, while Steve closed things up at night."

"What else do I need to know?" I asked. "What kinds of things have the detectives been asking you?"

"Their first thought was that Steve must have interrupted a robbery. Except that as far as I can tell, nothing was taken. The computers, Steve's wallet, his DVD player, everything is still here. Even the petty cash drawer behind the counter wasn't touched."

"What about the murder weapon?"

Candy shook her head. "The police didn't find a gun. And neither Steve nor I have ever owned one. So whoever killed my brother must have brought the weapon with him and then took it away again afterward."

About what I'd expected to hear. "Did Steve have any enemies?"

"Not . . . in a manner of speaking."

"Which means what, exactly?"

"You know." Candy flipped the eraser over and over between her fingers. "Calling someone an enemy seems pretty harsh. Of course, Steve got along with some people better than he does with others. He was a normal guy. That's the way life works."

"Sure," I agreed easily. "Tell me about the other people, the ones Steve didn't get along with."

Candy thought for a minute before continuing. "I guess I'd have to say that Adam Busch isn't terribly happy with us at the moment."

"And he is?"

"Our neighbor to the north." She turned in her chair and gestured vaguely in the direction of the window. "He seems to think that we're violating zoning laws by operating a business here."

"And are you?"

"Of course not. All our paperwork and permits are perfectly correct and up to date. But unfortunately, Mr. Busch is resistant to change. Up until not very long ago, this whole area of Stamford was residential. But you know how it is, the city's growing like a weed."

Alice and I both nodded. All of lower Fairfield County had changed enormously in the last twenty years, with Stamford leading the way when it came to development. Areas that had once been considered "country" now bordered towns that had expanded to meet them.

"We bought this land three years ago from an elderly couple who wanted to retire to North Carolina. Zoning around here had already been changed to allow for a commercial business on the property, but development hadn't yet begun to keep pace. When Mr. Busch found out we were planning to open a *kennel*"—Candy rolled her eyes— "he came marching right over and told us he wouldn't stand for it. As if it were up to him what we did on our own land."

"That was three years ago," I said. "Relations haven't improved since?"

"If anything, they've gotten worse. Which seemed crazy to Steve and me because now we're not the only business around here. The whole place has grown up, but since we were the first, it was like Busch blamed us for everyone that followed. He's gone to the city and lodged complaints about everything he can think of—the noise, the activity level, even the smell . . ."

Alice wrinkled her nose delicately. She sniffed several times, then shook her head.

"I know," said Candy. "I don't smell anything either. And we're right here in the middle of the place. He's several acres away. Believe me, we've tried hard to appease the guy, but nothing seems to help.

"To make things worse, Busch retired last year. So now he's got that much more time to devote to harrassing us. Steve was a pretty easygoing guy, but he was reaching the end of his rope."

I nodded. "So he had at least one enemy. Who else?"

"Well . . . maybe Lila Harrington."

"Who's she?"

"I guess you might call her a disgruntled client." Candy glanced briefly at Alice. "Not that we have many of those."

"Of course not," Alice said staunchly. She'd known Candy for less than a hour but she was already firmly on the woman's side.

"Tell me what happened."

"Lila has a female Shih Tzu named JoyJoy."

"Really?" I blinked. *JoyJoy?*

"I kid you not. JoyJoy is the love of Lila's life. She's like a member of the woman's family."

The name was awful, but I could well understand the sentiment.

"It turns out that Lila never had little JoyJoy spayed. And never bothered to mention that fact to us either."

"Don't you ask on the application?"

Candy flushed. "We do now."

"Uh oh," said Alice. She looked like she was trying not to laugh.

"It's not funny," Candy protested.

"I'm sure Lila didn't think so," I said.

"You'd be amazed how quickly two dogs can manage to get together under the circumstances. By the time we even figured out what was happening, Buster was on top of her and it was too late."

"Buster?" Now I was the one biting my lip and trying to keep a straight face. "I'm assuming he wasn't a Shih Tzu?"

"He's a Beagle . . . mix."

"A mutt?" Alice giggled. "JoyJoy hooked up with a mutt? The little hussy has no standards at all."

122

"Apparently not. Though the same can't be said of Lila Harrington. She threatened to sue us."

"On what grounds?"

"She said we were negligent in the performance of our duties. She had some lawyer convinced that JoyJoy was ruined for life. That once she'd mated with a mutt, she'd never be able to have purebred puppies."

"That's an old wives' tale," I said. "And one that doesn't even make sense. No one believes that anymore."

"Lila did. She was livid."

"What happened with the lawsuit?"

"After the lawyer did a little more studying up on things, he dropped her. I guess he'd taken the case on contingency and decided it didn't have a very good chance of success. Last I heard she was trying to interest someone else in representing her. And she's still madder than a hornet."

"That's two," I said.

Interesting that Candy had started this conversation by declaring that Steve was just a normal guy who pretty much got along with everybody, and yet in only a matter of moments, we'd managed to put that assertion to rest. I wondered what else she wasn't telling me.

"Anyone else?" I asked.

"Um . . . possibly."

This is the point where I usually sit quietly, waiting for the other person to become uncomfortable and break the silence. It's amazing what you can learn sometimes if you just don't push too hard.

I'd forgotten about Alice, however. She likes to talk entirely too much for a tactic like that to appeal to her. Alice has never met a silence she couldn't fill.

Now she leaned forward in her chair expectantly. "That sounds promising."

I reached my foot over and kicked her under the desk. Alice winced slightly and clammed up.

"I'm open to possibilities," I said to Candy.

"It's just that . . . Steve was my brother."

This time when she paused, neither Alice nor I said a word.

"And I hate to say anything bad about him, especially now that he's gone. But if you think it might help . . ."

"I do."

Candy sighed. "You met Steve, right? So you know he was a pretty good-looking guy."

"Right." I was pretty sure I could see where this was heading.

"And maybe he liked to flirt a little. You know, just a little harmless playing around with the ladies."

"The lady *clients*," I said, just to keep things clear.

"Yes . . . and . . . well, let's just say that some of them reciprocated. In fact, quite enthusiastically."

"So Steve was sleeping around," said Alice.

I was tempted to kick her again.

"Just once or twice," said Candy.

"Were these woman married?" I asked.

"I don't know. Some of them probably yes, others maybe no."

Some of them?

"So now we're moving beyond once or twice."

"I guess there could have been more."

"How many more?"

Candy looked up. "Steve was my *brother*. It's not like we talked about these things with one another. I'm just going by what I saw and what I guessed."

"So there's a possibility that someone's husband might have been angry at Steve?"

Candy nodded reluctantly.

"Maybe even more than one?"

"It could have happened," she admitted.

"Did you tell these things to the police?" I asked.

"No."

"How come?"

"Because I'm trying to save my business here, all right? I'm already losing clients after what happened and I can't think of a quicker way to alienate even more of them than by going public with things that should have been kept private."

Candy was fidgeting in her chair. She was on the defensive now. I liked that, it kept her talking.

Her movement disturbed Winston, though. The Corgi lifted his head and listened for a moment. Then he jumped down and padded away. Candy, intent on what she was saying, didn't even notice the dog's departure.

"Steve wasn't perfect, okay? He screwed up, and now he's gone. And I'm the one left trying to pick up the pieces. Right now, the best thing I can do for myself is save Pine Ridge and that's my number one priority."

Abruptly, Candy stood up. She braced her hands on the edge of the desk and leaned forward.

"So now you know everything. Are you going to help me or not?"

"I'm in," said Alice.

Lord love a duck, that woman was quick on the draw. I supposed that meant she was volunteering me again.

"Me too," I said.

11

"You got me into this," I said to Alice as we walked out. "So you're going to help."

"What do you mean? I don't know anything about solving mysteries. Besides, now that camp has started and Berkley's squared away, I'll be starting work on Monday."

"Tough luck."

I was feeling snarky, can you tell? Probably hormones again.

"You're not the only one who's busy," I said.

Alice stopped and held the door. "Oh right. I remember now. You're gardening."

She would bring that up.

"Among other things."

"Name one."

"There's Davey—"

"Camp."

"And Sam—"

"Working."

"The Poodles—"

"Keep each other company."

"Kevin," I said triumphantly.

"Big deal." Alice sniffed. "A baby. Millions of women have done it. Try having two in diapers at once. *That's* work. Besides, like I said, I don't know a single thing about clues, or suspects, or any of that stuff."

"You can learn. It's not nearly as hard as it looks. Mostly it's just a matter of paying attention to the little things other people miss. Take Madison, for example."

"Who?"

"Madison, the receptionist."

I nodded toward the teenage girl, who was currently standing on the other side of the parking lot. A delivery van was parked there, side door open. A young, well-built delivery man wearing a tight

T-shirt and equally tight jeans was unloading fifty-pound sacks of kibble and stacking them onto a handcart.

The two of them were talking while the man worked. He appeared to be taking his time handling the bags, and Madison's appreciative gaze followed every rippling move his muscles made.

Alice glanced over at the scene, then frowned as she turned back to me. "How do you know her name?"

"We've talked to her a couple of times. She was the one who called nine-one-one, remember?"

"Yeah, I guess. She's the office girl. So what?"

"So what if she was a suspect?"

Alice turned and had another look. This time with more interest.

"Is she?"

"I don't know yet."

"Who's the guy?" asked Alice. "It looks from here like those two are into each other. Maybe that's a clue."

"You see? Now you're getting the hang of things. That's how you figure stuff out."

"I guess I could do that," said Alice. She opened the car door and climbed in. "If I had time." The door slammed. "Which I don't."

"And yet," I said, getting in beside her, "you volunteered me."

"That's entirely different. Face it, Melanie. Solving mysteries is what you do. Maybe you've taken some time off recently for other things—"

"Like life?"

"Yeah, that. But now Kevin is here, and you're beginning to get back to normal. Which for you, apparently, is chasing murderers. Plus, you've quit your job—"

"I didn't quit, I'm on sabbatical."

Alice sighed. Loudly. "Semantics, okay? Besides . . . here's the deal. I really felt sorry for Candy. Who could help it? Now that Steve's gone, she's all alone. Someone has to step in and help her out."

"You're forgetting one thing," I said.

We'd reached the end of the driveway. Alice pulled through the white gate, turned on her blinker, and headed for home.

"What's that?"

"The first rule of investigating murders is follow the money."

"So?"

"There may not have been any insurance, but Candy still inherited. Pine Ridge used to be half hers, now she owns the whole place."

"She has a motive," said Alice. She sounded delighted by the discovery.

"That's right. So before you start feeling too sorry for her, don't forget that she could be a murderer."

Aunt Peg was the one who came up with the plan.

Which surprised exactly no one. Aunt Peg has a

129

strategy for every situation, and usually several backup ideas too. If she only had more relatives to manipulate, she could probably rule the world.

"You'll go undercover," she said the next afternoon as we were having lunch. Aunt Peg was holding Kevin on her lap with one hand and eating a ham and cheese sandwich with the other.

Here's the thing about having a new baby. Everyone stops by. Friends, relatives, people you once thought liked you for yourself, now turn out only to have eyes—and hands—for the baby. Since it had been three whole days since her last visit, Aunt Peg figured she was due again.

As is often the case, her arrival coincided with a meal. True to form, she'd brought dessert with her: Sarah Bernhardts, a sumptuous dark chocolate and marzipan confection from a bakery in downtown Greenwich. My mouth started to water as soon as I saw the signature box.

The first course that Sam and I came up with— homemade sandwiches on a choice of wheat or rye bread— looked pretty paltry by comparison. Thankfully, Aunt Peg was busy being entertained by Kevin and didn't seem to notice. I could have handed her a strip of beef jerky and she'd have put it in her mouth without protest.

"Do what?"

Okay, not a terribly articulate question but my mouth was full. As soon as I finished my sandwich, I could get to those candies.

"How much do you know about the staff and clients at Pine Ridge?" asked Aunt Peg. "Those are people whom Steve Pine spent most of his time with."

"Not much," I admitted. "Mostly just what Candy told me."

"Then you've got some work to do. You want to find out what makes that operation tick without anybody realizing that you're spying on them. What if Candy Pine pretended to hire you?"

"To do what?" This time the Sarah Bernhardts weren't to blame. Just complete and utter lack of comprehension.

"Let me think. There must be something she could pass you off as for a day or two, while you nose around."

"A consultant," Sam suggested. "Looking for ways to cut costs and trim down the business now that Steve's gone."

Aunt Peg shook her head. "Too adversarial. We want people to confide in Melanie, not fear for their jobs when she's around."

"What about a dog psychologist?" I said. "Maybe Candy could say she was bringing me in to work with some of their problem clients."

Aunt Peg shot me one of her looks. You know what I mean.

"Do you honestly think you could pull that off?"

"For a day or two, I don't see why not."

She was unconvinced. "Let's not get you in over

your head before you're even started. There must be something simple, something easy. . . . What about a web site?"

"Pine Ridge already has one."

"That works. Candy could tell everyone that now that things have changed, she wants to do an overhaul. You'll be designing the new web site, but first you want to walk around for a day or two and get a feel for the place."

"Perfect," said Sam.

Was he nuts?

"Perfect except for the fact that I haven't even the slightest clue about web site design," I said.

Trust me on this. Using Google was my idea of higher learning when it came to web-related activities.

"You can finesse that part pretty easily," said Sam. "After all, nobody is going to expect you to do any work right there. And it does give you a great excuse for being there and looking around."

Now I was the one who was unconvinced. It didn't do me any good, however, since I was also outvoted.

"If I'm going to be doing that," I told him, "then you'll have to keep an eye on Kevin for a couple of days."

"I can help," said Aunt Peg.

With everyone in agreement on the home front, I called Candy and ran the idea past her. She hopped on board enthusiastically and asked how soon I could start. So there we had it.

Undercover it was.

"I thought you had, like, a dog," said Madison.

Teenage grammar, it was a marvel.

I was tempted to ask Madison what she meant by *like a dog*. A cat? Maybe a squirrel? But I was supposed to be making friends and ferreting out information, so I refrained.

It was early Monday morning and I was back at Pine Ridge, presumably as an observer of the everyday operation. At least that was the brief explanation Candy had offered before leaving me to wander around on my own.

Now I was out in the front office watching clients drop their dogs off for the day. It wasn't hard to see that there was considerably less activity than there had been during the same time the previous week. Before Steve's murder had changed everything.

Today, there was no line of customers waiting to check in, and Madison wasn't working nonstop. She had plenty of time to shoot me curious glances.

Clearly, she was wondering what I was doing there. Not only that, but she was a little annoyed by my presence.

Which, frankly, was one reason why I'd remained in the front office, rather than leaving to check out the rest of the facility. The fact that Madison was suspicious of my motives was enough to make me wonder about hers.

"I do have a dog," I replied. "Actually, I have five."

"And you also design web sites?"

"Why not?" I tried out a cheery smile. "Everybody's got to do something, right?"

"I suppose. But . . ."

I waited for her to continue. She didn't. Madison had stopped looking at me too. Instead, she seemed riveted by the empty countertop.

"But what?" I asked finally.

"The old web site is fine. I don't see why it needs updating."

"That was Candy's decision," I said. "I'm just helping her out."

"It isn't fair."

"What isn't?"

Madison's eyes lifted. "She's cutting Steve out. That's what this is really about, isn't it? She wants to erase him from the web site like he was never here."

"I don't think—"

"It doesn't matter what you think," she said. "You don't know."

"Then tell me."

Her narrow shoulders rose and fell, a hopeless gesture. Steve had been gone less than a week and his loss was keenly felt. His absence left a large hole in the Pine Ridge community. Candy might have insisted on business as usual, but she couldn't mandate her employees' emotions to match.

"It doesn't matter now," Madison said unhappily.

"I'd still like to know."

"She was jealous of him."

"Candy?"

Madison's expression went blank. She was tuning me out.

"See? That's what I thought. You don't get it. Never mind."

I gave myself a mental kick. I'm a teacher, I'm used to dealing with kids. I know what they're like —vulnerable, emotional, mercurial in their moods. I should be doing better than this.

"Give me a chance," I said. "I'm new around here. I don't know how everything works. Or how it worked before. That's what I'm trying to figure out. Maybe you could help me."

"Maybe I already have a job."

She was all attitude now. Prickly and defensive. Still, I was betting that Madison wanted to explain, to tell me her side. Otherwise, what were we doing here?

I glanced over my shoulder, looked out the front windows, and didn't see any cars pulling in. Good. That gave me some time.

I leaned on the counter, closing the space between us and forcing Madison to acknowledge my presence. "Why was Candy jealous of Steve?"

"Because he was cool and she isn't," she said. "All you had to do was look at the two of them and you'd know that."

One look at Steve Pine, and you'd know that he was a teenage girl's fantasy. Candy had admitted that Steve liked to fool around with the clients. I wondered whether his flirting had carried over to the staff as well.

"I never had a chance to get to really know Steve," I said. "But from what I saw, he seemed like a nice guy."

"He was more than just a nice guy. He was smart; he was fun. He was a great boss. He wasn't always checking up on us to make sure we were working hard enough."

As I supposed—reading between the lines—Candy did.

"He understood that there was more to life than just slaving away at your job all the time. Like people might have outside interests. Or friends they need to talk to."

Madison pursed her lips in exasperation. "Candy makes us turn off our cell phones during work hours. Like she thinks anyone would actually do that, just because she says so. I put mine on vibrate and she never even knows. That was the difference between them. Everybody liked Steve. Steve *got it*."

At least it had appeared that way to Madison. Though she'd obviously missed out on one salient point. Not *everybody* had liked Steve.

"I guess you must have been pretty shocked by what happened."

"Well, like, *yeah*. Who would want to do something like that, especially to such a nice guy?"

"Do you have any ideas?"

Madison tipped her head to one side. "If I did—and I'm not saying I do—why would I tell you?"

"Why not?"

"Because I don't even know you, for one thing."

"Would you tell the police?" I asked.

"Not if I could help it. Talking to the police is *so* not my thing."

"But they did ask you questions."

"That doesn't mean anything." Madison was on the defensive again. "They questioned everybody who was here."

"I know," I said. "They talked to me too. Did you tell the detective about Candy being jealous of Steve?"

"What? And lose my job? I don't *think* so." Her eyes narrowed. "And you better not tell her either. If you do, I'll just deny ever saying it. I'll tell her you're a liar."

Good going, Mel. How to make friends and influence people.

Madison looked past me and out the windows. I turned and saw a silver-and-black Hummer pulling into a doublewide parking space.

A man I'd met briefly the week before got out of the vehicle. I couldn't recall his name, but when an Airedale hopped out after him I remembered that the dog's name was Logan.

It figured. If I didn't watch myself I'd turn into Aunt Peg.

"Looks like you have to go back to work," I said.

Madison was already pulling out a large index card from a stack on the counter. Roger Cavanaugh, I read across the top. That sounded right.

"We love Logan," Madison crooned as the door opened. She stepped out from behind the counter and leaned down to greet the new arrival. "He's our number one client. You've been here since the very beginning, haven't you, boy? We're always happy when you show up."

Since Logan and Roger were the first clients to receive such an effusive welcome, I assumed the display was for my benefit. Madison was telling me that we were through talking.

That was fine by me. The day was just beginning and I had plenty of other people to see.

12

Candy had invited me to make myself at home at the day care center, so I did.

Leaving Madison to her job, I walked down the back hallway, passing both executive offices. Candy's door was open. She wasn't inside, but Winston was. The Corgi was blissfully asleep on his corner chair, his little legs paddling in the air and keeping time with his dreams.

The door to Steve's office was still firmly shut. I hesitated briefly, then kept walking. Eventually I was going to want to go in there, but I didn't need to do so just yet.

Heading out the back door, I bypassed the paddocks—all of them still empty this early in the morning—and strode down the path to the Dog House. Inside, only about half the individual rooms were in use.

The playrooms were similarly empty, save for a pair of employees. Two young women, both dressed in the Pine Ridge uniform, were standing just inside a doorway, talking and giggling as I passed by. It sounded as though they were comparing notes on how drunk each of them had been the night before. Aside from glancing briefly in my direction, neither paid any attention to me.

I wondered if the two were slacking off, or whether there wasn't anything for them to do. I also wondered whether Candy was going to have to start laying off staff if business didn't start to pick up again soon.

As I'd hoped, Bailey was in the grooming room at the end of the hall. I pushed open the frosted glass door and slipped inside, being careful not to let out a fluffy white American Eskimo dog that was racing in dizzying circles around the linoleum floor.

Bailey was arranging some grooming supplies—clippers, scissors, a wide tooth comb—on a towel on the counter that ran along the back wall. She looked up when the door opened and offered me a shy half smile.

"Don't mind Pepper," she said, as the Eskie misjudged a turn and skidded into my legs, then bounced off and kept going. "He looks wild, but once he uses up some of his excess energy, he's really very friendly."

"Don't worry, he doesn't bother me a bit."

I stooped down and held out a hand. A wet black nose brushed my fingers briefly as the dog sped by again.

"Can I help you with something?" asked Bailey.

"I'm Melanie. We met last week?"

"Oh. Sure."

She sounded anything but sure. I tried again.

"My husband and I show Standard Poodles. You told me how much you'd like to try that yourself someday?"

"That's right, now I remember. Sorry, I meet a lot of clients here and I don't always pay that much attention." Her cheeks colored, the blush slipping up over her fair skin. "No, I mean I do pay attention, but mostly to the dogs not the peoplc. You know?"

I nodded. "You pay attention to what's important. And I didn't have a dog with me when I was here before."

"You don't have one now either," Bailey pointed out.

She leaned down and held her arms open wide. Pepper abruptly changed course and charged toward her. As dog and woman collided, Bailey straightened, scooping the Eskie up into her arms and depositing him on a nearby rubber-topped grooming table.

The maneuver was neatly done, and Pepper landed on his feet with his tail wagging. His pink tongue brushed a kiss across Bailey's chin before she reached around behind her and picked up a pin brush.

Some people have an affinity for animals and some people just don't. Bailey might not be entirely comfortable with me, but her rapport with Pepper was obvious. I'd trust her with one of my Poodles any day.

"I'm not here as a client," I said. "Candy's going to be updating the Pine Ridge web site and I'm going to work on the design. So I'm here as an observer to get ideas. Do you mind if I watch you work?"

"Suit yourself. Though it's probably going to be pretty boring."

"Been there, done that." I hiked myself up onto another grooming table and settled in to chat. "I have Poodles."

"I envy you that," said Bailey.

She separated the Eskie's coat and began to brush. Work like that could be done by rote: the

141

fingers busy, but the brain a million miles away.

"I've always wanted to try my hand at a continental trim, but we don't get too many Poodles here. Mostly they're the little ones and the owners just want something clean and fluffy, or else a Royal Dutch."

"Easier than the continental, though. Trust me, you'd change your mind up if you had to show them."

Thanks to the fact that we had dogs in common, Bailey was losing her reserve. "Yeah," she said with a smile, "I guess I probably would."

The door opened and a man stuck his head in. Mid-thirties, prematurely balding, sporting a paunch he didn't bother to try to hide. His white shirt had a streak of dirt across the front; his khakis were rumpled.

I'd seen him before. On my first visit to Pine Ridge, he'd been the man who was outside working in one of the paddocks.

"You want me to fix that cabinet now?" he asked Bailey.

"No, not while I'm trying to work in here. I thought you were going to do it first thing this morning before the dogs started to arrive."

He shrugged. "Didn't get to it."

"Yesterday?"

"Didn't have time."

"All right then." She sounded exasperated. "Tomorrow morning?"

"Could be."

He withdrew, shutting the door behind him. Bailey looked like she'd like to throw something. Instead, she picked up the brush and went back to work.

"Larry Holmes," she said, though I hadn't asked. "He does maintenance. Or at least he's supposed to."

"It looks like he's not very good at his job."

"You ask me, he's not very good at anything. Except maybe complaining about how hard he works. Things are constantly breaking down around here and it always takes forever to get them fixed. But whenever you ask Larry for help, he's too busy. I swear I have no idea what that man does all day. It will be interesting to see what happens to him now."

"What do you mean?"

"With Steve gone and Candy in charge, a new web site wouldn't be the only change I'd expect to see."

"Like what else?"

Bailey started to speak, then caught herself. "Oh, you know," she said vaguely. "Just stuff."

Stuff she didn't want to talk about apparently. Whereas griping about Larry came quite easily.

Just to keep her loose and talking, I said, "So who has worked here longer, you or Larry?"

"Like you mean, who has seniority?"

I wouldn't have put it that way exactly, but I nodded anyway.

"Larry's been here right from the start. At least that's the way I understand it. He and Steve had known each other for years. I think they were high school buddies or something. But then Steve went on to college and I guess Larry never got around to doing much beside hanging out and drinking beer."

Bailey shook her head. "If you ask me, Steve gave Larry a job here just to lend an old friend a hand. It certainly wasn't because he's good at what he does. I mean, maintenance? How hard is that? And if he ever got things fixed right the first time, they wouldn't keep breaking down."

"How about you?" I asked. "How long have you been here?"

"Not nearly as long as that. Maybe nine months?"

Her fingers continued to work their way gently through Pepper's long coat. When a dog was well-behaved, grooming could be soothing, almost hypnotic. Bailey was beginning to relax again.

"This place hasn't been in business all that long, but they had another groomer before me. I heard she got them in trouble and they fired her."

"What kind of trouble?"

"Some lady's bitch got bred by accident when it was here for grooming." Bailey looked up and giggled. "I guess I would like to have seen that. Anyway, the other girl got canned even though she didn't think it was her fault and now we have all sorts of new rules, like only one dog at a time can be

144

loose in here. The others have to be supervised by someone else or else in crates."

That had to be the tale of star-crossed lovers Buster and JoyJoy. A regular Romeo and Juliet. And Bailey was getting positively chatty. It was time to segue to a more difficult topic.

"I guess you must have been pretty upset about what happened to Steve," I said.

"Sure." Her eyes lifted briefly, then lowered to her task. "Who wouldn't be?"

"Do you have any idea why someone might have wanted to kill him?"

"Heck no. How would I know anything about that? The police are the ones who are supposed to figure that stuff out."

"I guess they talked to you about it."

"Just for a minute."

In my experience, police that had been called to a murder scene never talked to anyone *just for a minute*. Especially not someone who knew the deceased and had been in the vicinity when the body was discovered.

Eyes still cast downward, Bailey kept talking. "It's not like I had anything to tell them. Steve and I . . . that was over a long time ago. And anyway, it was just a fling. It's not like it meant anything."

I had started to hop down from my seat on the table. Now I froze in place.

Whoa, I thought. Back the train up. That was new. Steve and Bailey?

"You two had a fling?"

She shrugged as if it didn't matter. "I guess you didn't know Steve very well."

"I only met him once."

"Steve liked girls. And girls liked Steve. I think just about everyone here hooked up with him at least once."

"Really?"

"Yes, really."

Her exasperated tone made me feel old. Like I'd advanced beyond the age where I could understand what the younger generation was getting up to. But let's be honest here, I *was* a little shocked at her casual acceptance of the status quo.

"Didn't that make things a little awkward around here?"

"Like how?"

If I really needed to spell that out, I *was* out-of-date.

"Well, with so many of Steve's exes running around . . ."

"What?"

Bailey glanced up again. A smile played around the corners of her mouth. She looked as though the conversation was beginning to amuse her.

As long as she kept talking, I was happy to be of service.

"Like you think we were all fighting over him or something?"

"Or something," I said.

"Well, we weren't. Steve was good looking and all. And he could be a lot of fun. But I don't think anyone here kidded herself into thinking that he was the guy she was going to spend the rest of her life with."

"Oh."

As if that made everything all right. But then who was I to say? Maybe to them it did.

An intercom on the wall buzzed. Bailey stepped over and pushed the button. She and Candy spoke briefly about an Old English Sheepdog that was on its way back for grooming.

"Sorry," she said when the conversation finished, "but I'm running a little behind and I've got to get back to work."

"No problem." I slid down off the table. "Thanks for your time. It's been nice talking to you."

I was opening the door when Bailey said, "One thing?"

I turned and paused.

"Candy's probably going to remove Steve's name and picture from the web site. You know, because of what happened? But this place is still his vision. It's something that he founded and worked hard for. So if you have a choice, try not to let her do that, okay?"

"Okay," I said. "I'll see what I can do."

I left the grooming room and went back outside. I'd been too busy that morning to eat breakfast, but I'd stashed an apple in my car. I walked across the compound and around the front building to the parking lot and thought about what I'd learned so far.

The first time I'd met Steve and Candy, I'd liked them both. But the two employees I'd spoken to thus far both clearly favored Steve over his sister. Of course, they'd both been women and maybe that made the difference. It seemed like a miracle that things had run as smoothly at Pine Ridge as they did judging by what I was hearing about Steve's behavior.

Out front, the same delivery van I'd seen on my last visit was once again parked beside the building. Its side panel bore the logo of a local wholesaler: BYRAM PET SUPPLY was stenciled in block letters, with cartoon images of a puppy and a kitten peeking out from behind the words. Presumably, Pine Ridge received regular deliveries from the warehouse store.

The van's back doors were open, but I didn't see anyone in the vicinity. I wondered if the warehouse had sent the same delivery man as last time and whether he was inside talking to Madison.

Taking my time, I opened my car and got out my apple. It was warm but I bit into it anyway. Then I leaned against the car and waited.

It didn't take long. I was nibbling around the core when Mr. Muscles appeared. This time, however, it wasn't Madison who was chatting with him, but Candy.

Reaching the van, he slammed the doors shut, then

held out his clipboard for her signature. She bent over, started to write, and then stopped.

"Turn around," she said playfully. "I need to lean on something."

The man obliged. His back was strong and broad. Candy braced the clipboard against it and slowly signed. I could have written a paragraph in the time it took her to finish.

"Thank you, Cole," Candy said when she was done. "See you in a couple days."

He took the clipboard, tossed it onto the front seat, then climbed into the van after it. "You take care of yourself now. I don't want to hear that you're working too hard, okay?"

"I'll try."

Candy watched the delivery van pull away down the driveway, then went back inside. She never even noticed I was standing there.

Sheesh. And I thought my hormones were going crazy. I had nothing on this place.

13

By lunchtime, I had given myself a pretty thorough tour of the Pine Ridge facilities. I'm a skeptic by nature, but even so, I had to admit that my first impression still held. There was a lot to like about the establishment that Steve and Candy had built together.

At the top of the list was the fact that all the dogs I saw seemed genuinely happy to be at Pine Ridge and under the care of their staff. Tails wagged, eyes were bright and engaged. Puppies raced around the outdoor paddocks and danced on their hind legs. Staff members threw balls, climbed through tunnels, and played tug-of-war with the older dogs.

It was like Disneyland for dogs. Who wouldn't approve of that?

I was sitting outside early that afternoon when a member of the junior staff exited the Dog House carrying a grizzled, black and tan Dachshund in his arms. I watched as the tall, skinny teenager carried the dog into a nearby paddock and laid him down gently in the grass.

The Wirehaired Dachshund lifted his head and looked around but didn't rise. Instead, he sniffed the air a few times, then flopped over on his side in the sun. Almost immediately he began to snore. I could hear the small dog's labored breathing from some distance away.

When the boy who'd brought the dog outside walked over into the shade and leaned against the chain-link fence, I got up and strolled over to join him.

"Is he all right?" I asked, nodding toward the sleeping hound.

A Collie and a Weimaraner had begun to chase

each other noisily around an adjacent paddock. The Dachshund was oblivious. Even that much commotion didn't wake him up.

"Sure," said the teen. "That's just Nathan. He's old."

The name rang a bell. That first day when I'd been talking to Steve, he'd mentioned an eighteen-year-old Dachshund who was like a member of the family. This had to be him.

"Poor guy doesn't move around much anymore. Tell you the truth, I'm not sure he even knows where he is most of the time." The kid grinned. "But he likes to nap in the sun, so we bring him out here every day for an hour or so. It makes him happy, so why not?"

"Nice," I said. "I'm Melanie."

"Yeah, I know." His head bobbed in a nod. "Word gets around. Jason."

"Pleased to meet you, Jason. Have you worked here long?"

"Just since school let out."

"Summer job?"

"Yup, I'm saving money for college. It was either this or McDonald's, and I'm not the fast food type."

Jason was all limbs and angular features. His khaki pants rode low on narrow hips. An overlong belt, its tail looped up and still hanging, seemed to be all that was holding them in place. I thought about the careful way he'd handled the elderly Dachshund.

"You look like you enjoy working with dogs."

151

"Sure, who wouldn't? Besides, it beats cooking fries all day. I just hope . . ." He stopped. His voice trailed away.

"Hope what?"

"You know. LIFO."

I thought I was pretty good at keeping up with teenage slang, but that had me stumped.

"Life-oh?"

Jason shrugged. It was an attempt at looking care-free that he couldn't quite pull off.

"Last in, first out. I'm the new guy. When I started, I thought I was set for the summer. Now I'm not so sure."

"I guess that means things have changed since Steve died?"

"Not yet, but they're gonna."

"What makes you so sure?"

"I'm planning to major in business. Then get my MBA. But it doesn't take a corporate genius to see that business is down around here. I bet a third of our regulars have gone missing this week. And all Candy can figure out to do is update the web site? Man."

Jason shot me an accusing glance. "No offense, but I think she's got better things to devote her energy to right now."

"Like what?"

Jason held up a hand and ticked off his ideas on his fingers.

"How about making some reassuring calls to the

152

no-show clients, for one? Get them back on board first. Then think about taking out ads in some of the local papers to increase visibility. Or how about fliers to hand out at obedience clubs or stick on vets' bulletin boards?"

"All good ideas," I said. "Have you tried mentioning them to Candy?"

"Heck no. I just do the grunt work around here. Half the time I have a pooper scooper in my hands. I'm just the guy who's supposed to shut up and be invisible in the background."

Jason's tone hovered somewhere between resentful and resigned. Typical teen.

"Don't worry," I said. "You'll get where you're going, just not quite yet. Right now you're too smart for your age. Until you get more experience, chances are no one's going to take you as seriously as you think they should. But give it some time and that'll change."

"That's what Ms. Moynihan said."

"Who's she?"

"My AP English teacher. She's always telling me to slow down and try to appreciate what I have now, instead of trying to grow up right away."

"Good advice," I said.

"Maybe." He didn't look convinced. "Maybe not. Look what happened to Steve."

"What do you mean?"

"He was a real stop-and-smell-the-roses kind of guy. And look where he is now. Dead. And probably without accomplishing half of what he set out to do."

"Nobody plans to die young," I said. "Or to be murdered."

"He should have paid more attention to business," Jason said stubbornly.

"What makes you think he didn't? Until just recently, it looked as though this place was thriving."

"That's what you're supposed to think, isn't it? Customers want to see perfection, and that's what Steve was selling. No matter how much it cost to create the illusion."

I wondered whether Jason knew what he was talking about or if he was just showing off. He was clearly over qualified for his current job; but at the same time he was still immature enough to want to make sure that everyone around him knew it.

"Maybe it isn't an illusion," I said.

Jason shrugged. As if convincing me wasn't his problem, even though he was the one who'd raised the subject.

"Steve and Candy used to fight about money," he said. "I heard them when I was around, cleaning up. They never paid any attention to me."

There it was again, that thin thread of bitterness that underlaid his tone. Jason thought of himself as a person of consequence and no one was paying enough attention to him.

Until me.

Until now.

No wonder he'd spoken so freely. I was probably the first person at Pine Ridge to give him the notice he craved. Still, Jason was definitely a bright kid. And people who paid attention to what went on around them often learned useful things.

"What about money made them fight?" I asked.

"Splits, partners, who got what." Jason levered himself up and away from the fence. "It's always the same thing, isn't it? There's never enough to go around."

He walked out into the sun and scooped up the sleeping Dachshund. Cradled in Jason's arms, Nathan continued to snore. Boy and dog went back inside.

I'd seen enough for one day, I decided. And besides, I wanted to go home.

That was a first, I realized abruptly. Usually the adrenaline high attached to following a trail of clues or puzzling out a sequence of events had been enough to keep me engaged for hours. Once on track, I hated to be distracted from what I was doing. But not now.

For years, sleuthing had filled in the gaps in my life. It had also added an edge to what was otherwise a pretty mundane existence. But now it didn't seem as critically important as it once had. Now I got high on other things. Like being with my family.

Wow, I thought. Maybe this was what maturity felt like. If so, it wasn't half bad.

* * *

Out in front of the office building, Alice's Honda Accord was parked in the lot. There are a million silver Hondas in the world, but Alice's was instantly recognizable by the soccer ball decal affixed to the back window and the bumper sticker that read, MY BALLERINA CAN BEAT UP YOUR HONOR STUDENT.

One thing you have to love about Alice: nobody ever accused her of being politically correct.

As I was standing there, the office door opened and Berkley came barreling out. He was attached to Alice by one of those expando-leashes and the gadget unspooled quickly as he galloped on ahead. Fortunately, he made a pit stop at a bush bordering the parking lot; otherwise, she might never have caught up.

"High heels are hell," Alice said by way of a greeting. "Don't ever let anyone tell you differently."

She gritted her teeth, in either annoyance or pain. It was hard to tell which. "Especially not some cute, young, tight-bunned Italian shoe salesman who's never had to spend all day standing on his toes in his life."

"*Ay caramba!*" I said. "Serves you right."

Just for the record, I was wearing sneakers.

"Stuff that," Alice replied. She loaded Berkley into the car. "And besides, isn't that Spanish?"

"Close enough."

"Only if you're not Italian. Like these shoes."

She reached down, peeled them off, and tossed

156

them in the car with Berkley. The Golden eyed the delicate leather pumps with interest, especially the one that bounced off his shoulder before landing beside him on the seat.

"Don't you dare," said Alice.

Berkley pretended not to be listening.

I noted that and leaned in closer to keep an eye on him. Alice was busy shedding her blazer and unbuttoning the top button of her silk blouse. Her cheeks were flushed and there was a sheen of sweat across her brow.

"First days can be tough," I said.

"Just getting dressed is tough enough," Alice grumbled. "Who wears a suit in the summer anyway?"

"Lawyers?"

Her look indicated that the question had been rhetorical. I reached in through the open car window and rescued one of the shoes. Berkley was licking the sole lovingly. Another minute and he'd have the whole heel in his mouth.

"At least it looks like Berkley had a good day," I said. "I know you were worried about him not fitting in."

"Not fitting in?" Alice snorted out a laugh. "I was worried about him tearing the place apart."

As one, we glanced at the building. It was, not surprisingly, still standing.

"But they did a great job with him. From the moment I dropped him off this morning, you could see they weren't going to let him get away with behaving like an idiot. Right away, he began to pay attention. They probably handled him better than I do," Alice admitted.

"You're too much of a softie," I said. "Berkley doesn't think of you as the boss, so he doesn't respect you."

Alice thought for a minute. "Funny thing about that. I had the same problem at work this morning."

"Want to talk about it?" I asked.

Another rhetorical question. Alice looked like she was dying to sit down, kick off her shoes, and spill the beans. Though actually, now that I thought about it, the shoes were already off. A sharing of confidences could hardly be far behind.

"A stop at the Bean Counter would make my day," said Alice. "Race you there."

I hopped in my car and followed her out. My racing genes were in remission at the moment, but I'd be happy to come in second.

The Bean Counter was a coffee bar in North Stamford that served great gourmet sandwiches and pastries, and offered live music on weekends. It was also a joint venture co-owned by my younger brother, Frank, and my ex-husband, Bob. After a somewhat shaky beginning, the business had really taken off. Originally conceived as a local hang-out, it was now a popular gathering spot for everyone from dating teens, to young parents, to retirees.

Luckily for Alice and me, two P.M. on a Monday afternoon was far from peak time. We were able to find a parking space in the shade for Alice's Honda and a booth near the front window, from which we could keep an eye on Berkley, who remained in the car.

Frank, who could usually be found behind the counter, serving up coffee and local gossip with equal enthusiasm, wasn't on duty today. He, his wife Bertie, and their daughter Maggie were away on vacation. Two weeks by car, touring the country's national parks. The fact that I hadn't heard a word from Bertie in more than a week was hopefully an indication that things were going well.

Alice and I both ordered no-frills coffee. A plate of biscotti arrived on the tray with the two cups. Alice feigned innocence as to where they'd come from, then attacked them with relish.

I added a dollop of milk to my coffee, sat back, and waited until she was ready to start.

"Now I know why they call it work," she said finally. "And it's not because the stuff is so hard to do. It's because offices are filled with people who go out of their way to make your life miserable."

"Already?" I said. "You've only been employed for six hours."

"Six hours spent trying not to step on anybody's toes or choose up sides in their petty little office turf war."

"Welcome to the real world. You're the boss's

wife. Did you think they were going to welcome you with open arms?"

"I thought they would at least give me a chance to prove myself before making a judgment. But based on this morning, I'd have to say that there isn't a single person on the office staff who doesn't think I'm a potentially incompetent boob who only got her job because she's sleeping with one of the partners."

"Come on," I said with a laugh. "Surely it can't be *that* bad."

"I'm not even telling you the half of it." She stopped, sighed, then raked her fingers back through her hair. "You know, before the kids were born I was a damn good paralegal."

"I'm sure you were."

"But it's been ten years since I was a member of the workforce. Maybe my brain has atrophied in the meantime."

"Somehow I doubt that."

"I don't know which was worse, the fact that they all acted like they were humoring me, or that I just knew that they were talking about me behind my back. Do you know what I did all morning?"

I shook my head, sipped my coffee, and let her rant.

"Filing! That's it. Idiot work. A second-grader could have done it. They said they wanted me to ease my way into the job. I'm supposed to be a paralegal. Hell, I *am* a paralegal. And I never got within fifteen feet of an actual lawyer."

"Joe included?"

"Joe." She spat out the name.

I was glad I wasn't going to be having dinner at their house tonight.

"Do you know what he did?"

I shook my head again. Trust me, words were superfluous on my part.

"He asked me out to lunch. To lunch! To celebrate my first day of work."

"What a jerk."

Alice's brow lowered menacingly. "Don't start with me, Melanie. I mean it. I'm in no mood."

"I can see that."

"Here I was doing everything I could think of to fit in with the rest of the staff, and Joe does the one thing that's guaranteed to set me apart."

"I'm sure he didn't do it on purpose."

"What he didn't do was *think*. I might as well just have a sign taped to my forehead that says PARTNER'S WIFE."

"Better than an *L*," I commented.

"Not necessarily," Alice grumbled, but I could tell that she was finally running out of steam. She took the last piece of biscotti and stuffed it into her mouth. "So now you know how my life is going."

"Change is hard."

"Fortune cookie wisdom."

"If the shoe fits . . ."

The same thought struck both of us simultaneously. Alice had slipped a pair of flip-flops on her feet. Her Italian leather pumps were still in the car with Berkley.

"Oh Lord," she moaned.

"Think of it this way," I said. "If he got them, at least you'll never have to wear them again. Your feet will thank you."

"I better go," she said. "It's just about time to pick up the kids."

She started to rise, then sat back down. "I guess I never asked about you. Everything okay? Anything we need to talk about?"

"Nothing that can't wait." I reached out and scooped up the check. "Well, one thing . . . Amber Fine?"

Alice frowned. "What about her?"

"Bob wants to know where her husband is."

"Don't we all."

I looked at her in surprise. "You mean you've never met James either?"

"Met him? If it wasn't written on the mailbox, I wouldn't even know his name."

"Try to find out."

"Yeah right. Why would I want to do that?"

"You gave me Candy's problems to solve. I'm giving you Bob's."

"No fair," Alice protested.

I ignored her grimace and walked over to the counter to handle the check.

"Tell me about it," I said.

14

When I got home, Sam had everything under control. Not that I'd ever doubted his ability to cope. The man was an organizational marvel. Actually, he was a marvel of many kinds. How I got so lucky I have no idea.

Kevin spent the rest of the afternoon napping, then decided when we put him to bed that night that sleep was superfluous. Sam and I took turns rocking, soothing, putting him back down in his crib, but nothing made the slightest difference. Kevin was ready to party and he couldn't understand why we didn't feel the same way.

By four A.M. when Sam and I were both bleary-eyed, not to mention a step slow in getting out of bed to respond each time Kevin began to wail, Eve decided to help out.

Faith had been Davey's guardian since the moment she arrived. The big Poodle slept every night curled up at the foot of his bed. So when a second child joined the family, Eve followed in her dam's footsteps. Her nights were spent stretched out on the rug beside Kevin's crib, a constant, supportive presence.

As long as she felt we were on top of our duties,

Eve remained quiet and out of the way. But as soon as we began to slack off—and in the Poodle's mind, that meant letting Kevin cry for more than a few seconds before swooping in to pick him up—she made her displeasure felt.

Now she came trotting into our bedroom, stood beside the bed, which put her nose in line with my face, and stared at me accusingly.

I opened one eye. "I know," I mumbled. "I'm coming."

Apparently my response wasn't satisfactory. Eve grabbed the quilt between her teeth, braced her feet, and pulled.

"Hey," Sam said sleepily from the other side of the bed. "Give a guy a break." Then he stopped and listened, hearing the sound of Kevin's cries for the first time. "Oh."

He started to swing one leg over the bed. I pulled him back.

"My turn," I said. "I'll go."

Sam didn't argue. His head flopped back down on the pillow. "Then give me back my covers."

"Eve has them."

He turned and looked at me.

"She thinks I'm too slow."

Sam groaned and passed a weary hand over his face. "She'd be slow, too, if sleep was just a fond memory."

"Mom?"

Davey appeared in the doorway. His bedroom was

at the other end of the hall. Kevin's cries almost never woke him up. Faith was at his side. That meant the other three Poodles had to get up and mill around too.

Join the party, I thought. I was probably getting punchy.

"How come Kevin's crying?" Davey asked.

As if on cue, the wails crescendoed.

"I don't know," I said.

Believe me, if I had known, I would have fixed the problem before now.

"Maybe he's hungry."

"Nope," said Sam.

"Needs a new diaper?"

"Doubt it," I said. "But I'll check."

I threaded my way through the pack of canine bodies and headed for the door.

"Maybe he's bored," said Davey.

"It's the middle of the night," I said grumpily. "He's supposed to be bored."

"He supposed to be asleep," said Sam. "And that isn't working either."

Then suddenly, miraculously, the noise ceased.

I stopped in the doorway, waiting for the next round. It didn't come.

After a minute, Davey yawned. His eyes slipped half shut. He turned around and headed back to his room, with Faith padding along behind him. In the morning, he probably wouldn't even remember he'd been up.

I looked at Eve. "Satisfied?" I asked in a whisper.

She slipped past me like a shadow and went back to the nursery. The other three Poodles lay back down.

I fumbled my way to the bed and fell in next to Sam. He pulled me close and piled covers on both of us. My eyes were closed before my head even found the pillow.

Wonderful quiet. Blessed peace. Who knew how long it would last?

I wasn't about to waste a second.

The next morning, fortified by two strong cups of coffee, I dropped Davey off at camp, then headed in the direction of Pine Ridge. So far, everyone I'd spoken to had professed to be surprised and saddened by Steve's death. It was time to take a new approach. I needed to start talking to people who hadn't felt so kindly toward the day care facility owner.

The first person Candy had mentioned in that regard was an unhappy neighbor who lived to the north of Pine Ridge. Adam Busch's house probably wouldn't be hard to find; and she'd said that he was retired, so hopefully he'd be home. I wondered if he'd be willing to talk to me about what had happened.

As it turned out, Mr. Busch was not only willing, he was delighted. He seemed to think it was about time *someone* was interested in listening to his side of the story.

"Come in, come in," he said expansively, throwing his door open wide as I stood on his doorstep. "Let's go out back to the deck where we can talk. You want something to drink, some iced tea maybe?"

He didn't remember me, I realized, though I'd recognized him immediately. We'd spoken briefly on my first visit to Pine Ridge. Busch was the impatient man in the gold Lexus who'd come whipping into the parking lot as I was leaving.

Up close, he was short and slight, with weathered skin and wispy gray hair that barely covered his freckled scalp. His eyes were a washed-out shade of blue, and thick jowls bracketed his mouth, dragging it down into a permanent frown.

Just judging by the expression on his face, I could see how the Pines might have found him to be a troublesome neighbor. He looked like someone for whom disgruntlement was a way of life.

I declined Busch's offer of refreshments and followed him through his medium-sized, ranch-style house that was neat as a pin. I doubted it was the kind of place where either pets or children would be welcome.

On the other side of the house, we walked outside onto a small raised deck that overlooked the back of the Pine Ridge property. From our elevated perch, we could see over the solid cedar fence that marked the perimeter. The facility's buildings and paddocks were clearly visible. I didn't hear any noise, however, and the only scent was that of the honeysuckle climbing on a nearby trellis.

Busch waved me to a padded seat in the shade and settled down quickly opposite me. He rubbed his hands together, looking eager to get started.

"You're not from the press by any chance, are you? *Stamford Advocate*? *Greenwich Time*?"

"No, I—"

"Town official? Zoning office? That's good too."

"I'm afraid not," I said.

My second denial brought him up short. As if he'd suddenly, and belatedly, realized that he'd invited a stranger into his home for no good reason.

"Then what do you do?"

Not the easiest of questions to answer right at the moment. Mother? Teacher? Sleuth? I wondered which answer would be most likely to make a good impression. None seemed terribly promising.

"I'm a concerned neighbor," I said after a moment's pause.

That would be *neighbor* in the broad sense. After all, I did live in Stamford too. No need to mention that my home was a half-dozen miles away.

"I assume you're aware of the recent tragedy that occurred at the Pine Ridge Canine Care Center?"

Busch snorted. "Hard not to be, seeing as I live right here. Good riddance to bad rubbish, that's what I say. Steve Pine got what was coming to him. Before *those people* arrived, this was a decent place to live. Now I guess nothing that happens around here would surprise me."

"You sound as though you think the Pines were the ones who attracted a bad element to the area."

"What else would a reasonable person think? Especially as he's the one who ended up dead. Him and his sister and that other guy in with them, they all came over here before they even started construction on that place. Trying to make nice and act friendly—as if a social visit was going to make me overlook the fact that they were building a commercial business right in my backyard."

Busch was growing agitated, working himself up into a frenzy of annoyance. He bounced up out of his chair and began to pace as he spoke, striding back and forth across the length of the deck.

"That was the beginning of the end right there. Next thing I knew, friends and neighbors who had lived here for years were selling out and moving on. I told them they ought to stay and we could fight progress together—"

"But—"

"But nothing," Busch overrode my objection. He was the kind of man who liked to hear himself talk. And pontificate. "Money talks, isn't that what they say? People got paid to sell out and leave their homes behind and they did. A row of nice houses gets bought up and next thing you know there's a strip mall where they used to be. Like anyone in their right mind would consider *that* progress."

Busch wasn't just mad at the Pines, I realized. He was equally perturbed with his ex-neighbors. But unfortunately for Candy and Steve, they were the only ones who'd remained in the vicinity for him to vent his wrath on.

"With all the commotion they've got going on over there, people coming in and going out at all hours, who would want to live next to that? Once Steve Pine sweet-talked the zoning board and got permission to put up a business in a residential area, the rest of us might as well have given up."

"But you didn't," I said quietly.

Busch stopped pacing and stared out across his yard at the facility next door. The sight seemed to fuel his ire. His knuckles grew white as his hand gripped the wooden railing.

"No," he said. "I didn't give up. That's not the way I do things. I'm not a quitter. I take a different approach. Seems to me, the only thing left to do now is to try to make those folks as miserable as they've made me."

"Murder makes people pretty miserable," I commented.

"Murder?" Busch spun around to face me. "Hell, you think that's what I'm talking about?"

"It sounds as though you were mad enough to consider it."

"Maybe I was, but it doesn't mean I did. Peaceful protest, that's my way. I'm a product of the seventies. Make love, not war. You're probably too young to remember that."

I knew the reference; anyone would. But that didn't mean I was convinced. There'd been nothing peaceful about his earlier rant.

"You're overlooking one thing," I said. "The Stamford zoning board is what's responsible for your problems, not Steve and Candy Pine. Once they changed the classification for this area of town, it was inevitable that development would follow."

Busch stared down at me. His eyes were hard.

"You didn't tell me when you knocked on my door that you were on their side."

"I'm trying not to take sides. I'm just trying to find out what happened."

I'd been referring to Steve's murder, but Busch misunderstood. In his mind, his problems were bigger and more important than anything else.

"I'll tell you what happened," he said. "Once again, the little guy got bulldozed. You talk about the zoning board. You think I didn't go down there? Hell, back when I still had neighbors, I even rounded up some of them and we put in an appearance at the town meeting. You want to know what happened?"

I nodded, just to make myself feel like I was part of the conversation. Why not? He was going to tell me anyway.

"Nothing happened, that's what! We all got together and went down there on a cold February

171

night and nobody listened to a damn thing we had to say. Oh, they let us say our piece all right, but all they were doing was humoring us. In the end, the vote still went unanimous the other way."

Busch closed his hand in a fist and pounded it down on top of the railing. The entire deck shuddered from the blow.

"I know how things work, it's not like I was born yesterday. The town officials get in cahoots with the developers. They tell you they're making decisions for the good of the town and all the time they're getting kickbacks under the table. One man can't stand in the way of progress, they told me. Well, that's a crock. I'm standing here now, by God."

A drop of spit flew from between Busch's lips. No wonder Steve Pine had given up on trying to reason with the man. Busch was so enamored with his own agenda and his own version of events that nothing else even made an impression on him.

The notion of this man keeping his protests to a peaceful level was becoming harder and harder to swallow. I hoped the police had interviewed Busch after Steve's murder and that they'd been subjected to the same sort of vitriolic rant. That might move their investigation along.

"Thank you for your time," I said, rising.

"No problem." Busch frowned. "Where'd you say you were from again?"

"I didn't, actually—"

" 'Cause I was thinking that I've seen you some-where before. Maybe at a town meeting?"

"I don't think so."

I retreated through the sliding glass door and headed for the front of the house. I wasn't sure I wanted to be around when Busch's memory finally kicked in.

"Hey, wait a minute!" he said abruptly.

My hand was on the doorknob to the front door. I froze.

"Now I remember. I saw you last week. You were over at *that* place." He jerked his head in the direction of Pine Ridge. "You're one of *them.*"

The condemnation in his tone made it sound as though he were talking about mutant life-forms. Or perhaps aliens. I twisted the knob and yanked the door open.

Busch followed me out onto the flagstone walk. "So this is what it's come down to, is it? Now they're sending spies over here to keep an eye on me?"

The accusation was so patently ridiculous that I paused in my headlong rush to the curb where I'd left my car. Jeez, the guy was a one-man bundle of con-spiracy theories.

"Nobody's spying on you," I said. "Not the govern-ment, not the town, and certainly not the Pines."

"Then what are you doing here?"

I exhaled slowly. Now that I had my car keys in my hand and I'd managed to put some space between us, I was feeling a little more comfortable.

"To tell you the truth, I came to see if you knew anything about Steve Pine's murder."

Busch laughed. The sound was harsh and unpleasant. "Like who did it?"

"Something like that."

"I don't know who it was, but I'll tell you this. You find the guy, you send him over here to me and I'll pin a medal on him. What do you think about that?"

I think you're a jackass, I replied silently.

There didn't seem to be any need to say the words aloud.

15

Well, that had gone well.

Not only had I not learned anything of value beyond the fact that Adam Busch had a very short temper, but I'd left our encounter on the run. I was pretty sure that that humiliating turn of events had to be a first.

After Busch went back inside his house, slamming the door behind him for good measure, I sat in my car and considered what to do next. If I returned home, I'd probably end up involved in some dull domestic chore. It seemed I could make better use of my time by seeing what else might be accomplished while I was out.

The only other person Candy had mentioned by name as having had a grudge against Steve had been client Lila Harrington, owner of JoyJoy, the amorous Shih Tzu. I wondered if she might be as eager to tell me her side of things as Adam Busch had been.

Usually I think of cell phones as the bane of Western civilization. I carry one but talk on it as infrequently as possible. Occasionally, however, even I find their services useful.

I had programmed Candy's number into my phone earlier and now all I had to do was push a couple of buttons to get connected.

"Hey," I said, when she picked up. "It's Melanie. I need you to give me some more information about Lila Harrington. I was thinking of paying her a visit this morning."

"Why would you want to do something like that?"

I would have thought the answer was obvious. Candy, however, seemed to be waiting for a reply.

"You asked for my help," I said.

"I know that."

"So this is how I help."

"I thought you were going to be hanging around here." Candy sounded petulant.

"I did that. Yesterday. And I'll probably do it again in the future. But you want me to explore all the possibilities, don't you?"

"I guess."

"So tell me something about Lila. Where does she live? Where does she work?"

"Do you have to start with her?"

Actually, I hadn't. I'd started with Adam Busch. But somehow this didn't seem like the right time to bring that up.

"Is there a reason that I shouldn't?" I asked.

"Lila can be . . . difficult."

"All the more reason to like her as a suspect," I said cheerfully.

"You don't understand."

"Then explain it to me."

It was beginning to sound like this conversation might take a while. I started up the car, looked both ways, then eased out away from the curb.

"Lila grew up in Greenwich. On Round Hill Road."

The address implied wealth. And perhaps a sense of entitlement. But let's get real, I thought. If Lila Harrington had been so far above the rest of us mere mortals, wouldn't she have had her maid watch over little JoyJoy rather than dropping the Shih Tzu off at Pine Ridge?

"She won't want to talk to you."

"Then I'll leave," I said reasonably.

"She'll be mad."

"So what? From what I heard, she's mad at you and Steve already. That's why I want to talk to her."

"What are you going to say?"

"I don't know yet," I said honestly. "I thought I'd just . . . wing it."

"Wing it? What does that mean? Lila Harrington isn't the kind of woman you want to meet with unprepared."

I blew out a sigh. "Fine. Then prepare me. Tell me what kind of woman she is."

I reached Long Ridge Road and pulled cautiously into traffic, heading north toward the Merritt Parkway. It seemed like a pretty safe bet that I'd be on my way to Greenwich by the end of the conversation.

"Think old money. Junior League. Young Republicans. Round Hill Country Club."

"Got it," I said.

I'd grown up in a middle-class section of Stamford. It was impossible to live that close to Greenwich and not be acquainted with the expensive habits and excesses enjoyed by many of the neighboring town's residents. But still, there was something wrong with the picture Candy was painting.

"So if that's the case," I said, "why was Lila Harrington leaving her dog with you? Pine Ridge is a day care center, which implies that Lila must have a job. What happened to all the old money?"

"I guess I forgot to mention that part. Most of it seems to have run out. In fact, if the age of her Mercedes is anything to go by, it's been gone for a while."

Now things were making more sense.

"But trust me, none of that matters. Even if she does have to work for a living, Lila still conducts herself like she thinks she's related to the queen. She has a boutique on Greenwich Avenue that sells Chanel, Dior, Versace, stuff like that. The shop is called Grosvenor, maybe you've heard of it?"

"Nope, sorry." Bloomingdale's was more my style.

"Anyway," said Candy, "you can't just go over there and drop in on her."

"Why not?"

"She'd be horrified, that's why not. And she'd end up blaming me."

Obviously patience was called for here. It's not a commodity I have a huge supply of, but I gave it my best shot.

"We're talking about a woman who already doesn't like you," I said again. "That's why I'm going to see her. So I'm afraid I don't understand why you care how she feels."

"I care because Lila said she was going to sue us. She threatened to put us out of business for good."

"Suing people has become America's favorite pastime," I said.

"But Lila was serious!"

I moved the Volvo into the left lane, flipped on my signal, and drove up onto the parkway. "Maybe, but she hasn't actually done it yet. She's still in the threatening stage, right?"

"So far, yes. Which is exactly why I don't want you stirring things up and making her mad all over again. If you'd seen how upset she was . . . It was crazy. Her anger was all out of proportion to what had happened. Threats I can handle, I'm a big girl. But I don't have the money to defend a lawsuit. Especially not right now."

"Listen to what you're saying. Lila was furious at you and Steve. She made a bunch of threats. But she probably didn't have the money to mount a lawsuit either. So think about this: maybe she found another way to get even."

There was silence on the other end of the line.

"Still there?" I asked after a few seconds had passed.

"Yes." Candy sighed. "And I guess I see why you're doing this. But try not to make things any worse than they already are, okay? I mean it, Melanie. I've got enough trouble around here without that."

"Got it," I said, and snapped the phone shut.

No use in mentioning that stirring up trouble was what I did best.

Grosvenor was located near the bottom of Greenwich Avenue, tucked in between the movie theater and a gourmet ice cream shop. Considering the boutique's proximity to my favorite bakery, it was surprising I'd never noticed it before.

One glance, however, at the headless, bone thin, mannequins in the small shop's front window revealed the reason why. Couture dresses, fashioned from soft, luxurious fabrics draped the skinny-to-the-point-of-anorexic forms. Not only did I not possess the budget to patronize such a shop, I didn't have anywhere near the required figure either.

I pushed open the door and walked inside. The place even smelled expensive. Mingled scents of leather, silk, and cashmere were overlaid with a hint of jasmine. I wanted to close my eyes and just inhale, but I doubted that would make a good first impression.

Instead, I closed the door behind me as my shoes sank into the white, deep-pile carpeting. White, in a store. What were they thinking? Almost immediately I answered my own question. The customers who shopped at Grosvenor were the kind of women whose shoes never had a chance to get dirty.

The single, medium-sized room was furnished more like a sumptuous parlor than a store. Two Queen Anne–style loveseats sat on either side of a graceful butler's table with cabriole legs. Cherry-wood racks, built into the damask-covered walls, held a collection of dresses, blouses, and skirts in fabrics so weightless that they seemed to float on their wooden hangers.

Sizes appeared to range from zero to six. The color palette was restricted too. I saw clothing in every shade of beige from ivory to taupe. And black. Those were the only choices. Amazing.

"Good morning, may I help you?"

While I'd been standing there, staring around

like a tourist in a foreign country, a slender woman in her forties had slipped into the room through a door in the back wall. She looked at me inquiringly.

If this was Lila Harrington, it was easy to see why Candy had been intimidated. The woman was tall and trim; her makeup, hair, and manicure were all flawless. She was wearing layers of cashmere that swayed around her gently as she walked.

She probably would have been pleased to know that the clothing hung on her every bit as well as it did on the mannequins in the window. And although she was overdressed for the weather outside, air-conditioning had reduced the temperature in the shop to slightly frigid. I imagined she felt rather cozy, while I was feeling underdressed in more ways than one.

"I'm looking for Lila Harrington," I said.

"I'm she." The woman tipped her head up and to one side, a gesture of disdain that wasn't hard to read. "Whatever you're selling, I'm afraid I'm not interested."

I suppose I should have been insulted. Certainly I was meant to be.

I wondered if Lila had ever watched *Pretty Woman*. Didn't she know that shoppers with platinum credit cards and a desire to acquire anything deemed fashionable and au courant came in all guises these days?

"Perfect," I said, "because I'm not selling anything."

"Then perhaps you were looking for the ice cream shop next door?"

"Not now." My smile was beginning to feel a little strained. "But maybe I'll go there next. Thank you for the recommendation."

"Anytime." She flicked an imaginary speck from the carved wooden back of one of the settees.

As if dust would have the nerve to settle in this place.

"I'd like to talk to you about Steve and Candy Pine," I said.

I was hoping to catch her by surprise, but Lila's face betrayed no emotion at all. Either my ploy had failed, or the woman had a serious yen for Botox.

"I'm afraid I don't have time for that."

Her tone sounded both bored and dismissive. I guess she thought that would be enough to make me take the hint. It wasn't.

"I can see why not." I walked over to a loveseat and sat down. "Obviously you're overwhelmed with customers. I can wait."

"There's no need."

"Trust me. There is."

The latest issue of *Vogue* was sitting on the coffee table. I picked it up and began to thumb through the pages. Even for someone with a distinct lack of interest in high fashion, there were worse ways to spend time. Some of the photography was great.

Besides, after all the sleep I'd missed the night

before, I was still tired. Eventually, if she kept me waiting long enough, maybe I'd take a little nap.

"You can't just sit there," Lila said in her haughtiest voice.

I looked up. "Why not?"

"Seats are reserved for clients."

"Okay. When any show up, I'll give them mine."

"I'm sure you don't mean to be odious."

I couldn't imagine why she thought that.

"Actually, I think I do. Or maybe persistent is a better word."

I put down the magazine. "You know, you'll save us both a lot of time if you just talk to me now."

"I don't have to talk to you at all."

"Quite right," I agreed mildly. I picked the *Vogue* up again and went back to browsing.

Five minutes passed, then ten. I was engrossed in an editorial proclaiming charcoal gray to be the new black when Lila cleared her throat loudly.

"Tell me what you want from me," she demanded.

"Nothing difficult. Just a few answers."

"About Steve and Candy Pine?"

"That's right."

"I'm afraid I can't help you. My lawyer has advised me not to discuss any pending litigation."

Great jargon. And probably a load of bull. I took a shot.

"I don't believe you have a lawyer," I said.

"You may believe whatever you like."

"Why don't you call him then, and ask? I'm sure he won't mind if you talk to me."

For the first time since I'd entered the shop, I saw the merest flicker of uncertainty cross Lila's face. If there really was a lawyer, she was probably weighing how much such a call might cost. You know, in billable hours where nothing comes cheap.

"Look," I said reasonably, "I'm not here to upset you. I don't want to cause trouble. All I want to do is to hear your side of the story. To find out what happened to JoyJoy when you entrusted her to the Pines' care."

"That part's easy enough. It's public record. Poor little JoyJoy got herself knocked up."

Public record? Like maybe there was a government office keeping track of canine pregnancies?

I stopped just short of shaking my head. It looked as though Candy had been right about one thing. Lila had gone more than a little overboard in her reaction.

"And you feel that the Pines were to blame for that?"

"Of course they were to blame." Color flushed Lila's cheeks. "They were the ones who hired that incompetent dog groomer Shannon. If she'd been paying attention to her job like she was supposed to, nothing would have happened.

"All JoyJoy needed was a simple bath and blow-dry. Just like a visit to the beauty salon. I wanted her to smell nice and fresh when I picked her up that afternoon, that's all."

"I see." I tried to sound sympathetic. Anything to keep her talking.

"As for Buster, that opportunistic *cur,* who knows what he was in for. Maybe to get his grasping little claws trimmed back. As soon as he laid eyes on my darling girl, he jumped right on top of her. Poor thing, she never even had a chance to defend herself."

Poor thing, indeed. I'd seen bitches that didn't want to be bred. And they were more than capable of defending themselves.

"So you saw this happen?" I asked. "You were there?"

"No, but I heard all about it later. When I arrived to pick JoyJoy up. As soon as I saw her, I could tell that she'd been traumatized. And then that awful Steve Pine had the nerve to try to make light of things. As if there was anything remotely funny about what had happened. All I could think was, isn't that just like a man?"

Not Steve's smartest move under the circumstances. Perhaps if he'd have taken a different tack, he might have succeeded in diffusing Lila's anger. Instead, he'd only made things worse.

"Even so," I said. "Accidents happen."

"This was no accident. It was negligence on the part of the facility, plain and simple."

"You weren't there. What makes you so sure?"

Lila gazed at me down her nose. "I'm not without resources, you know. After the Pines brushed me off as if JoyJoy's misfortune meant nothing to them, I took matters into my own hands. I engaged a private investigator to do a little nosing around the premises."

I gulped. That was unexpected news.

"What did he find out?"

"That Shannon, the idiot groomer, was known to spend a great deal of her time flirting with her lunk of a boyfriend. That if she'd been attending to business like she should have been, those two dogs would never have gotten together."

I sat up straight. "What boyfriend? Who are you talking about?"

"You know. The big dumb one. Larry something-or-other. The man who does maintenance around the place."

I hate it when someone takes me by surprise.

"So you see, the facts make it clear that I was right to be upset. Steve and Candy need to be held accountable for what they did to me."

"Don't you mean to JoyJoy?"

She waved a hand. "In the end, it's all the same, isn't it? I was the one who had to clean up the mess they'd made. And now they're going to pay."

I rose from my seat. "If it's Steve you're after, you're too late."

"So it seems." Lila smiled. It was the first time I'd seen her look happy since I'd arrived. "Payback's a bitch, isn't it?"

She ushered me toward the door. Now that I

mostly had what I'd come for, I went willingly.

After the chill of the shop, the air outside felt warm and clammy. Or maybe it was the company that had left a bad taste in my mouth. At any rate, I felt a sudden urge for ice cream.

Luckily, I'd never need to fit into the kind of clothing I'd seen in Lila's shop, so I went for the double scoop.

16

The Greenwich Kennel Club was scheduled to hold its annual dog show that weekend. The event was a popular fixture on the springtime circuit and had been in existence for more than three quarters of a century. The show owed its continuing success to a dedicated committee that consistently offered good judges and a workable venue, and to kennel club volunteers who pulled together to ensure that everything went off without a hitch.

Thanks to their efforts, the event attracted a wide range of exhibitors who traveled from all over New England and the Mid-Atlantic states to attend. But for us, the Greenwich show—actually held this year in Norwalk—was a local event, and that was cause for celebration.

That was the good news. The bad news was, none of us had a dog that was ready to show.

A small glitch like that, however, wasn't enough to put a damper on Aunt Peg's enthusiasm. She phoned the night before and proposed a family outing to the dog show that would double as a further learning experience for Davey.

Having started his education at home, Aunt Peg now meant to continue it in the milieu in which he would be expected to perform. The two of them would pull up a couple of chairs and watch the junior showmanship classes together, with Aunt Peg providing commentary about what each of the entrants was doing right and wrong.

I thought an outing to the Greenwich dog show sounded like a dandy idea. While there, I planned to reconnect with my sister-in-law, Bertie, a professional handler who would have a small string of dogs at the show. She, Frank, and Maggie had returned from vacation at the end of the week, but I hadn't yet had a chance to see them.

Sam, meanwhile, would be glued to the Poodle ring. With more than a hundred Poodles entered in all three varieties, the competition promised to be fierce.

Not only that, but having recently retired Tar, his specials dog, Sam, like the rest of the Standard Poodle exhibitors, was on the lookout for the up-and-coming young dog that would prove to be his replacement. While the competition itself would be interesting, the ringside speculation was sure to be even more so.

So we were all in a jovial mood when we arrived at the showground on Saturday morning. For once, we didn't have to pull up to the grooming tent and unload a carful of equipment. Any mother who's ever complained about having to lug around a diaper bag or baby seat ought to try showing a Standard Poodle. Trust me, you'll emerge from the experience with a heightened appreciation of what packing light really means.

Davey skipped on ahead as we approached the grooming tent. The Poodle classes were scheduled to start in late morning, so the exhibitors were already in place under the tent, preparing their dogs for the ring. Between brushing, banding, trimming, and spraying, the process can easily take several hours depending on the size of the dog and the skill of the groomer.

Meanwhile, all I had to do was manage one small baby who, at the moment, was sound asleep in a sling that hung from my shoulders. Compared with how hard everyone around me was working, I felt like I was on vacation.

The persistent whine of blow-dryers, powered by a battalion of generators that sat just outside the tent, masked our approach. Bertie, bending over a grooming table, busy brushing an apricot Miniature puppy, didn't hear us coming until we were almost upon her.

Then she looked up and smiled. Her luminous greeting lit up the tent and caused more than a few men in the vicinity to drop what they were doing and stare. Bertie, tall and gorgeous with a figure that could halt traffic, didn't even notice. She'd had that effect on the opposite sex for so long that she took it for granted.

"Welcome home!" I cried, swooping in close for a quick hug.

Both of us were careful not to jostle Kevin into wakefulness. Bertie lifted the flap of fabric and took a quick peek inside.

"I've missed you guys," she said, hauling Sam to her and hugging him harder.

The Mini puppy opened one eye to observe the festivities. When it lifted its head, Davey reached up tentatively and let the Poodle sniff his fingers. He knew better than to touch any hair.

"How's my best guy doing?" Bertie asked Davey. "I hear I'm going to be having some competition in the show ring soon."

"Nah." Davey blushed slightly. "It's just junior showmanship."

"*Just* junior showmanship?" Bertie leaned in close and dropped her voice. "Better not let Peg hear you say that. She's already been by twice this morning and I don't know when I've seen her more excited. She can't wait for you to get started."

"Really?"

"Really. You should go find her and see for yourself. What time do your classes start?"

"Not til this afternoon."

"Still," said Bertie, "I bet Peg will find plenty of interesting things to show you in the meantime."

"Can I?" Davey looked up eagerly at Sam and me.

"Sure," said Sam.

I gave him a none-too-gentle nudge.

Those are the kinds of questions that mothers and fathers respond to differently. You know, the ones that seek permission for your children to go wandering off alone in strange places?

"What?" said Sam. He managed to look innocent.

On the other hand, I thought, Davey *was* pretty mature for his age. And he'd been coming to dog shows for years, so he was familiar with many of the exhibitors and the layout of the venue.

I exhaled and said, "Nothing."

I slipped my cell phone out of my pocket and handed it to Davey. "If you can't find Aunt Peg, come right back, okay? And call us if you need anything. In fact, call us when you find her so we'll know where you are—"

"Got it," cried Davey.

He tucked the phone away and was off like a shot. He zigged and zagged through the setups under the tent like a pro.

I stared after him.

"At least you didn't tell him not to talk to strangers," said Bertie.

"That was coming next." I sighed. "He didn't wait around to hear it."

"He'll be fine," said Sam. "When I was his age, I had my own paper route. My parents never knew where I was."

"I'll bet you had to walk miles through the snow in the cold and the dark to deliver those papers," Bertie teased.

"Smart ass," Sam said with a grin. "I had a bike."

"You look great," I said to Bertie. "Vacation agrees with you."

She nodded and went back to work on the puppy. "Imagine the three of us cooped up together for ten days in that car. I guess that's how you find out what your marriage is made of."

"And?"

I pulled over an empty table, hopped up on it, and sat. Kevin, curled over on himself and snoring softly, never even stirred.

"It was heaven," Bertie said happily. "We turned off our phones, left the computer at home, and spent our nights in these little lodges that didn't even have television."

"Wow," said Sam. "Just like the pioneers."

"I guess I deserved that," Bertie said with a laugh. "Tell me what you guys have been up to while we were gone."

"Obviously you already heard about Aunt Peg's plan for Davey."

"Yup, Peg was here earlier and I wasn't kidding. She's really looking forward to getting him off to a good start in the dog show world. He hasn't even been in his first Novice class and she's already talking about Westminster."

That was Aunt Peg, all right. She'd never been one to do anything by halves.

"Davey will keep her busy," I said. "And I bet the two of them will have a ball together. Which will be great considering that she's probably despaired of me ever amounting to much."

"Not so fast," said Sam. "Don't forget, you finished Faith and Eve."

His show of support was touching. And appreciated. Even though we all knew that the two Poodles in question—one bred by Aunt Peg, the other whose breeding she'd meticulously planned—were both good enough that a monkey could have handled them to their championships.

"What else is going on?" asked Bertie.

Sam cleared his throat and looked at me to answer. As usual, my life was the one that was spiced with all the unexpected twists and turns.

"This could take a while."

Bertie gestured toward the stacked crates that formed the boundaries of her setup. Each held a dog, waiting to be prepped and shown.

"I've got time."

So Sam took himself off to watch the Rottweiler judging, and I settled into my seat and told Bertie the story of the Pine Ridge Canine Care Center. At least as much of it as I knew so far.

Bertie knew Alice, the women had met previously

on several occasions, and she even had a passing acquaintance with Berkley. It was the concept of doggie day care that she found to be utterly foreign.

"People really *do* that?" she asked.

"Apparently so. Until very recently, Pine Ridge was thriving."

"But why even bother to own a dog if you're just going to leave it with someone else every day?"

I gazed around balefully. The dogs sitting in crates around us, the ones who made up Bertie's livelihood and kept her in Prada and perfume, all belonged to someone else.

"That's entirely different," she said.

That's the good thing about talking to Bertie. We know each other so well that we don't have to spell everything out. Often a look will do.

"Maybe," I said, "but the end result is the same."

"Not really, because these dogs are here for a purpose. Most are competing to finish their championships. When that's accomplished, they'll go home. The specials dogs may live with me longer, but eventually they'll go back to their owners too."

Okay, so she had a point.

We moved on.

"The thing is," I said, "Alice seems to think I have something like a special knack for solving mysteries—"

"Alice seems to think?"

I let that one rest too.

"Okay, here's the problem. I'm supposed to be figuring out who killed Steve and I don't have any idea."

"You'll come up with something," Bertie said confidently. "You always do."

"That was then."

Her fingers flew through the Poodle's coat, untangling snarls and straightening the golden hair. "Then when?"

"You know, before I had Kevin. Back before sleep was just a fond memory and I could still count to ten without having to stop in the middle and regroup."

Bertie glanced over. I could tell she was biting back a laugh.

"Surely things can't be *that* bad."

"Worse. He never sleeps."

"I hate to break it to you, but that's not entirely true. In case you haven't noticed, he's sleeping now."

"That's precisely the problem!" I wailed. "He sleeps all day and he's up all night. He sleeps in the car, he sleeps when I'm carrying him, he sleeps in his swing."

"Movement," said Bertie.

"I know. We figured that part out too. And his crib is still as a stone."

"What about a cradle that rocks?"

I nodded sadly. "Great idea, until we fall asleep and stop rocking it. Then he wakes up again."

"I see your problem."

195

"Seeing is good. Solving would be better."

Bertie didn't offer any ideas. She just switched from pin brush to slicker, moved from the puppy's body to his legs, and kept grooming. Which, as far as I was concerned, wasn't productive at all.

"You're a mother," I said, after five unhelpful minutes had passed. "How did you get Maggie to sleep at night?"

"Magic."

"Pardon me?"

Bertie stopped brushing. She straightened and looked at me.

"I don't know. She just came that way. I used to hear about all the problems other parents were having and wonder why we were different. Maggie just did everything right, right from the beginning. There was no rational way to explain it."

She shrugged. "Just, you know . . . magic."

"That doesn't help." I'm sure I sounded more than a little grumpy.

"I didn't figure it would." Bertie nodded over my shoulder. "Here comes Terry. Why don't you ask him? Terry knows the answer to everything. He probably knows the secret to the universe."

That wasn't strictly true, of course. Terry only *thought* he knew the answer to everything.

"Do I hear people talking about me?" he asked happily. "Are you saying nice things?"

Terry was one of my best friends. We had met

years earlier when he joined the dog show community as assistant and partner to top professional handler Crawford Langley.

He was funny, and brash, and impossibly handsome; with baby blue eyes and hair that changed color more frequently than Britney Spears's. Terry liked to shop and his wardrobe was infinitely better than mine, a fact he liked to remind me of with annoying frequency. I maintained that my vocabulary was better than his, but it seemed small consolation by comparison.

Terry knew all the best vacation spots and the finest wines. He was always tuned in to the choicest gossip. Of course, it wasn't uncommon for him to have had a hand in creating at least some of it.

He cut my hair, he watched my back, he made me laugh. In short, he was the ideal male friend. Except that he got bitchy when ignored. But hey, nobody's perfect.

"Of course we were saying nice things," I told him. "Would we talk about you any other way?"

Bertie smirked as Terry leaned in to give me a smooch. He was obviously on his way back to Crawford's setup from the show ring as he was carrying a Norfolk Terrier under one arm and had a pin brush sticking out of his back pocket.

One kiss was never enough for Terry; he had to aim for the second cheek too. It wasn't an easy maneuver for either of us, considering the burdens we were both toting.

Then he glanced down and jumped back. "There's a baby in there."

"I know. I put him there."

"Well keep it away from me!"

"Why?" Bertie asked. "Do you think he has cooties?"

"Don't be ridiculous." Terry sniffed, as only he can do. *"Cooties!"*

"Why then?" I asked.

I really was curious. Crawford and Terry had sent flowers and a charming card to the hospital when Kevin was born. And of course I'd spoken to Terry since, but this was the first time we'd seen each other.

No big deal, I thought. I'd been busy. He'd been busy. But now I began to wonder what was up.

"He's too little," said Terry. "If I look interested, next thing you'll be making me hold him. And then what will I do if he breaks?"

"He won't break," I said.

"Sure, you say that now. Afterward, you won't be so happy."

I glanced at Bertie, who shrugged.

"He didn't want anything to do with Maggie either."

"It wasn't my fault. Every time I looked at her she cried. *Women.* No wonder I'm gay."

"Kevin's a boy," I mentioned.

You know, in case that might help.

"When he learns to bark and needs a good grooming, let me know. Until then, he's all yours."

"Thank you," I said sweetly. "I think I'll keep him."

"Motherhood agrees with you," Terry said, considering.

He plopped the Norfolk down on an empty tabletop and leaned against a bank of crates. I didn't see Crawford anywhere. Presumably that meant Terry had a few minutes to talk.

"Except for . . . you know."

Trust Terry never to give a compliment that didn't have strings attached.

"What do I know?" Always a dangerous question, but even more so when Terry was in the vicinity.

He puffed out his cheeks and sketched a round figure in the air with both hands.

"Are you calling me *fat?*" I asked incredulously.

"If the muumuu fits . . ."

"Five pounds," I said.

My tone might have been a little sharp. Kevin stirred in his sling. I reached up and patted his back, lulling him back to sleep.

"That all?" Terry cocked a brow.

I wanted to slug him.

Bertie looked like she might do it for me.

"If I were you, I'd change the subject," she said. "Before somebody strangles you with a leash."

Terry nodded. He had a narcissistic streak a mile wide, but he knew good advice when he heard it.

"Now there's a topic Melanie can relate to," he said lightly. "Anybody died recently?"

"Now that you mention it."

"Oh." He looked crestfallen. "I was only kidding. I haven't heard any bad news on the dog show grapevine recently. I assume it's no one I know?"

"You'll never believe this," said Bertie. "It was some guy who owned a doggie day care place in Stamford with his sister."

"Not Steve Pine."

Bertie and I both stared at him.

Small world, huh?

17

I probably shouldn't have been surprised, but *come on*.

It wasn't difficult to accept that Terry knew everyone in the dog show world, and to understand that his charm could pry state secrets from a sphinx. After all, the dog community was, at its core, a rather small, enclosed universe where die-hard exhibitors revolved around one another in an endless circuit of show rings.

But Steve and Candy Pine operated in an entirely different milieu. The dogs they dealt with wore bandanas looped around their necks and probably needed their ears cleaned. The Pines lived in the real world, which on a daily basis was pretty far removed from Terry-Land.

Terry looked at Bertie's and my faces. They confirmed his guess.

"It was Steve, wasn't it?"

I nodded. "He was shot in his office last week. The police have no idea why."

"I'm so sorry." Bertie sounded stricken. "I never would have been so flip if I'd realized it was someone you knew."

"Don't worry about it," said Terry. "I'm not upset. I'm sure Steve Pine was a nice enough guy, but I never actually met him."

Things were growing more curious by the minute.

"So where'd you come up with the name?" I asked.

"Candy," Terry replied.

"Bad for your teeth," said Bertie, "but I probably have some sugar-free gum in my tack box."

"I think he means Candy Pine," I said.

"Precisely. Crawford met her last year at a seminar on holistic health care in Armonk. Being the only two dog people in the room, of course they immediately hit it off. Candy stopped by our place a couple of times after that. She loved looking around the kennel and checking out the way we had things set up."

Crawford had been a star on the dog show firmament for as long as Aunt Peg; his Bedford Kennels, located in mid-Westchester County, was a showplace. The list of dogs whose careers Crawford had launched and managed from that venue was long and impressive. The facility, the equipment, and the services provided were all state of the art.

Even though Candy's business concentrated on a different aspect of dog care, it was easy to see how she could appreciate Crawford's meticulous approach and his attention to detail. Given their mutual love of dogs, I could readily understand that she might enjoy poking around such hallowed ground.

"I met Candy for the first time a couple of weeks ago," I said. "And I only met Steve once. A friend of mine was looking for a place to leave her Golden Retriever during the day. She asked me to check things out at Pine Ridge. If you've been socializing with Candy, you probably know her better than I do, so I'm surprised you never met Steve."

Terry laughed out loud. "What a warped view of family relationships you must have if you think grown siblings are likely to share the same interests or spend their time hanging out together."

Put that way, he had a point. My brother and I had existed in a state of wary détente for years and had only in recent times discovered that we could actually be friends. A state of affairs that Bertie, who cared deeply for both of us, was largely responsible for.

"According to Candy," said Terry, "Steve was into fly fishing, number-crunching, and women, not necessarily in that order."

"What about dogs?" asked Bertie. "Considering

what he did for a living, I'd have thought that was a given."

"That was where Candy came in. Getting involved in doggie day care was her idea—at least to hear her tell it. Steve was the one with the head for business. He wanted to buy that piece of land and hold it while it appreciated. But coming up with the right way to put it to profitable use in the meantime, reaching out to the dog-owning public in Fairfield County, that was all Candy."

"Are you sure?" I asked, thinking back to the first time I'd been to Pine Ridge. "Steve was the one who initially showed me about the place, and he made a huge point of telling me about how attached he was to the dogs and how providing them with the best possible care was very important to him."

Terry held up his hands. "Like I said, I'm only repeating things I heard from his sister. So you're not exactly getting an unbiased view. But according to her, Steve was a born salesman. And nothing was more important to him than making money and growing that business. I wouldn't be surprised if he was just telling you what he thought you wanted to hear."

Interesting, I thought. Especially in light of the fact that Candy hadn't mentioned anything like that to Alice and me.

"Well, they built a great facility," I said. "And while some of the things Pine Ridge offers might be a little over the top, all the dogs I saw looked pretty happy there."

"Over the top how?" asked Bertie.

Terry looked interested, too, as well he might. Excess was his middle name.

"Inside, the dogs aren't kept in pens, they have private rooms. Each one contains a couch for them to lie on and a TV to watch if they're bored."

"TV?" Bertie giggled. "Really?"

"I kid you not. Apparently, the dogs like to watch game shows and *Animal Planet*. They have their own remote controls so they can pick what they want to see."

"How anthropomorphic," said Terry.

"Pardon me?"

I knew what the word meant, I was just surprised to hear Terry use it.

He looked at me and stuck out his tongue.

I probably deserved that. But considering how many different ways he finds to criticize me, big words were about the only thing I had left to hold over him. It would be a crying shame if I lost that advantage, too.

"It sounds to me," said Terry, "like they set the place up to make the owners feel good about it, not the dogs. I can't imagine a dog actually *choosing* to sit around all day watching TV."

"I don't know," said Bertie. "Beagle really likes the cooking channel. She'll watch for hours if I let her."

Beagle, name to the contrary, was a cat. Go figure.

"Last time I saw Candy was probably a couple of months ago, and she sounded like she was getting really fed up. Maybe stuff like that was the reason why."

"Fed up?" I repeated. "With what? Steve? The business? The clients?"

Terry tipped his head and gave me a look. "Let me guess. You've gotten involved, haven't you? You're trying to figure out who killed Steve Pine."

Like that was a given.

Oh hell, I thought. Who was I kidding? It probably was.

"Candy asked me to," I said in my own defense.

"Did you give her any choice?"

"Now, now," said Bertie. "Let's not be snide. I'm sure Melanie is just trying to be helpful."

"That's me," I said. "Ever helpful. And ever cheerful, too, don't forget that. So tell me about Candy being fed up. What's the story there?"

"Apparently now that they had the business up and going, she didn't like the way Steve was running things. And that was part of the problem, too —the fact that Steve thought he was in charge. Candy felt she had to keep reminding him that the place and everything they'd built together was just as much hers as his. I suspected, though she never said as much, that maybe she was thinking about getting out and starting over somewhere else."

Terry stopped and shrugged. "But don't take that

as gospel, because obviously it didn't happen. So maybe I was just reading more into the situation than was there."

"Or maybe not," I mused. "After all, look how things turned out. Candy didn't leave, but she's the one in charge now."

I would have carried that thought further but Kevin began to stir. He lifted his head, stuck it out of the top of the sling, and had a look around. His deep blue eyes, so like Sam's, blinked at the sights. The expression on his small, round face was almost comical.

In the setup next door, a Kuvasz was having its luxurious white coat blown dry. On the other side, a Bloodhound was snoozing on a tabletop that was slightly too small for its body. Front legs and long ears draped over the side. Dogs were barking, people were talking, the tent top was flapping in the breeze.

Business as usual for a dog show, but possibly a bit much for his three-month-old brain to process. Then he tipped his head back, looked up at me, and smiled. It was a big, toothless grin that conveyed his delight in the entire scene. Kevin lifted his hands out of the cover of the sling and waved them emphatically in the air.

"Eeeeee!" he squealed happily.

"What did he say?" asked Terry.

"I'm not sure. Probably a combination of 'feed me' and 'change my diaper.' "

"Yup." Terry reached over and swept the Norfolk up off the table. "That's my cue. I'm out of here."

"Chicken!" Bertie called after him.

Terry flapped his elbows and kept going.

While Bertie went back to grooming, I attended to baby business. The grooming table doubled as a changing table, then Kevin sucked down a bottle of formula greedily. His short legs kicked up and down in delight as he ate. Two burps later, and we were good to go.

Which was just about the time Sam reappeared.

"You planned it that way, didn't you?" I asked as he reached over and took Kevin from my arms.

"Sure." Sam laughed. "Perfect timing."

Father and son smooched and rubbed noses. Then Kevin reached up, grabbed Sam's ears, and pulled. His hands were small, but his grip was surprisingly strong.

"Youch!" said Sam, gently disentangling himself. "This kid's a lethal weapon. I think we may have to cut his nails."

"He missed you. That's his way of telling you he wants you to take him for a walk."

"Can do."

Sam cradled Kevin under his arm like he was a football, or a small dog on his way to the show ring. The baby responded by shrieking with delight. Next row over, the Bloodhound opened its mournful-looking eyes, raised its head, and had a look.

Kevin immediately wriggled his way around and

flapped his hands in the hound's direction. Given half a chance, he'd love to pull those ears too.

"Oh no, you don't." Sam quickly angled the baby the other way. He could read his son's thoughts as easily as I could.

"Have you seen Aunt Peg?" I asked. "Is Davey with her?"

"They've staked out a couple of seats over by ring three. The junior showmanship classes are getting ready to start."

"I think I'll wander over and have a look." I unhooked the baby sling, rolled it up, and stuffed it inside the diaper bag, which I'd shoved into an opening between crates. "Are you all set?"

"Are you kidding? We menfolk are going for a stroll around the grounds together. Don't ask me how I know this, but apparently there's nothing as appealing as a man with a baby. We'll be fighting off the women with a stick."

Bertie looked up from her grooming and laughed. "So that's why Frank volunteers to take Maggie with him when he's out running errands. And here I thought he was just being a nice guy."

"Sorry, bud." I stood on my toes to give Sam a peck on the cheek. "But I suspect most of the women you run into today will be too busy with their dogs to even notice you."

Sam and Kevin headed one way and I went in the other. Ring three was across the field and down at the other end of the row.

Drawing near, I could see that the first of the junior showmanship classes was already in progress. The Novice Junior Class was for boys and girls between the ages of 9 and 12, who had not already won three first place awards against competition. It was the class in which Davey would make his debut at the end of the month.

There were six handlers in the ring, three girls and three boys. All of them looked older than Davey and all were handling small- to medium-sized, smooth-coated dogs. They had lined up in order of speediness: a Chinese Shar-Pei was in front, followed by a Bull Terrier, a Basset Hound, a French Bulldog, a Dachshund, and a MinPin. Davey and Custer would have made an eye-catching pair in such sedate company as that.

I saw Peg and Davey sitting ringside, their two heads tipped together as they conferred about the class, and slipped into an empty seat beside them.

"There you are," said Aunt Peg. "It's about time. Where have you been?"

"I was talking to Terry and taking care of Kevin. What'd I miss?"

"Nearly half the class. Fortunately, Davey and I have carried on without you. We're enjoying a wonderful educational experience."

Easy for her to say. Aunt Peg can be a little overbearing. Sometimes she doesn't know her own strength.

I leaned over and caught Davey's eye behind my aunt's back.

He looked at me and winked.

Okay, so things were going well. That was good to know.

In the ring, the judge was putting the junior handlers through their paces. The boy with the Bull Terrier was moving his dog in an L pattern. The girl with the Basset had her dog stacked and ready to be examined next. The MinPin at the end of the line was dancing and hopping on its hind legs. Its inattentive handler had yet to notice that the little dog was tangled in its leash.

"So," I said, lowering my voice to conform to ringside protocol, "who's going to win?"

"The class isn't over yet," Aunt Peg said crisply.

As if that mattered. Aunt Peg already knew the answer. In fact, she'd probably known within the first minute after the six handlers had walked into the ring. Don't ask how she does it, it's a mystery to me too.

Davey leaned across in front, and whispered, "It's the boy with the Frenchie."

Aunt Peg pinched his arm. He grimaced but didn't withdraw. "The girl with the Basset will be second. The MinPin is last."

Well, we could all see that. Now, despite frantic gesturing on the part of a woman—presumably a parent—standing ringside, the little black-and-tan dog was rolling in the grass while his hapless handler stared off into the distance.

"I'm better than that," Davey scoffed.

"You most certainly are," Aunt Peg agreed. "But let's hope we've set our sights higher than being better than the worst in the class."

"If I was in there, I would win."

"Not yet." Aunt Peg shook her head slowly as she considered the options. "That boy with the Frenchie is really quite good."

The child in question was now free baiting his dog at the head of the line while waiting for the judge to approach. Large bat ears pricked at attention, the brindle bulldog followed the boy's every move. The two made a formidable team.

"But don't worry, we'll get you there. We still have two more weeks to practice."

"Besides," I said staunchly, "all those kids are older than you. And they've obviously been doing this for much longer than you have. You can't expect to win your very first time out."

"Yes, I can." Davey was supremely confident in his abilities. Some of Aunt Peg's self-assurance must have been rubbing off on him.

Speaking of Peg, I'd obviously done something to tick her off because now she angled her elbows outward, nudging both of us back into our seats. That effectively cut off my communication with Davey since her body now blocked the way between us.

"Some cheerleader you turned out to be," Aunt Peg grumbled under her breath in my direction.

"What do you mean?"

"I'll have you know I'm not teaching my nephew

to handle a dog merely so that he can walk into the ring and lose."

"Of course not, but—"

"If you're going to begin to spout some nonsense about self-esteem, and finding his own way, and doing the best he can, you might as well save your breath."

"He's only nine years old," I protested.

"And I'm sixty-four. What's your point?"

For once, I refused to back down.

"If you make him think that winning is the only possible outcome, you're setting him up for disappointment."

"No," said Aunt Peg. "I'm setting him up for success."

In a perfect world, maybe.

In the ring, the judge was awarding the blue ribbon to the boy with the French Bulldog. The Basset stood behind him in second.

"What are you going to do if he loses?" I asked.

"Pick up the pieces," Peg said firmly. "And try again."

Davey leaned across and pushed his way between us. "Stop arguing," he said. "I'm gonna win. And that's final."

Oh great, I thought. Add it to the list. Now I had something else to worry about.

18

On Monday morning I went back to Pine Ridge. I was hoping to talk to Candy again; I wanted to discuss a few of the things I'd learned since our last conversation. Like the fact that Steve's and her working relationship hadn't been nearly as amicable as she'd made it out to be. Or that in recent months she'd considered leaving Pine Ridge and striking out on her own.

But I arrived to find the facility in the midst of a minor crisis. Madison, the receptionist, had been bitten by a Jack Russell Terrier during check-in, and Candy had bundled the bleeding teenager into her car and driven her to the emergency room.

I got the story from Jason, who was filling in for Madison behind the front counter. Judging by the look of abject boredom on his face when I maneuvered the door open with one hand and pushed Kevin's stroller into the reception area with the other, he would have preferred to be just about anywhere else rather than inside, answering phones.

"Cool," he said, as I walked in. "Is that a baby?"

I hoped that was a rhetorical question. Either that, or Jason needed his eyes examined.

"His name is Kevin," I said.

I propelled the stroller several feet into the room, then stepped back to close the door. It's amazing how many extra steps are added to even the most basic procedures when there's a baby involved.

"You do know we only do dogs here, right?"

"I kind of figured that. He's just along for the ride."

Jason stepped out from behind the counter. His legs were long and he crossed the room in three quick strides. Squatting down in front of the stroller, he positioned himself at eye level with Kevin.

"Hey, little guy, whatcha doin'?"

"He doesn't talk yet," I said, but I gave Jason points for trying.

Kevin shrieked and waved a hand in the air.

"Sure he does. He just has his own language."

I smiled. Despite my better judgment, I liked this kid.

Jason looked up. His hand came up and scooped the bangs back off his face. "Can I hold him?"

I started to say no, then remembered the gentleness with which he'd handled the elderly Dachshund.

"Do you have any experience with babies?"

"Two younger brothers. Plus, I used to baby-sit."

"From babies to dogs," I said. "Why'd you switch?"

"That's easy." Jason grinned. "Dogs don't talk back. I'll be careful. Honest."

I unclipped Kevin's harness and lifted him out of

the stroller. Jason reached out his hands. To my surprise, Kevin did the same. It was like watching two halves of a magnet pull toward one another.

So I delivered the baby into the teenager's arms. He cradled him like a pro.

"Is Candy around?" I asked.

"Nope, sorry. She had to go out."

"Do you expect her back soon?"

Jason was rocking now, swaying back and forth from one sneaker-clad foot to another. In another minute, he'd probably be dancing around the office. Kevin looked like he was enjoying himself enormously.

"I doubt it. She had to take Madison to the emergency room. You know what hospitals are like. They could be gone all day."

"The emergency room?" My breath caught. "I hope it wasn't something serious."

"The way Madison was whining and wailing, you'd have thought it was the end of the world," Jason said with a smirk. "Some lady was checking in a Jack Russell. Her name is Bella, she's new here."

I noted the way he'd remembered the terrier's name, if not her owner's. Aunt Peg would like this boy too.

"I guess Madison reached out to lift the dog over the counter. Any idiot could have told her that was a bad idea, bringing a strange dog right up toward her face like that."

Good one, I thought, and added a few more mental points to his score.

"I wasn't here, so I don't know exactly what happened next, but Bella must have gotten upset about something and she nipped Madison on the chin."

"That doesn't sound so bad," I said, relieved.

"It didn't look that bad either. I mean, don't forget we're talking about a girl who already has a couple of holes punched in her face." Jason shook his head. "So what's another scrape or two on top of that? Instead of complaining, she should have just stuck in another earring and gotten over herself."

Could be Jason had a point.

"I take it Madison was more upset about what happened than you are?"

"Man, that girl screeched like an angry bobcat. I was out back and even I heard her screaming. Everybody came running. The lady, you know, the owner? I thought she was going to start crying. The only one who wasn't upset was Bella. She was running around the floor, chasing her stubby little tail."

I could picture the scene. "Then what happened?"

"The lady left and one of the girls from the back came and got Bella. Then Candy took Madison away and told me to fill in until they got back. So here I am stuck inside sitting behind a desk when I should be out doing something useful, you know?"

I knew.

Jason waggled his index finger in front of Kevin's hands, encouraging the baby to reach up and catch it. "How's the web site coming?"

"What . . . oh . . ." For a moment, I'd forgotten I was supposed to have a cover story. "It's fine. How's business around here? Picking up?"

"I guess so. I mean, it's not like we're full or anything. But we seem to be getting supplies delivered every other minute—kibble, canned food, rawhide bones, stuff like that—so I figure if Candy's doing that much ordering, she must be planning to build the business back up again."

"Have you stopped worrying about losing your job?"

"For the time being, anyway. And that's good news, right?"

"Good news," I agreed. I held out my hands.

"Ah, come on. Not yet. The kid likes me."

He was right, Kevin did. Whether it came to handling dogs or babies, Jason was a natural. And to think, eventually he'd have his MBA and all that talent would go to waste in the business world.

"If Candy's not here, there's no point in my hanging around the office. I think I'll go out back and take another look around, maybe see if I can pick up a few more ideas."

Next item on my agenda was locating Larry, the maintenance man. Thanks to Lila Harrington, his girlfriend had been fired from her grooming job. I wondered how angry Larry had been at Steve Pine when that happened.

There wasn't any need to explain that to Jason, however. Instead, I reached over and lifted Kevin out of his arms. Both of them relinquished the contact reluctantly.

"He doesn't like everybody," I said. "You're good."

Jason's ears grew red. An Adam's apple bobbed in his skinny neck. "I know."

I strapped Kevin back into his seat. Distracted by a set of plastic keys, he picked up the toy and began to shake it vigorously.

"If Candy returns anytime soon, will you tell her I'm out back and I'd like to speak with her?"

"Will do."

Jason opened the door and held it wide so I could push the stroller through. As the baby passed by, he leaned down and gave an exaggerated wave.

Kevin blinked and lifted his own hand. For a moment, I thought he was going to return the wave. Then instead, he flicked his wrist and sent the set of plastic keys flying.

Jason caught them on the fly and handed them back to me. "What'd you say his name was again?"

"Kevin."

"Nah, that's too plain for a kid with an arm like that. How about Kev-man? Or the Kev-ster?"

"Kevin," I said again. "He likes his name."

Jason laughed. "That guy's easy. He likes everything."

Except sleep apparently.

I found Larry out back.

It wasn't hard to do. I'd intended to look for him inside the Dog House or to ask Bailey for a lead, but both proved to be unnecessary. As soon as I pushed Kevin's stroller around the side of the office building, I saw him.

The maintenance man was sitting on a bench, beneath an oak tree that supplied shade to a nearby paddock. He was sipping on a can of Bud and staring off into the distance. Perhaps he was pondering how long Candy might be held up at the hospital, as I was pretty sure this wasn't his normal mode of behavior when the boss was around.

The stroller's wheels crunched on the gravel walk as we approached. Larry glanced briefly in our direction, then turned away again, dismissing us. He looked annoyed at the interruption.

"You must be lost. Clients belong in the front building. That's the office. You just missed it."

"Thanks for the directions, but I know where I am. I was looking for you."

"I don't think so." He took another swallow of beer.

"You're Larry Holmes, right?" I was talking to the back of his head. At this rate, pretty soon there were going to be two of us who were annoyed. "You're the man who does maintenance here?"

"You got something you need fixed?" Finally, he shifted his body to face me. "Put it on the list in the office and I'll get to it. As you can see, I'm on a break here."

The paddock closest to Larry's bench held a pair of Akitas, one white, one black. The big, powerful dogs were scrambling around the enclosure, chasing each other through a set of wooden climbing blocks. Kevin clapped his hands and squealed with delight at the show.

I wheeled the stroller closer to the fence and parked it in the shade. Then I went back to Larry.

"Look, lady, I don't know who you are—"

"Melanie Travis." I held out a hand.

Larry stared it. He didn't offer his. "That wasn't a question, okay?"

"Just trying to be friendly." I withdrew my hand.

"I don't need any more friends."

I took a deep breath and tried a different approach. "Candy asked me to speak with you."

Larry looked mildly interested. "Yeah? Why?"

"I'm updating the Pine Ridge web site for her. I'm supposed to talk to everyone, find out what they do, and gather impressions about what should be included."

The brief spark of interest faded. "Candy isn't here."

"Yes, I know. Jason—in the office—told me that when I arrived."

"That kid."

I waited for Larry to elaborate. He didn't.

"What about him?"

"I don't know what he thinks he's doing here. He ought to have an internship at Merrill Lynch or Ernst & Young. Then we wouldn't have to listen to how smart he is all day long."

"Internships don't pay," I pointed out. "I believe he's working here because he needs the money."

"Yeah," Larry agreed sardonically. "I guess there's a lot of that going around."

"Jason was feeling pretty insecure after Steve Pine died. He was afraid Candy might cut back and he'd lose his job."

"Summer help." Larry shrugged. "What can you expect?"

This guy was a prize. If a problem didn't relate directly to him, he didn't want to know about it. I decided to steer the conversation in a more personal direction.

"So I guess that means you weren't concerned?"

"For my job? Hell no."

Larry helped himself to another slug of beer. As he lowered the can, his eyes narrowed.

"Unless you've heard something? Is that what this is about?"

I shook my head. "I haven't heard a thing. Well, except . . ."

"Except what?"

Larry turned the rest of the way around in his seat and straightened. I had his attention now. He even seemed to have forgotten that he hadn't wanted to talk.

"It's just that I heard a story about a girl who got fired over something that didn't seem very important. A groomer, maybe? I think her name was Shannon. So I guess that makes me wonder how secure anyone's job is."

"Yeah, Shannon." Larry frowned. "She got a raw deal all right."

"You knew her?"

"Sure, I knew her. Still do. She and I are livin' together."

"Oh," I said, with what I hoped was a convincing show of surprise. "Then you must know all about what happened."

"Yup. I was here at the time. It was all a big fat fuss over nothing. Some snooty lady's hussy fur ball came in for grooming and got herself bred instead. The bitch should have been spayed and she wasn't. I don't see how that made it Shannon's fault."

"It does sound like she wasn't to blame," I said sympathetically.

I wasn't the best actress, but Larry wouldn't notice. He wanted me to take his side.

"It sounds like Steve's reaction was way out of line," I said. "How come he got so mad?"

"That was Steve's way. Everybody thought he was Mr. Sweetness-and-Light because that's what he wanted people to think. But that was only as long as everything was going according to plan—his plan. Believe me, that guy had a temper on him.

And when something came up that he didn't like, he wasn't afraid to use it."

Looking at Larry, who'd polished off his beer and was now easily crushing the can with his big hand, I wondered if the same could be said about him.

"I guess you've probably known Steve for a while."

"You could say that. He and I grew up together. We met in middle school."

"And all these years later you ended up working together? What a coincidence."

"Not really. We'd stayed in touch over the years. Steve went away to some fancy college in New York, but we still saw each other whenever he was here. I started at UConn but found out pretty quickly that higher learning wasn't going to be my thing. I wanted to be out in the workforce earning money, you know what I mean?"

"Sure." Right then, I'd have agreed to anything that would keep Larry talking.

"When Steve got the idea to open this place, I was the first guy to come on board."

"What about Candy?"

"She was family, that was different. Steve had to let her be a part of things. But he brought me in because he knew I could be a big help with what he was trying to accomplish here."

Larry's version of events didn't jibe with what I'd heard from other people. That didn't particularly surprise me. It did, however, make me want to hear more.

"It must have been hard the way things turned out," I said. "You and Steve being old friends, and then you ended up working for him."

"It wasn't like that," Larry said quickly. Then he stopped and reconsidered. "Well, maybe it was a little. Steve was the hometown boy who went away and made good. I was the hometown boy who just . . . stayed home. But when we had a chance to partner up on this deal—"

I stopped and stared. "You and the Pines are partners? I didn't realize that."

Larry looked uncomfortable. "Things didn't exactly work out. We talked about going in together, but this land and all the improvements? That stuff doesn't come cheap. Steve was looking for another investor, but . . ."

"You didn't have the money," I guessed.

"You got it. I told Steve I'd provide my share in sweat equity, you know what that is?"

I nodded.

"But that wasn't good enough for Mr. Bigshot. He wanted some classy businessman with a big wallet. Some guy who could be convinced to hand over the dough and keep his opinions to himself."

"And did he find that guy?"

"This place is here, isn't it? It's not like Steve and Candy had the start-up money to do this on their own."

So Pine Ridge has a silent partner, I thought. Yet another pertinent fact Candy had neglected to mention.

"Who'd they bring in?" I asked. "Does the investor ever stop by to see how things are going?"

"Sure. He comes by just about every day. Twice even. Once to drop off his dog and once to pick it up. His name is Roger Cavanaugh. Look down there at the last pen. See the big red-and-black dog? That's his."

The big red-and-black dog was Logan, the Airedale who'd nearly bowled me over on my second visit to Pine Ridge. I remembered his owner too. He'd driven a Hummer and looked like a man with money. Score one for first impressions.

I wondered if Steve had been annoyed at the way things turned out. Whether he'd resented the fact that the guy he'd brought in merely to shore up his finances was now around all the time—and maybe looking over his shoulder and second-guessing his decisions.

In his stroller by the fence, Kevin was beginning to get restless. It was time for me to move on. I threw out one last question.

"Are you sorry Steve Pine is dead?"

Larry scowled. "What kind of thing is that to ask?"

"Considering how he treated you and your girlfriend, it seems pretty fair."

"Fair? Give me a break. I'll tell you the same thing I told the police. Steve and I were pals, buddies. Sure we had our differences at times, but we would have been friends to the end. And that's the way it was."

It was a nice little speech. Pat, convincing even.

And yet somehow I didn't believe a word of it.

19

Larry's mention of the police got me thinking. I wondered what Detective Minton and his cohorts were up to.

Along with the rest of Stamford's residents, I'd read about the aftermath of the murder in the local newspaper. I'd devoured articles written about the early stages of the investigation when the police had been filled with confidence that they would bring Steve's murderer to justice within the week.

But since then, nothing.

Both the media and the authorities were being curiously silent. I couldn't even find so much as a single update on how the investigation was progressing.

I wondered whether Detective Minton was following the same trails I was. If he wasn't, it would make sense for us to pool our information.

I considered picking up the phone and calling him, but I hesitated. There was a good reason for that. The authorities and I have what might politely be called a checkered history.

The problem—as I've learned from past experience—is that the police aren't happy when other, non-authorized people do their job for them. They're especially annoyed when those people occasionally beat them to the punch.

But here's the thing. People—suspects, witnesses, interested bystanders—talk to me. People who wouldn't dream of opening up to the authorities seem to find me much less threatening.

Maybe it's because I look like somebody's mother. (Check.) Or maybe they think I look too dumb to put all the pieces together. (Go figure.) Or maybe they think that the things they say to me won't get them into trouble. (Sometimes, but not always.)

I'm not exactly sure why what I do works, but it does.

Try explaining that to a police detective, however. In the past, my conversations with the authorities have tended to include phrases like "obstruction of justice" and "interfering with police business." Which is why now I mostly try to keep a low profile.

Still, it would be nice to know what they were doing to solve Steve's murder—if only so that we didn't have to cover all the same ground twice. Now that I have a new baby, I'm into all the time-saving measures I can find. Which left me conflicted about what to do.

So I did what I always do in times of confusion —I called Aunt Peg.

"Good morning!" she sang cheerfully into the phone.

"You're in a good mood."

"Why wouldn't I be? The sun is shining, the birds are singing . . ."

Good Lord, I was talking to Pollyanna.

"I need your advice," I said.

I figured that would put a halt to the flow of sugar-coated imagery, and it did.

"Of course you do, dear. That's what I'm here for. Where are you?"

"I'm in the car," I said. "I just left Pine Ridge and we're heading home."

"We who? Is Kevin with you?"

"He's in the backseat."

"Put him on."

As you might imagine, that was a problem. Bear in mind, I've been known to put Poodles on the phone, so the fact that Kevin didn't talk wasn't the issue. Simultaneously accomplishing that maneuver and keeping my eyes on the road, however, was.

"I'm driving," I said, just in case she'd missed that fact earlier.

"My, my, you are in a snit today, aren't you? No wonder you need my advice."

"I am not in a snit." Though the longer this conversation continued, the closer to snittiness I was beginning to feel. "I'm trying to figure out who killed Steve Pine."

"Still? I'd have thought you'd be done with that by now."

I sighed. Then counted to ten. After that, I figured I might pray for patience.

I never got that far. By the time I reached the number eight Aunt Peg was back.

"Are you still there?" she chirped.

"I'm counting."

"How does that help?"

"It keeps me calm," I said.

"Calm? What good is that? I thought you said you were trying to solve a murder. What you need is motivation, zip, get-up-and-go."

A pep talk, Aunt Peg style. Damn the torpedoes and full speed ahead.

"That isn't what I called for advice about."

"Oh well then, carry on. I'm all ears."

Rather than trying to navigate the Volvo while I laid out the details for Aunt Peg, I pulled off the road into a nearby garden shop. There was an empty parking space in front of a tiered row of shelves that were filled with brightly colored impatiens.

As the car rolled to a stop, I opened all the windows. Now Kevin could look at the flowers while Aunt Peg and I talked.

"As you can probably imagine, I've been talking to a lot of different people," I began.

"Suspects," Aunt Peg said happily. She likes to get

right to the point and there's nothing she enjoys more than a good puzzle.

"Well, yes . . . but mostly I'm still just gathering information."

"Such as?"

"For one thing, Steve Pine was apparently quite a womanizer including having had flings with members of the staff and some clients."

"Any disastrous breakups?"

"None that I've heard about so far."

"You might want to keep digging in that direction. Go on."

"Apparently Steve and Candy had a third partner in the business. A money man named Roger Cavanaugh. What's interesting about that is that Candy never mentioned anything about him to me."

"Is this Mr. Cavanaugh happy with their partnership arrangement?"

"I haven't spoken to him yet. I'm hoping to do that this evening."

Before leaving the day care center earlier, I'd stopped back in the office and gotten Cavanaugh's home address and phone number from the files. Jason had still been on duty, and luckily it hadn't occurred to the teenager to question my request. He'd simply looked up the information and handed it over.

"Another thing Candy never mentioned is that she and Steve had been arguing a lot recently. There were disagreements over money, as well as whose vision the facility should conform to."

"A rather intriguing omission," said Aunt Peg. "I assume she stood to inherit the business from her brother. Does Candy possess a gun?"

"She says no."

"Do you believe her?"

I paused and thought. "Mostly. I guess so."

Not exactly a ringing endorsement but as much as I wanted to offer for the time being. "Speaking of guns, Madison, the receptionist at Pine Ridge, is an enthusiast."

"And you know this how?"

"The first time I was there, she was sitting at her desk flipping through a gun magazine."

"Not the kind of employee likely to make the best first impression on incoming clientele." Aunt Peg sniffed.

"Agreed. Also there are other employees at Pine Ridge who are unhappy for one reason or another. One is Larry, the guy who does maintenance. He was a lifelong buddy of Steve's—"

"Who now finds himself in a subordinate position?"

"Precisely. Not only that, but his live-in girlfriend was fired by Steve earlier in the year for letting a client's Shih Tzu bitch get bred by accident, when she had been dropped off at Pine Ridge for grooming."

"Ouch," said Aunt Peg. "Who was the other partner in crime? Not a Shih Tzu, I take it?"

"Buster, the Beagle mix."

"Oh my. That does complicate things."

"And here's another complication. The owner of the Shih Tzu in question had threatened retaliation. She blames Steve and Candy for ruining her lovely pet."

"She ought to blame herself for not getting the bitch spayed." Aunt Peg has little patience with dog owners who don't live up to their responsibilities. "Anyone else?"

"Adam Busch, a disgruntled neighbor, and owner of one of the few residential properties remaining in the area. He's convinced that the Pines are to blame for the downfall of his neighborhood."

"That's quite a list."

"Tell me about it."

"So who's the guilty party?"

In Aunt Peg's world, things were always just that simple.

"If I knew that," I said, "I'd be talking to Detective Minton instead of you. Which brings me to my question."

"There's a question? You should have started with that."

"I did. I told you I needed advice."

"So you did. Well, I'm all warmed up now. Shoot."

"Does any of this sound convincing enough to you that you think I should march myself down to the police station and have a chat with the guy in charge of the case?"

Aunt Peg thought about that. I used the time to lean around and check on Kevin. He'd pulled off one of his socks and was entertaining himself by stuffing it into his mouth. It wouldn't have been my first choice for oral gratification, but he seemed happy.

"Let's recap, shall we?" Aunt Peg said after a minute. "Steve and his sister didn't always agree on the direction the business should be heading. Not all the employees at Pine Ridge are happy campers. Several clients appear to have had their differences with the Pines too. A neighbor, who should be angry at the zoning board, has instead directed his ire toward a more accessible target in his own back-yard. That's the sum total of the information you want to trot down to the police?"

Put that way, it didn't sound all that impressive. Aunt Peg's sarcasm didn't help either.

"Umm . . . right."

"Do yourself a favor," she said. "Don't bother."

Well, that put me in my place. As I was sure it had been intended to.

"Anything else?" Peg asked cheerfully.

"No."

"Then put my new nephew on. I've been waiting long enough."

I reached around and handed Kevin the phone. He stared at it for a moment, then spit out the sock and aimed the new prize toward his mouth. I rescued it just in time and pressed the receiver to his ear.

Aunt Peg was talking. I couldn't hear what she was saying, but Kevin gurgled happily in reply.

After a minute, I took the phone back.

"Still there?" I asked.

"Kevin says he wants a Poodle of his very own," Aunt Peg told me.

"No, he didn't. I was sitting right here."

"Do you understand everything he says?"

"No, but—"

"Trust me," said Aunt Peg. "He wants a dog."

"We already have five."

"Then one more will hardly matter, will it?"

I was so undone by that leap of logic that, for a moment, I couldn't think of anything at all to say. Which gave Aunt Peg the last word.

As usual.

I spent the afternoon puttering around. Really, there's no other word for it.

I looked after Kevin and did some work in the garden. I went grocery shopping and stopped to pick up Davey from camp on the way home. While Sam put dinner together on the barbeque, I groomed Faith.

Sad to say, my Poodles were looking pretty scruffy. Keeping up a Standard Poodle coat is a labor-intensive endeavor, but I'd always taken pride in my dogs' appearances. As retired show champions, I figured they'd earned the right to be comfortable while still looking neat and well cared for. And that meant regular grooming—clipping, scissoring, and a bath and blow-dry—at least once a month.

But Kevin's arrival had changed all that. Any schedule I'd formerly adhered to had quickly been thrown out the window. My "spare time" now consisted of minutes grabbed here and there. Long enough to sit down with a cup of coffee maybe, but not nearly enough time to do a Poodle coat justice.

As it was, Faith got her face, her feet, and the base of her tail clipped. I brushed through her coat and did some minor reshaping. The bath would simply have to wait.

After dinner, I told Sam I was going out for a little while.

He lifted a brow. "Anywhere in particular?"

"Faith and I are taking a walk. Can you watch the kids?"

"Sure. Unless you want company. Then we'll come along."

"Not this time. There's a guy I have to see."

Sam cleared his throat. Tipped his head. Considered the situation. "Should I be worried?"

"He has an untrained Airedale and a moustache," I said. "And on top of that he drives a Hummer. What do you think?"

Sam was convinced that everyone who drove a Hummer had an Arnold complex. So he got my point.

"Plan to be gone long?" he asked.

"I guess that depends how talkative Roger Cavanaugh feels. I need to ask him some questions about Pine Ridge. And I found out earlier today that he only lives about a mile from here. It's a beautiful evening. I figured Faith and I would take a stroll over and see if he's home."

"You don't want to call first?"

"And give him a chance to decline? No thanks." I grinned. "I like the element of surprise."

Sam just shook his head. "You have your phone with you?"

I patted my pocket.

"Battery charged?"

He knew me so well.

I got out the phone and had a look.

"Yup, we're good."

Sam looked down at Faith. The Poodle gazed up at him adoringly.

"You take care," he said.

Faith wagged her tail. It was a firmer promise than he would have gotten from me and Sam knew it.

20

I'd really like to think that I'm good at what I do, but the truth of the matter is, some days you just get lucky.

It was, as I'd told Sam, a beautiful evening for a walk. There aren't any sidewalks in the area of north Stamford where we live, but there's ample room for strolling. The houses are set back from the road on spacious, tree-lined lots, and the streets see little traffic. It's the kind of neighborhood where mothers can still send their children out to play on a summer night without worrying that something will happen to them.

As Faith and I walked along the edge of the road past low stone walls and manicured hedges, we saw a couple kids in a yard eating ice cream and, farther down, two more tossing around a baseball. We also passed numerous loose dogs. A black Lab, a Boxer, and a mutt of indeterminate origin were all out investigating the evening's sights and sounds.

Faith knew better than to strain at her leash, but I did hear her whine softly. It had to be hard being the only dog who was required to behave when all the others in the vicinity were running free.

So I debated. At that point, we'd been walking for ten minutes and not a single car had gone by. Not only that, but Faith was great at obeying voice commands. Even if we weren't physically attached, I knew she wouldn't stop listening to me.

I reached down and unsnapped the leash. Faith looked up at me in surprise.

"Go on," I said. "Have some fun. Just watch out for cars and don't get into any trouble."

With a delighted yip, the big Poodle flipped her tail high in the air and took off. Within seconds, she'd joined up with the Lab and the two of them were playing tag—scooting, running, and chasing each other from one large yard to the next.

I'd paused to pull the paper out of my pocket and check Cavanaugh's address when a third dog appeared to join the game. A series of short, mid-pitched barks alerted me to the new arrival and I looked up to find that the Airedale, Logan, now had Faith on the fly.

For a moment I was tempted to call her back to my side. Then she feinted and ducked, spinning a quick circle that brought her up behind the other dog. Now it was her turn to chase and Logan's to run.

With her rounded topknot and pom-ponned tail, Faith might have looked dainty, but she was no wuss. In a game of canine give-and-take, she gave as good as she got. She caught up with Logan and gave him a strong nudge with her chest that sent him flying head over heels.

The Airedale rolled in the grass and came up

grinning. He caught his balance and shot back after her. The Lab, now panting heavily, saw his chance to pull out of the game and flopped down under a tree.

I broke into a jog as Faith and Logan went barreling down the road together. Both dogs were drunk with the sheer delight of freedom and racing to see who was fastest. I knew that Faith would return to my side eventually, but in the meantime, I didn't want to lose sight of her.

Two houses up, the front door to a slate gray Georgian Colonial drew open. Roger Cavanaugh appeared in the doorway. He leaned out and looked both ways, up and down the street.

"Hey, Logan, where are you? Time to come home, boy!"

Good thing Aunt Peg wasn't with me. Otherwise, Cavanaugh would have been in for a lecture on the dangers of letting a dog roam unattended. Fortunately, I could overlook such a transgression.

He stepped outside onto a front walk that was lined with a riotous display of colorful spring flowers. The only way my garden was ever going to look that good was in my dreams.

Last time I'd seen him, Cavanaugh had been wearing a suit. Now, while he still had on a button-down shirt, he'd opened the collar and rolled back the sleeves. Light wool trousers had been replaced by pleated shorts, and his feet were shoved into a pair of worn deck shoes.

I'd imagined him as a man without a family. Otherwise, why would he leave his dog at day care? The spotless yard and the single car sitting in the driveway near the garage seemed to support my assumption. As did the fact that he was the one in charge of retrieving the recalcitrant Airedale.

Cavanaugh spotted Logan and Faith as they shot across his neighbor's lawn. He fitted his fingers to his lips and gave a loud whistle. The Airedale didn't even lift an ear in response. Either he didn't think the hail was intended for him or else he didn't care.

I increased my pace and was now running to catch up. With luck, pounds were melting away with every step.

Cavanaugh saw me coming and walked out to the road to meet me. When I slowed to a walk ten feet away, I had a stitch in my side. Yet another reminder that my pre-pregnancy body was nothing more than a fond memory.

The dynamic duo zigged and zagged across the street and began to lope figure-eights around a pair of tree trunks. Long pink tongues lolled from both their mouths. In another minute or two, they'd have succeeded in wearing each other out.

"Is that your Poodle?" Cavanaugh asked.

"Yes. If I call her, she'll come. Will your dog follow?"

"Who knows?" He shrugged. "Maybe. He's a terrier. They have minds of their own."

Especially when their owners haven't bothered to train them, I thought snidely.

I checked both ways for cars. The road was still empty.

"Faith, come!" I called.

The Poodle's head came up. She skidded to a stop. After casting a regretful look in Logan's direction, she turned away and began to trot toward me.

Having lost his running partner, the Airedale slowed his pace, then stopped too. He looked around, confused. Clearly, he was wondering what had brought his game to such a precipitous end.

"Call him," I prompted.

Cavanaugh just stood there.

"Go on," I said. "Then when he comes you can tell him what a good dog he is."

"If he was a good dog," he grumbled, "he would have come five minutes ago."

But he whistled again anyway, and after a moment's hesitation, the Airedale scrambled to catch up with Faith. The two dogs crossed back to our side of the road. When Faith approached, I gave her an enthusiastic pat and snapped the leash back onto her collar.

She wriggled with delight and pressed up against my side. Since Kevin was born, Faith and I haven't spent nearly as much time together as we used to. I missed our walks and I was sure she did too.

Cavanaugh, meanwhile, threaded his fingers through Logan's sturdy leather collar. He hauled the

241

Airedale to his side and pushed him into a sitting position. Then he looked up and stared at me thoughtfully.

"Don't I know you from somewhere?"

"Pine Ridge," I said. "We met there—briefly—a couple of weeks ago."

"Right." He nodded. The crease in his brow eased. "That's it. I knew you looked familiar. I don't know whether it's a curse or a blessing, but I never forget a face."

"Count yourself lucky. I have an aunt who's not great with faces, but who never forgets a dog."

Cavanaugh laughed out loud. "That's pretty funny. There's something that would be a curse. Never forgets a dog, indeed."

He chuckled by himself for a full thirty seconds. I hadn't realized I was that witty. Logan, meanwhile, took advantage of his owner's distraction to stand up and wander away.

"Sorry," he said when he'd finally stopped, "but I don't remember your name."

"Melanie Travis."

I would have introduced Faith, too, but he didn't seem like the type to appreciate the gesture and I was afraid it might set off his laughter again.

"Pleased to meet you. I'm Roger Cavanaugh. Some coincidence. I guess you must live around here?"

"Not too far," I replied. "Although our meeting tonight isn't exactly a coincidence. I walked this way on purpose. I was hoping I might be able to ask you a few questions."

Cavanaugh went from jovial to wary in the blink of an eye. "Could be, I guess. It depends what they're about."

"Pine Ridge Canine Care Center. And Steve and Candy Pine, and why Steve might have gotten himself killed."

Before I'd finished speaking, Cavanaugh was already shaking his head. "Just because I leave my dog there a couple times a week, I don't know what makes you think I'd know anything about that."

"If that was the extent of your involvement with Pine Ridge, you probably wouldn't." I tried out what I hoped was an ingratiating smile. "But that's not what I've heard."

He shoved his hands in his pocket and rocked back on his heels. "Who've you been talking to? Candy?"

Under the circumstances, that seemed to be the answer likely to win me the most points, so I nodded.

"Yeah, well, sometimes she says more than she should."

"I understand that you're a partner in the business."

"A *silent* partner. At least that's the way the deal was described when it was brought to me. Silent means I don't have to get involved in the day-to-day running of the place. And it especially means that when something goes wrong, it's not my problem."

Yeah right. Cavanaugh might profess a lack of concern, but I wasn't buying it. He hadn't gotten this house or that Hummer by being stupid.

"Considering that you have a financial interest in Pine Ridge," I said, "I would think that you might find the recent events there to be pretty upsetting."

"In what way?"

"For one thing, Steve was running the place, and now he's gone. That has to affect the business, and maybe the viability of your investment."

Cavanaugh shrugged. The elaborate movement looked more scripted than careless.

"Steve was good. He really kept on top of things. But Candy's no slouch either. I don't have any reason to believe that the facility will suffer under her management. In fact, maybe just the opposite."

Interesting, I thought. None of the employees I'd spoken to would have agreed with him.

"I don't suppose you've thought about stepping in and taking a management position yourself?"

"Why would I want to do something like that? For one thing, I already have a job. For another, I don't know anything about taking care of dogs."

That was easy enough to believe. Case in point: since the last time Cavanaugh had paid any attention to his own dog, Logan had lowered his nose to the ground and sniffed his way halfway down the block.

Faith, meanwhile, was lying down in the grass beside my feet, her long, slender muzzle resting lightly on her front feet. I could see her dark eyes moving; she was following the Airedale's progress. But she made no attempt to get up and join him.

"Besides, that's not the way the deal went down. Steve and Candy had all the manpower they needed. What they didn't have enough of, was cash. That's where I came in. I like to keep an eye out for a likely investment and Pine Ridge rang all the right bells. But my involvement in the place was financial, nothing more. That's the way the Pines wanted it, and the arrangement suited me as well."

"It sounds like everyone knew what they were doing," I said. "So what went wrong?"

"What do you mean?"

Did he really have to ask?

Apparently he did. Cavanaugh was waiting for me to reply.

"Steve's dead. To me that indicates that there must have been a problem somewhere."

"I guess. But I wouldn't assume that it had anything to do with the business. Steve had a life outside of work, you know. Friends, girlfriends . . . that guy had an eye for the ladies, and they didn't ignore him either, if you know what I mean. It wouldn't surprise me if that's what got him into trouble."

"Any particular lady friend strike you as trouble?" I asked curiously.

Cavanaugh quickly shook his head. "That's not the kind of thing I would know. Steve might have thrown out the occasional tidbit concerning his social life, but he didn't offer details and I didn't ask for them. As long as Pine Ridge was running smoothly, that's all I cared about."

I wasn't entirely convinced of that, but Cavanaugh clearly didn't intend to elaborate. He looked down, then around, and even checked behind himself. When he realized Logan was missing, he swore under his breath.

"Over there," I said, gesturing down the block. The Airedale was lifting his leg on a neighbor's tree.

"Damn dog. Logan, you idiot, get over here!"

"He's not going to come if you're already yelling at him," I said mildly. "Why would he?"

"Because he's supposed to do what he's told!"

Faith flattened her ears against her head at the man's tone. Frankly, I felt the same way.

"Try calling him nicely. You want to offer him an incentive to come to you."

Cavanaugh cast me a withering glance. "What are you, some kind of dog whisperer?"

Aunt Peg would have laughed at that. Though I doubted she would have found anything funny about the casual disregard with which Cavanaugh attended to his pet.

"No," I replied, "just someone with a little dog experience."

Not surprisingly, Logan hadn't answered his owner's call. Cavanaugh left us and strode toward the dog. Long, angry steps carried him down the side of the road.

Faith rose, and she and I followed. At this point it seemed more likely that Logan would return to the Poodle than to his owner.

Which was exactly what happened. The Airedale went gamboling right past Cavanaugh and came to us. I snagged his collar as the two dogs reacquainted themselves.

"Take a deep breath," I said when the man walked back to reclaim his dog. "There's no point in getting mad at him now. Either he doesn't understand or he doesn't care what you want him to do. And that's a training issue. Yelling at him isn't going to help."

For a minute, it looked like Cavanaugh was going to argue with me. Then he shrugged.

"You're probably right. The breeder told me terriers could be a little hard to manage when I got him, but I figured I could handle that."

"You can. You just have to find more time to devote to working with him, that's all."

Now that his temper had cooled, I let Cavanaugh have the dog. Logan looked delighted to see his owner. He jumped up and planted his dirty feet on the man's chest.

Cavanaugh didn't correct him. Instead, he reached up and ruffled the dog's ears. No wonder Logan's manners were lacking.

"So it sounds like you were happy in your partnership with Steve and Candy," I said. "You weren't having any problems with them at all?"

"Not in the least." Cavanaugh pushed the big terrier back down to the ground and prepared to leave. "Steve told me he'd make money for me and he did. What's not to like about a deal like that?"

I watched man and dog walk away. Too bad Cavanaugh didn't pay as much attention to his pet as he did to his business dealings. The two of them would have been in much better shape.

21

The next morning, I went back to Pine Ridge. This time, before driving over to the other side of Stamford, I called first. I may not always get things right the first time, but at least I'm capable of learning from my mistakes. That ought to count for something.

Fortunately, Candy was indeed at the day care center. She told me she could block out some time for me at ten o'clock.

Madison was, once again, in her usual spot behind the counter in the front office when I arrived. There were two stitches in her chin and an area of purple bruising along her jawline. She hadn't made any attempt to cover up the injury with a bandage or makeup. Instead, she seemed rather pleased by the response it was generating.

"I heard you had some excitement here yesterday," I said.

The girl tilted her head back so I could check out the damage for myself. "I'm telling everybody, 'You should see the other guy.'"

"The other guy only weighed fifteen pounds."

"Yeah, but they don't know that," Madison said with a grin.

No doubt about it, she was enjoying the extra attention. This was the most cheerful I'd seen her.

"Some lady this morning actually slipped me a card with a number on it for an abuse hotline. Can you imagine? She must have thought I let some stupid boyfriend beat me up."

"She was trying to be helpful," I said mildly.

"I don't need anyone's help. I can take care of myself."

"Good to know. Would you tell Candy I'm here?"

Madison waved a hand toward the door in the back wall. "She's expecting you. She said to tell you to just go on back."

In the ten days since I'd last been down that corridor, not much had changed. The door to Steve's office was still firmly shut.

I wondered whether Candy had been back inside that room since her brother's death. Presumably, she'd needed access to the books and records that Steve had been in charge of. Hopefully, she'd employed the cleaning service recommended by the police. The longer she ignored both those tasks the worse they were going to be.

On the other side of the hall, the door to Candy's office was slightly ajar. As I raised my hand to knock, I saw that she was talking on the phone.

Winston, lying on his chair in the corner, lifted his head and looked at me. The Corgi's move alerted Candy to my presence and she waved me into the room.

"I'm going to have to get back to you on that," she was saying. "No, I'm afraid I don't have that answer for you right now."

As before, there was no place to sit down in the small room. I opened the closet, got out a folding chair, and set it up.

Receiver still pressed to her ear, Candy smiled, gave me a thumbs-up for remembering the drill, then bounced her fingers and thumb open and shut to indicate that the party on the other end of the line refused to stop talking.

"I know that," she said after a minute. "And I will get you that information as soon as possible. But now I'm afraid I have to go. Yes. Yes. Good-bye."

She slapped the receiver back down in the console and grimaced. "Sorry about that."

"Problems?"

"God, yes. But it's not like that's anything new. Take it from me, running your own business is just one headache after another. At least when Steve was here, I had someone I could delegate all the crappy office work to."

That was a different spin on their working relationship. I wondered if history was being rewritten now that Steve wasn't around to refute his sister's claims.

"Was that how it worked between the two of you?" I asked as I sat down. "Were you the one in charge?"

"Sure—at least in my own mind." Candy had the grace to smile at the fact that I'd called her bluff.

"On the other hand, Steve probably would have told you that he was delegating all the crappy kennel work to me. We each knew our own strengths, and luckily for us, the way the partnership came together both of us could work in the area we were most comfortable in."

"Speaking of your partnership," I said, "I'm wondering why you never mentioned that you and Steve weren't the sole owners of Pine Ridge."

Candy looked at me. She blinked, then frowned. I'd taken her by surprise and she didn't know what to say.

"I've spoken with Roger Cavanaugh," I told her.

"Oh . . . right, Roger."

"Why you didn't say anything about him when we talked before?"

"I don't know. Everything was crazy then." Candy shrugged. "It wasn't related to what was going on. It didn't seem important."

"You're kidding," I said.

"What's the big deal? Roger is just the money guy. At any rate, that's what Steve used to call him. It's not like we're something special to him. He has investments all over Fairfield County."

"Maybe so, but apparently he has a sizable amount of money sunk into this place. Which means that Pine Ridge's success matters to him. Maybe he had a disagreement with Steve about how things were being managed."

"Oh no, that wouldn't happen." Candy sounded quite sure.

"Why not?"

"Roger doesn't know a thing about dog care and he doesn't want to. The day-to-day stuff is totally left up to Steve and me, which suited us just fine. The last thing either of us needed was someone second-guessing our decisions and checking to see what we were up to."

That jibed with what Roger had said himself. Still, I couldn't resist pushing a little further.

"Yet, he's here every day when he drops Logan off and picks him up."

"Roger's out front, that's all. Most days, Steve and I never even see him. It was just a convenient coincidence that we could provide a service he needed. No big deal."

"Okay," I said. "Next thing. Tell me about Steve's will."

Last time I'd asked this question I hadn't thought

I needed to hear all the details. Since then, I'd changed my mind.

"He left his share of Pine Ridge to you, right?"

Candy nodded. Her short curls bobbed up and down.

"It's like I said before. When we opened the business, we knew we needed to cover ourselves for any eventuality, so we had a lawyer draw up both wills at once."

"Where did Roger Cavanaugh fit in?"

"I keep telling you, he doesn't. At least not in the way you're thinking. Roger's financial contribution bought him forty percent of the business, plain and simple. Steve and I each owned thirty percent. So even though Roger had the largest single share, as long as Steve and I agreed on things—which we almost always did—we could just outvote him. Which meant that we were the ones in charge."

"Now things have changed," I pointed out. "Now you're the majority shareholder. And you don't have to answer to anyone."

For a minute, Candy didn't say anything. Her eyes grew watery. Her mouth quivered. Over in the corner, Winston raised his head and whimpered softly.

"I see where you're going with this," Candy said finally. Her breath caught on a sigh in her throat. "But you have to believe me. I'd give anything . . . anything in the world . . . not to be in charge. If I had one wish, it would be to have my brother back and everything just the way it was."

She certainly sounded sincere. And Winston agreed. The Corgi hopped down off his chair and trotted around behind the desk. Candy dropped down a hand and fondled his ears.

"Even so," I said. "Things weren't perfect between the two of you. I know you and Steve argued about money."

"Of course we argued." She sniffed once, hard; then her spine stiffened. "We were related, for Pete's sake. And much as I loved Steve, sometimes he could be the biggest ass in the world."

Candy peered at me across the desk. "You have a brother, right?"

"Yes." And although I loved Frank dearly, there were times when he could be an ass too.

"And?"

"No, we don't always get along."

"You see?"

I did. But that didn't mean I could let the matter drop.

"Were you and Steve having money problems?"

"Not in a manner of speaking, no."

"Which means what, exactly?"

"This place is bringing in a decent amount of money. Perhaps not quite as high as the original projections; but still, we're operating in the black. The problem was that Steve and I didn't always see eye to eye on how funds—you know, operating capital—should be allocated. So yeah, maybe we had a fight or two about it, but so what? We both wanted what we thought was best for the business, which was what made us good partners."

"Any chance you might have considered leaving here and going out on your own?"

Candy went very still. "Where did you hear that?"

"It came up in a conversation," I said carefully.

Terry had been one of my best sources over the years. No way was I going to get him in trouble.

"Someone I talked to was speculating that maybe you weren't happy here."

"Your *someone,*" Candy spat out the word, "was wrong."

"You sure?"

Abruptly Candy stood. She straightened her arms, braced her hands on the desktop, and leaned in my direction. Given my position on the folding chair, she towered over me. Just as I was sure she'd meant to.

"What are we doing here?" she asked.

"We're talking."

"Really? Is that all? Because that's not what it feels like to me. I think you're trying to accuse me of killing my brother."

I gazed up at her and kept my voice calm. "Did you kill him?"

"No!"

"Then why should you mind answering a few questions?"

"Because you're making me feel like I'm a suspect."

"There's a reason for that. Like it or not, Candy, you *are* a suspect."

She shook her head vehemently. I plowed on anyway.

"The very fact that you were Steve's heir ensured that anyone investigating his murder would examine your relationship. That's not just the way my mind works. I'm sure the police are thinking the same thing."

Candy was still shaking her head. As if the act itself could transfer some of her conviction to me.

"I can't believe this. I thought you were trying to help. And now I find out all you've done is waste a lot of time trying to build a case against me."

"That's not true," I said mildly. "Why would I want to do that? What I *have* been doing is asking questions and gathering information. And these are the kinds of things people have been saying to me. That's why I came here this morning—to hear your response."

"To hear my defense, you mean."

Semantics. I shrugged. Then looked at her across the desk.

"For what it's worth, I don't think you did kill Steve."

That part was based on nothing more than gut instinct. But what the heck, it had served me well in the past.

"What do you mean 'for what it's worth'?"

"I'm not the police. I'm not the one you're going to have to convince of your innocence."

Candy sank back down into her seat. Anger gone, she looked deflated.

"Detective Minton calls me every other day. He says he just wants to check in. I think he's checking to see if I'm still here."

"Don't leave the country," I intoned solemnly.

"Are you kidding? That guy doesn't even want me to leave town."

We both shook our heads.

"Let's start with the assumption that I'm innocent," said Candy. "I hope you've managed to come up with some other suspects."

"I'm working on a couple of things," I said vaguely. There didn't seem to be any point in revealing how little I'd actually accomplished. "Is there anyone else you can think of whom I should talk to? Maybe someone you might have forgotten to tell me about last time?"

Candy sat and thought. As I waited, I watched Winston go and retrieve a rawhide bone from a stash of toys beneath the window. He dragged it over next to her chair and began to chew.

"What about Steve's exes?" I asked. "Is there anyone in particular who comes to mind? Someone whose relationship with him didn't end amicably?"

"Steve didn't have relationships," Candy said with a snort. "He wasn't a commitment kind of guy."

"All the better. What about someone who was upset over the way their fling ended?"

"I don't know . . . Steve was usually pretty careful about stuff like that. Mostly, he tended to get involved with women who understood the parameters going in."

"Mostly?"

"Sometimes shit happens," said Candy.

"Like what?"

"There was this one girl named Shannon Ritter. She used to be a groomer here—"

Ding, ding, ding. Either we were having a fire drill or alarms were going off in my brain.

"Oh," I said aloud. "I've heard about her."

"She was a screwup. Not Steve's finest moment by anyone's standards. He ended up having to fire her."

"Because of the personal issue, or because of what happened to JoyJoy?"

"Probably both," Candy admitted. "Even before she messed up with Lila's bitch, things were getting a little sticky around here. It had become pretty clear that Shannon really needed to go."

"Now she lives with Larry Holmes."

Candy's eyes widened. "She does?"

"He never mentioned that to you?"

"No," Candy muttered. "Idiot."

"That's probably why he didn't tell you."

The phone on Candy's desk began to ring. She picked up, listened for a few seconds, then lifted the receiver away from her ear, and said, "Sorry, I have to take this."

I stood up, refolded my chair, and stashed it back in the closet. I'd reached the office door when Candy's voice stopped me. "Melanie?"

I turned. She still hadn't gone back to her call.

"Despite our differences, I loved my brother. I would never have hurt him. You have to help me prove that." Her voice shook, making the plea all the more forceful.

I nodded and let myself out.

22

On the way out, I saw the delivery man from Byram Pet Supply again.

This time Cole was flexing his muscles unloading boxes of grooming equipment. As he piled them onto a handcart, he was also passing the time flirting with Bailey. For a facility that didn't do full-time boarding, Pine Ridge certainly seemed to run through a lot of supplies. And Cole, with his tight T-shirts and dark eyes, had the knack of making the most of every drop-off opportunity.

"It's pathetic, isn't it?"

I turned to find Jason standing behind me. And I feigned innocence.

"What's pathetic?"

"That guy. All brawn and no brains."

There was a thread of naked envy in Jason's tone. And why not? Cole seemed to bask in the admiring gaze of just about every girl at Pine Ridge. Jason, probably not so much.

Once a teacher, always a teacher, however. And there was a lesson just begging to be taught here.

"How would you know?" I asked. "Have you ever even spoken with him?"

"I don't have to. Just watching is bad enough."

"For all you know, he could be a PhD candidate working his way through graduate school by driving a truck."

"With that build and a name like Cole Demarkian? Give me a break. He's nothing more than a low-level achiever whose mother spent too much time watching soap operas."

Much as it annoyed me that the teen was making snap judgments, it irked me even more that he was probably right. Cole appeared to be a likable guy, perfectly competent in his job, but I wouldn't expect to see him running a Fortune 500 company anytime soon.

He and the groomer were talking with some animation now as he unloaded another box and placed it atop the stack on the cart. Bailey was shaking her head, but she followed Cole around the side of the building heading in the direction of the Dog House.

"Bailey doesn't seem to mind his lack of qualifications," I said.

"Bailey is not what I'd call selective." Jason snorted dismissively. "She'd probably flirt with a Cocker Spaniel if it had the right equipment."

"I heard that," said Bailey.

She reappeared around the corner and marched over to where we were standing. Her arms were crossed over her chest. She did not look happy.

"And I'll have you know that you're not only rude, but you're wrong. I didn't come out here to flirt with Cole, I came to tell him that there must be some mistake with the order. I didn't ask for any more grooming supplies. Not only that, but I don't have room for them back there. Ever since Steve died, all the ordering and stuff has gotten all screwed up. Like that's any big surprise. But now I've got to go find Candy and ask her what the heck she thinks she's doing."

"Candy's in her office," I said. "I left her there just a few minutes ago."

"Thanks." Bailey gave Jason a level look. "Don't you have some work you ought to be doing?"

"Yes, ma'am."

The teenager ducked his head. The motion secmed less an act of contrition than a move designed to cover the fact that he was laughing.

He hurried away around the building. Bailey left and went into the office. I headed toward my car and considered my next move.

I wondered where Shannon was working these days. The easiest way to find out, of course, would be to walk around back and ask Larry. But I didn't want to involve him in what I was doing if I didn't have to.

For one thing, he'd probably warn Shannon I was coming. For another, he might insist on being present when I spoke with her. And I had little doubt that Shannon would be more open in discussing her relationship with Steve if her new boyfriend wasn't part of the equation.

Which led to Plan B, the Yellow Pages. Even though Shannon had left Pine Ridge, it seemed logical to assume that she was plying her trade as a dog groomer somewhere else in the vicinity. It was just a matter of figuring out where.

As I was climbing into the Volvo, my phone rang. Alice's name popped up on the screen.

"Hey," I said. "How's the job going?"

"Don't ask. Where are you?"

"Leaving Pine Ridge. Why?"

"Perfect. Let's meet for lunch. How about the Bean?"

I checked my watch. "It's eleven o'clock."

"Fine," Alice snapped. "So we'll be fashionable and do brunch instead. See you there."

Since she'd hung up without giving me a chance to refuse, I figured that meant I was going to the Bean Counter. I called Sam to see if he and Kevin wanted to join us.

"Why are you eating lunch now?" he asked predictably enough.

"Because Alice asked and she sounded desperate."

"Oh yeah." Sam laughed. "Desperate women. That sounds like my kind of scene."

"No, really. Maybe she needs advice. You're always good at that."

"I am?" He was still laughing. "You never do a single thing I say."

"But I always *listen*," I said.

"I think I'll take a pass. Tell Alice I said hi and bring home a half-dozen blueberry scones."

So I went to the Bean by myself. The coffee-before-work crowd was long gone. The lunch bunch had yet to appear. I had my choice of parking places in the nearly empty lot.

"Hey Mel!" Frank said as I walked in the door. "Long time, no see."

My brother was behind the counter futzing around with the espresso machine. Wet hands held high and out to his sides, he walked out onto the floor and gave me a hug with his elbows. Really, you had to see it.

Since my hands were fine, I gave him a proper hug back. It was nice that we finally had that kind of relationship.

"Where are the kids?" he asked. "I bet Kevin's grown at least another couple inches since I last saw him."

"He has. You and Bertie ought to come over some

night and see for yourselves. Davey's at camp; Kevin's home with Sam. I've been out running errands."

"And I'll bet you needed a midmorning break. Grab a seat." Frank waved to the row of now-empty stools that ran along the front of the counter. "Coffee?"

"Not just yet. I'm waiting for Alice Brickman. Joey's mom, remember her? We're lunching today."

"Great idea. Come in early. Beat the crowd. You know, the one that actually eats at lunchtime?"

"Shut up," I said fondly, and took a stool. "Has anyone ever told you that your counter-side manner could use some help?"

"No. Most people are so in awe of my culinary skills that they wouldn't dare complain."

"Right. Like you actually baked those pastries yourself."

"Shhh!" Frank held a finger up to his lips. "You don't want to ruin your brother's mystique."

"Mystique? You? You must be joking."

The door slammed shut behind me.

"Stop squabbling you two," said Alice, walking up to the counter. "I get enough of that at home with Joey and Carly."

Having come straight from the office, Alice was dressed in a navy linen suit worn over a white silk shell. Low heeled pumps completed the outfit. She was wearing tasteful makeup, and her hair was pulled back into a bow at her nape.

"Wow," said Frank. "You look great."

On other occasions when their paths had crossed, Alice had probably been dressed much like me—in clothing whose sole purpose was to withstand wear-and-tear and not show stains. You know, the basic mother's uniform. No wonder he was impressed.

"Thanks," said Alice. "And aren't you a sweetheart to say so? Unfortunately, great looks aside, I feel like crap. You don't happen to have anything stronger than coffee tucked away behind that counter, do you?"

"Sorry. We don't have a liquor license. How about green tea? It's supposed to be very soothing."

"Soothing is good. Soothing might help. Bring it on."

Alice and I chose a booth near the front window. When a waitress delivered our drinks, we ordered without bothering to consult a menu. Cobb salad for me, a Reuben sandwich for Alice.

I lifted a brow. "That seems like an unlikely choice."

"It does, doesn't it?" Alice pulled off her jacket, folded it neatly, and laid it on the seat beside her. "I feel like I'm splurging on my last meal. Either that or stocking up on protein before heading into battle."

"That sounds ominous. Who are you thinking of doing battle with?"

"Oh, it's Joe, of course." Alice sighed. "Who else

could make me so mad that I just want to kill him?"

"The other people you've been working with for the last week?"

"Yeah," she agreed. "Them, too. Somehow this whole going-back-to-work experience seems to have brought out my latent homicidal tendencies. How do other women manage this stuff?"

"About as well as you are."

I picked up my green tea and had a sip. It tasted good, but soothing was a stretch. Or maybe I was just too wound up to notice.

"Has it occurred to you that maybe you're trying to do too much at once? Rather than testing the water, you've thrown yourself back in the deep end. You've got Joey at camp, Carly at Silvermine, Berkley at Pine Ridge, and along with all the other things like shopping, cooking, and housework, now you're working 25 or 30 hours a week. It's no wonder you're feeling a little frazzled."

"Frazzled doesn't even begin to describe it. And to top it off, everybody at Plummer, Wilkes is still treating me with kid gloves. As if they think I'll be totally unable to cope with any assignment that involves the slightest use of either technology or brainpower. Sometimes I wonder why I'm even there."

"You're there because you got tired of being 'just a mother.' You thought it was time to reenter the real world."

"Like that's happening."

"It will," I said. "Give it time. You've only been there a week. They've hardly even had a chance to get to know you yet."

"At this rate, I'm not sure they ever will. Yesterday I put in nearly a full day at the office, then ran out and picked up the kids and Berkley, and barely managed to make it home before Joe did. And do you know what he said when he walked in the door?"

"Nope." Considering Alice's current mood, guessing seemed like a dangerous option.

"He asked me what was for dinner."

"That wretch!"

Alice reached across the table and poked me. "Cut it out. You're supposed to be on my side."

"I am on your side. Really." And I could well imagine what had gone wrong, even if Joe hadn't been able to. "I hope you handed him a take-out menu and a phone."

"There might have been some screaming first. I'm afraid I sounded like a banshee. You know, those wailing demons in Irish folklore? The kids were probably hiding under the furniture."

"You were tired," I said.

"Either that or possessed." Alice flopped back in her seat and closed her eyes. "Lord, what am I doing sitting here complaining to you? I forgot. You used to be a single mother. You did all this and more."

"Things seem more clear-cut when you don't have a choice," I said pragmatically. "And it's easier once you get into a routine."

She opened one eye. "You're lying to make me feel better, aren't you?"

"Not entirely."

"Now I feel pitiful."

"And yet you still look great. Even Frank noticed."

"Even Frank?"

He was my brother. I just shrugged. It seemed like enough of a comment.

"I've lost three pounds," said Alice. "It's probably stress."

"Or lack of dinner."

There was a beat of silence, then she burst out laughing. "You're really not going to let me take myself so seriously, are you?"

"Not if I can help it."

Our food arrived and we both dug in eagerly. A couple of minutes passed before either one of us paused for breath.

"Let's change the subject," I said. "Talk to me about something besides work."

"Amber Fine."

"Good choice." With everything else that was going on, I'd pretty much forgotten that I was supposed to be snooping around in Bob's neighbor's life. "What about her?"

"I took her a bundt cake."

"A bundt cake?"

"You know, those round, curvy cakes you make in a mold? Mine was pistachio."

"I know what they are, I just wouldn't have the

slightest idea how to make one. You're a woman of many talents."

"I'm a woman who can read the directions on the back of a box," said Alice. "Trust me, it's no big deal. Davey could probably make one if he was so inclined."

Perish the thought.

"Okay, so you took Amber a cake. That was very neighborly of you."

"That's what I thought. Also, you know, better late than never. Did you know that woman has *nine* cats?"

"Really? She only had six when we lived there. She must have had a litter of kittens."

"Maybe you ought to talk to her about spaying and neutering."

I held up my hands. Like maybe I was warding off evil.

"Not me. I've got my own problems. What did you find out about James?"

"For one thing, he isn't just a figment of her imagination. She showed me her wedding pictures. They've been married three years."

"Right. And separated for how long?"

"I didn't have the guts to ask. I did, however, manage to do a little snooping around. You would have been proud of me. I looked for things that might indicate that a man was actually living there."

"Newspapers piled on the table and wet towels lying on the floor?"

We smiled together.

"I got nothing," Alice continued. "The woman's a neat freak."

"With nine cats around, I imagine you'd have to be."

"Says the person who lives with five big dogs."

"Point taken. Now back to James. What did he look like?"

Alice thought for a minute, then said, "Ordinary."

"That doesn't help."

"Maybe it does. Think about it. Maybe he has been around some and we just never noticed him. That could be the case. In fact, I bet it probably is."

I put down my fork and looked at her. "Another possibility is that you're trying to wiggle out of your assignment."

"Well, okay, you're right, that could be the case as well. But come on, I baked the woman a cake. What more do you want from me?"

"Oh please. You already told me all you did was read a box."

"And add eggs. Don't forget that part. That was important."

To the bundt cake, I'm sure. To me, not so much.

"So we're back to square one."

"Square two," said Alice. "I've seen pictures. That should count for something."

"Bob suspects Amber sliced James up and buried him in the basement."

"Bob has a terrible imagination." Alice shook her

head. "It's a good thing you divorced him."

"I think so too," I agreed. Without that step, I'd have never met Sam.

"What about Steve?" asked Alice.

"He's definitely dead."

"I *know* that. But you were supposed to be figuring out who killed him. How's that going?"

There was only one thing I could think to say. "Slowly."

"And you had the nerve to criticize me."

"Maybe I should bake Candy a cake," I said mildly.

"Make it a bundt," said Alice. "They do the trick every time."

23

Fortunately, Shannon Ritter wasn't hard to find. I let my fingers do the walking through half a column of telephone book listings and at the sixth grooming salon I called, the person who picked up the phone offered to get her for me. I declined and asked instead what hours she worked.

"Eight to five," the woman said shortly. "Just like the rest of us."

I'd returned home after visiting Pine Ridge and seeing Alice, but now it looked as though I'd be heading out again. Sam was working, so Kevin was with me. Riding in the car ranks right up there among his favorite things, so he didn't mind a bit.

Beautiful Petz turned out to be a storefront operation in a strip mall on the Post Road in west Norwalk. I had Kevin's stroller with me, but once again it was easier just to wrap the sling around my shoulders and pop him inside.

The car windows had been open during our drive, and when I went to get Kevin out of his car seat I saw that most of his wispy blond hair was standing on end around his head. Unfortunately, my efforts to smooth the strands down into place with my fingers only created more static. When I began to laugh, Kevin joined in, clapping his hands with glee. Punk baby it was.

A bell above the door chimed as we entered the store. I doubted that any of the groomers scattered around the big room could hear it over the high-decibel roar of blowdryers and rock music, but one lifted her head and glanced my way.

"We don't take walk-ins," she said.

Without waiting for a reply, she turned her attention back to the fluffy little dog on her table. It looked more or less like a Cockapoo, but the groomer was scissoring in the lines of a Bichon.

"I don't have a dog," I said. "I'm here to see Shannon Ritter."

"What?"

I took a couple of steps closer.

"Shannon Ritter?" I yelled.

272

Kevin stirred within the sling, and I gave his back a reassuring rub.

"She expecting you?"

I shook my head.

"She's busy."

The groomer lifted a hand and pointed with her scissors. A girl in the back of the room was lifting a wet Cocker Spaniel out of a tub. The black dog was draped in towels, only its muzzle and nose were visible.

Shannon looked younger than Larry by at least a decade. Baggy overalls covered most of her body, but she was thin enough that her shoulder blades stood out in stark relief beneath her thin T-shirt. Long red hair was piled in a messy knot on top of her head. Her roots needed touching up.

I started to walk back to see her. The groomer at the front table held up her arm to bar my way.

"No customers allowed past the yellow line. Company rules. Safety, you know?"

Like what? I might accidentally trip over a grooming table and fall in a bathtub? I sighed and stepped behind the line of tape on the floor.

Shannon was now placing the Cocker in a wire crate. She shut the door and directed the flow of a nearby blower to start the process of drying his coat. This looked like an opportune time to grab her.

"Would you mind getting her for me, please?"

The groomer rolled her eyes. I crossed my arms

over my chest. Or as close as I could come with Kevin there.

We'd reached a standoff.

The woman sighed in exasperation. I couldn't hear the sound, but her body language was eloquent enough to convey her meaning.

Then she swiveled around and screamed, "Shan! Lady here to see you!"

Jeez. I could have done that.

Shannon gave me the once-over from the back of the room.

I gave her a friendly little wave in return.

Shannon didn't look impressed. "What's she want?" she yelled.

"Dunno." An exaggerated shrug punctuated the reply.

It was like watching the Three Stooges have a conversation.

"I need to talk to you," I said.

"Like, now?"

"Like, yeah."

When in Rome and all that.

With a last glance at the Cocker, now lying on the floor of the crate and cringing beneath the rush of hot air, Shannon opened a nearby cupboard, grabbed her purse, and threaded her way through the other tables to the front of the store.

"Come on outside," she said.

I was only too happy to follow. After the barrage of noise in the grooming salon, the sound of traffic

274

on the nearby Post Road seemed almost soothing.

Shannon stepped to one side. The shipping store next door had a striped awning that provided a welcome strip of shade across the sidewalk. She'd slung her purse over her shoulder and her hand fumbled inside it briefly before emerging with a cigarette and a lighter.

In a gesture that was both practiced and economical, she lit up, inhaled deeply, and leaned back against the concrete building. I was guessing she did this a lot.

"So," she said. "What?"

"I want to talk to you about Steve Pine."

"Shit." She frowned. "I thought it was something important."

"His death isn't?"

"Not to me."

I was hoping she'd elaborate, but unfortunately the cigarette made a great oral substitute. Shannon sucked on that thing so hard that I wouldn't have been surprised to see it disappear into her mouth.

I considered my options and decided to play dumb. "I guess that means you two didn't have a good working relationship?"

"We didn't have a good any-kind-of-relationship." Her eyes narrowed. "And this is your business why?"

"Candy asked for my help—"

"She would." Shannon snorted. "Candy can't get anything done on her own. Larry—he's my guy, he

275

works there—says the place is falling apart now that Steve's not around to run things. Probably only a matter of time until it goes under."

Deliberately I angled my body away from hers. Kevin didn't need to breathe in any of her second-hand smoke. Shannon noted the move, glanced down inside the sling, and exhaled in the opposite direction.

"I guess you wouldn't be sorry to see that happen," I said.

"None of my business anymore. I imagine you heard I got fired. That's probably why you're here, right? To see if I was mad enough to sneak back over there and shoot Steve?"

Cigarette dangling from between her lips, Shannon laughed as if the thought was highly entertaining.

"Were you mad enough?"

"Nah. Why would I be? So I lost my job, big deal. I'm working again. One place is as good as another, you know?"

"You're bathing dogs," I said. "That's grunt work. I bet it doesn't pay as much as grooming."

"So I'll work my way up again. There's always plenty of turnover."

The cigarette was already half gone. I had no illusions about why Shannon hadn't already left and gone back inside. The nicotine fix was the draw, not me. Which meant I only had another minute or two.

"Is one boyfriend as good as another too?"

"What does that mean?"

"You and Steve had more than a working relationship."

"Maybe . . . once upon a time. That was over a while ago."

"That's not what I heard."

"Yeah?" Shannon straightened abruptly. Her face leaned in close to mine. "Well, you can tell Candy from me that she has a big mouth. And that brother of hers? He wasn't the angel she thought he was. Nowhere near. You should hear some of the stories Larry tells about things the two of them did together when they were younger."

"I heard they'd been friends for a long time. I guess that must have been pretty awkward for you."

"What?"

"Going from one to the other."

"It wasn't like that." She shook her head vehemently. "Not at all."

"Larry didn't mind?"

"You must be kidding. Larry got lucky when he got me, and he knew it."

Who says America's youth is lacking in self-esteem?

"So now the two of you are living together."

Shannon averted her eyes briefly. "For now. You know, until I get my shit together."

"And then what?"

She pulled the stub of the cigarette out of her

mouth, dropped it to the sidewalk, and ground it beneath the heel of her shoe. "Then I guess we'll have to see, won't we?"

She started to leave, then paused. "You'll see Candy again, right?"

I nodded.

"You want to take her a message from me?"

"Maybe."

"Just tell her . . ." Shannon's expression softened. "Just tell her I'm sorry about what happened."

It wasn't the message I'd expected.

"I can do that," I said.

I stopped and picked up Davey at camp on the way home. Then Sam called and told me to grab some Chinese food while I was out. Enough for four, he specified. So I stopped and did that too.

We arrived home to find Sam and Aunt Peg having drinks out on the deck. Aunt Peg took one look and held out her arms. I delivered Kevin into them.

"He needs a bottle," I said.

"I know how!" cried Davey. "Let me."

Sam followed him back inside to supervise, and I sat down on the chaise next to Peg.

"You look worn out," she said. "Aren't you sleeping?"

"No." I probably sounded a bit testy. I nodded Kevin's way. "You can blame him for that. And why does everyone keep commenting about how I look?"

"People care about you."

"They never cared this much before," I grumbled.

"Maybe you never noticed before."

Aunt Peg bounced her knee up and down. Kevin jiggled, threw his hands up in the air, and laughed a throaty little chuckle.

"I thought new mothers were supposed to glow," she said.

Aunt Peg, who never had children herself, is sometimes a little hazy about the particulars.

"That's pregnant women. I was glowing last year."

"Really? I don't remember that. How's your suspect list coming? I seem to recall there were several more people you were going to interview."

I nodded. "Roger Cavanaugh, the silent partner, for one. I saw him last night."

"And?"

"He didn't have anything earth shattering to report. He said his contribution to Pine Ridge was strictly financial, and that he'd been perfectly pleased with the way his investment was being managed by the Pines."

"Harrumph," said Aunt Peg.

The sound was meant to convey disapproval with what I'd accomplished without actually adding anything to the conversation. As you might surmise, I've heard it before.

"And then this afternoon I spoke with Shannon Ritter."

"Which one is she?"

"Current girlfriend of Larry the maintenance man, ex-girlfriend of Steve Pine, and the groomer who was responsible for letting JoyJoy the Shih Tzu get bred to Buster."

"*JoyJoy?*"

I swear I could be passing along state secrets and if there was a dog anywhere in the mix, she'd zero in on that first.

"That was her name."

"It's ridiculous."

Aunt Peg jiggled Kevin again and his head appeared to nod in agreement. No doubt, she did that on purpose.

"I'm sorry, I didn't name her. I'm just the messenger. And it would help if you could focus on the important things."

Aunt Peg frowned. She turned her head fully in my direction and stared at me with a look that went straight down her nose.

"I would be delighted to do so, if only you would tell me what those are. There's a method to mystery solving, you know. At this point you're supposed to be narrowing things down, not blithely enlarging the list as you go along. Have you eliminated *anybody* as a suspect yet?"

Blithely? Come on, *blithely?* That was a low blow. If there was anything blithe about what I'd been doing, I had yet to discover what.

"Well . . ." I admitted reluctantly. "I guess Candy Pine."

"Steve's business partner and closest relative? The woman who, I assume, inherited the majority of his assets? Interesting choice. And what's the reason you've decided she's innocent?"

Like I hadn't seen that coming.

"Instinct," I said with more fervor than I was actually feeling. "I'm going with my gut."

"Good Lord, that's brave of you. When I follow my gut, it usually leads me straight to the refrigerator. And speaking of which, didn't someone promise me dinner?"

"I did." Sam appeared in the doorway with a bottle in his hand. "Moo shu pork, beef with broccoli, kung pao chicken. All coming up as soon as I take care of this guy." He leaned down and scooped Kevin up out of Aunt Peg's arms. "It's a beautiful evening. I thought we'd eat outside."

I jumped up. "I'll set the table and pour the drinks."

Aunt Peg followed me inside to help. While Davey was preparing Kevin's bottle, Sam had fed the Poodles. All five had their noses buried in their dishes when we walked into the kitchen. Faith lifted her head briefly, wagged her tail in greeting, then went back to eating.

I stood there for a minute, watched the big black dogs inhale the kibble and stew mix, and thought about the fifty-pound sack of dry dog food we had stored in our pantry. Even with five dogs to feed, it lasted for quite a while.

"What are you staring at?" asked Aunt Peg. Her gaze roamed from one Poodle to the next, checking to see what she'd missed.

"I'm thinking."

"About what?"

"Kibble. In fifty-pound bags."

"A very economical arrangement. Anyone with more than a mouth or two to feed should buy their dog food that way."

"I know."

I opened a cupboard and pulled out four place-mats and napkins. I was still thinking. Aunt Peg continued to look at me curiously.

"Ten years ago," I said, "when Uncle Max was still alive and Cedar Crest Kennel was at its peak, how many Poodles did you have?"

"Quite a few." Aunt Peg stopped and considered. "We kept many more good ones to show in those days. And sometimes had three or even four litters in a year. Max loved the new puppies. He was always sure that each litter was going to contain our next superstar."

Considering the number of top Standard Poodles Cedar Crest Kennel had produced over the decades, Max had probably been right about that more often than not.

"How many?" I asked again.

"Maybe twenty-five, perhaps even as high as thirty at times. That seems like a tremendous num-ber now, but with both of us as involved as we were, it never felt like a lot of work. Why do you ask?"

I shook my head. I didn't want to lose my train of thought.

"I'll tell you in a minute. Just bear with me first. Next question. When you had that many dogs to feed, how much kibble did you go through?"

"I'd have to think back . . ."

"Wait. Before you do that, here's a better question. How many times per week did you have dog food and other supplies delivered?"

"Per week?" Aunt Peg sounded surprised. "Certainly less than once. I seem to recall we had a regular monthly delivery. In most cases, that was more than sufficient to meet our needs."

Once a month? I pulled out a kitchen chair and sat down. Aunt Peg took the placemats and napkins out of my hands and went outside to set the table herself. Meanwhile, I kept thinking.

Judging by what I'd seen, Byram Pet Supply was making deliveries to Pine Ridge several times a week. And according to what Steve had told me on my first visit, they cared for about as many dogs per day as Aunt Peg had had in her kennel. Not only that, but Pine Ridge's dogs went home at the end of the day. So why was Cole always there, and how could they possibly be going through so many supplies?

"You look like you're on to something," said Aunt Peg. Hands filled with silverware, she passed by on her way outside again.

"I think maybe I am."

"Kibble?"

"That's part of it."

"Not the most important part, I hope." She sounded skeptical.

"I don't know yet. Maybe. At any rate, it's worth following up."

"What is?" asked Sam.

He and Davey were back. Kevin was nowhere to be seen. Presumably, they'd read the baby a story and put him to bed. Early nights like this probably explained why he got us all up at the crack of dawn.

"Dinner," said Aunt Peg. She looked around at the three of us. "I'm starved and no one's offered me so much as a potato chip yet. Are you people going to feed me or not?"

"Coming right up," I said. This time my gut was following Aunt Peg's.

Dinner it was.

24

The next day was Field Day at Davey's soccer camp. Both Sam and I were planning to attend. Before the event began in late morning, however, there was just enough time for me to make a quick trip down to Byram to talk to Cole Demarkian.

Byram is a small section of Greenwich, Connecticut, tucked into the southwest corner of town. It's the final outpost of Fairfield County before the New York border, and the area owes its commercial identity more to neighboring Port Chester than to the chic shops and upscale boutiques that characterize the rest of its hometown.

Byram Pet Supply turned out to be a warehouse store, housed in a large, square, concrete building, and located in a high traffic area between the Post Road and the shoreline. Early on Wednesday morning, the parking lot out front was almost empty.

Aside from my Volvo, the only other vehicles I saw were three identical white cargo vans, each sporting the company logo. Hopefully, the fact that they were still sitting there meant that Cole hadn't yet left the store to begin his day's deliveries.

I'd just dropped Davey at camp and Kevin was home with Sam. So the trip to the pet supply store had seemed like a perfect opportunity to grab a little more quality time with my number one Poodle, Faith. She was riding shotgun beside me on the front seat. When I opened my door and got out, the Poodle waited politely for an invitation to join me, then gave a small yip of delight when one was forthcoming.

I clipped a thin leather leash to Faith's collar, then opened the door to the store and let her precede me inside. There were fish tanks to the left of the entrance area and birdcages on the right. Half a dozen yellow canaries popped up in the air, startled from their perches by our appearance. They chirped loudly as they zoomed around their enclosed space.

The store was one big, wide-open room. From where we stood I could see the back wall about an acre away. It was stacked from floor to ceiling with the practical stuff: bags of dog and cat food. Before a shopper got that far, however, he would first have to pass by tempting displays filled with pet toys, books, and grooming supplies.

For the devoted pet owner, this place was consumer heaven.

That early in the morning, the row of check-out counters stood idle. Aside from the frantic chirping that continued unabated, all was quiet. The smell of kitty litter hung in the air.

I was debating which way to head first when a young woman wearing a dark green WE LOVE YOUR PETS! apron, stuck her head around an end-cap midway back. According to the sign that hung from the ceiling above her head, the aisle she was working in was devoted to FERRET SUPPLIES.

"Can I help you?" she asked.

"Yes, I'm—"

Then the woman caught sight of Faith. She came flying around a display of colorful ferret cages with names like Critter Trail and Habitat Playground. The name tag affixed to the top of her apron identified her as Penny. It also told me she was HERE TO HELP!

"Wow, what a great dog! Standard Poodle, right? She's a big one! What's her name? Who does your grooming? She looks so soft! Is she friendly? Can I touch?"

It was hard to know which question to address first. But while I hesitated, Faith did her part impeccably. She walked forward, touched the woman's outstretched hand with her nose, and wagged her tail back and forth above her back with all the serene majesty of a queen greeting a loyal subject.

"Her name is Faith," I said. "And, yes, you can touch her. She's very friendly."

Penny slid her hand along Faith's muzzle until her fingers reached the Poodle's ears. She gave an experimental scratch. Faith tipped her head and leaned into her.

"Some coat." Penny lifted her hand to stroke the long, smooth ear hair. "I'll bet she's a lot of work."

"She is. But she'd be the first one to tell you that she's worth it."

We smiled together.

"We get a lot of Poodles in here," Penny said. "But mostly it's the little ones. Not to mention all the other crosses . . . Cockapoos, Pekepoos, Poogles. You name it, we see it."

"Poogles?" I said reluctantly. I hadn't heard that one before.

"You know, a Beagle Poodle cross?"

I tried to imagine a mixture of those two breeds leading to something good, and simply couldn't. I wasn't being Poodle-centric. I was pretty sure that Beagle breeders would have felt the same way.

"It's the age of the designer dog," Penny continued brightly. "Why be restricted to the already existing breeds when you can just create your own? All the celebrities have them now."

"They do?"

"Sure. Don't you read *Star* magazine?"

"Umm . . . no."

"If you like, I'm sure I can find you a book in our collection about creating your own designer dog. A big Poodle like that"—she beamed down at Faith who responded, once again, by wagging her tail—"could really make some beautiful puppies. You wouldn't believe how many possibilities there are. Labradoodles, Goldendoodles, Boxerdoodles. You can even register them now. Pretty soon, they'll be like whole new breeds. You'll even be able to show them in dog shows."

The mind boggled.

"No, thank you," I said as politely as I could manage. "I don't need a book."

An aspirin maybe. But not a primer on how to create more mixed breed dogs.

"You sure? Because Faith really is a beauty. And I bet you could find someone right here in Greenwich with a Lab or a Golden Retriever they'd be willing to stud out. Then it only takes two months until you get a litter. You come back in and put a cute picture up on our community access bulletin board and the puppies will be sold before you know it. Easy money!"

"I don't think so," I said.

My tone was clipped, but Penny didn't seem to notice. She was still smiling, as if she didn't understand how I could fail to see the beauty of her excellent plan.

"Do you have any idea how many unwanted dogs there are in the United States already?" I asked.

"No, but—"

"Tens of thousands. Pounds and shelters are filled with them. Some are mixed breeds and some are purebred. And I'm sure they were all cute puppies once. Most likely the majority of them were bred by people who didn't put any more thought or consideration into having a litter than you're advising me to."

Penny retreated several steps. That probably meant that the expression on my face wasn't particularly pleasant. Not surprising, considering that this conversation was pushing most of my buttons.

Easy money? Designer dogs? She was lucky I didn't have smoke coming out of my ears.

"Jeez," she said. "You could have just said you weren't interested."

I'd already done that. And Penny had rolled right over my first several objections. I wondered how many other dog owning customers the saleswoman had managed to seduce with her cheerful advice and her get-rich-quick ideas. Hopefully not very many.

"Actually, I'm looking for someone," I said. "Cole Demarkian. I believe he drives one of your delivery trucks?"

Penny shrugged. "I work out front. I wouldn't know anything about what goes on in the back."

The rebuff was clear. I'd criticized her grand plan; now I was on my own.

"Maybe there's someone else I could talk to?"

Her eyes flickered briefly toward a swinging door in the back wall.

"Thanks," I said and headed that way.

Faith caught up in one stride and fell in step at my side.

"Wait!" Penny hurried after us. "You can't go in there. That area is for employees only."

"Cole Demarkian," I said again. My pace slowed slightly. "Curly dark hair, big muscles, very good looking?"

If the effect Cole had on the women at Pine Ridge was anything to go by, Penny had to know who he was. He didn't seem like the type of guy who was likely to go unnoticed by any females in the vicinity.

"I just need to ask him a few questions."

Penny frowned. "I guess you could try around back. The guys usually hang out there while they're waiting to get their delivery schedules for the day."

"Thanks."

Faith and I exited the front of the store and followed the parking lot around the side of the build-

290

ing. A loading dock with two bays, its garage-style doors currently sitting open, took up the near end of the back wall.

Approaching the chest-high platform, I saw a middle-aged man carrying a clipboard and a mug of coffee. He spotted me and came over.

"Whatcha need?" he asked.

"Cole Demarkian."

"Hang on." He turned and yelled over his shoulder into the bay. "Yo, Cole! Come on out here."

After a moment, Cole appeared in the open doorway. Tight jeans, form-fitting T-shirt, a shadow of stubble across his strong jaw. Yup, Cole was ready for work, all right.

"Lady here is looking for you."

Cole strode out to the end of the loading dock. As the older man went back inside, Cole leaned down, grasped the edge of the platform, and hopped down to my level. The movement was easy and fluid. Cole looked good in motion and he knew it.

He squinted at me briefly, his gaze dropping to Faith and then lifting again. "I'm sorry. Have we met?"

"Not exactly. But I've seen you at the Pine Ridge Canine Care Center in Stamford. I know you make deliveries there."

"Sure. I stop there a couple of times a week. It's on my route."

"So you must have known Steve Pine."

"Sure," Cole said again. A varied vocabulary didn't

291

seem to be his strong suit. "Were you a friend of his? I'm real sorry about what happened."

"Actually, I'd only met him once. But after he died his sister, Candy, asked me to do a job for her."

"What's that?"

Faith stepped forward to give Cole a sniff. He reached down, patted the top of her head, and murmured, "Hi, girl," under his breath as he was waiting for my answer.

I have an automatic fondness for people who like my dogs. Besides, Faith's a pretty good judge of character.

"Candy asked me to help figure out who murdered Steve," I said.

Cole sized me up again. His expression was somewhat skeptical.

"So you're like, what? A police detective?"

"No, strictly amateur," I replied. But that raised an interesting point. "Speaking of which, did the police ever question you about what happened?"

"No. Why would they? It's not like I knew anything. I didn't even find out Steve was dead until a couple days later when I made my next delivery. I went inside to have him sign the papers and Candy had to do it instead."

"So Steve was the one you usually dealt with when you made deliveries?"

"Sure. Steve was *the man*."

"Meaning?"

Cole shrugged. "He was just a good guy, easy to be around. Easy to work with. You know?"

"So I guess you wouldn't have any idea why someone would want him dead?"

"None at all." Cole was firm. "I figured it had to be some kind of freak accident."

A man found dead in his office . . . shot once in the head . . . no murder weapon to be found. It was hard for me to see how that could have happened accidentally, but to each his own.

"You seem to make quite a few deliveries to Pine Ridge."

"Couple times a week, I guess. But that's not up to me, I just do what it says on the roster."

"Has the number of times you go to Pine Ridge changed recently?"

Cole thought for a moment. "Could be. Now that you mention it, it does seem like I've been over there more often than usual lately. Used to be I'd stop there every ten days or so. Now it's more like twice a week."

"Has Candy changed something? The pattern of ordering, maybe?"

"Like I said, I wouldn't know anything about that part. I just get told what to put on the truck and where to take it. That's all."

Cole was losing interest in my questions. Fortunately, he had Faith to keep him occupied. He patted the front of his T-shirt, inviting the big Poodle to jump up on him.

She cast a quick glance at me, seeking permission for what was normally a forbidden act. I nodded absently.

Faith was every bit as graceful as Cole. She hopped up lightly and braced her front paws against the taut muscles of his chest. While he waited for me to continue, Cole ran his hand up and down Faith's sides. The Poodle wriggled with delight at his touch.

Human or canine, Cole had a way with the ladies, all right.

"So you're stopping at Pine Ridge more often now," I said. "What about the size of the deliveries? Has that changed or remained the same?"

"I guess about the same. It's not like I pay attention to what each customer gets. To me, all that matters is how many handcart trips it takes to unload. At Pine Ridge that's three, pretty much every time."

"And yet you're stopping there more often," I said slowly. I thought about Bailey, waylaying Cole in the parking lot and trying to stop the flood of supplies that she didn't have room for. "Which means you're actually delivering two or three times as much stuff as you were in the past."

"I guess." Cole shrugged again. "If you say so."

Forget what I'd told Jason about the possibility that the delivery man was a PhD candidate. Cole had enough brain power to handle his current position, but there wasn't going to be much left over.

"And yet," I said, thinking aloud, "the number of clients has dropped since Steve died."

"You don't have to worry about that part," said Cole.

I looked up. "I don't?"

"No. Steve and I talked about that once. Probably a year ago. He had this process built into his bookkeeping system to handle that kind of fluctuation. It was something he designed himself."

"And he talked to *you* about it?" I asked, puzzled.

"Sure. Like I said, Steve was pretty easygoing. He got along with everyone and when he talked to you, it was almost like he was taking you into his confidence. He told people things, made them feel like they were part of what was going on."

I had no idea where Cole was going with this, but I certainly wanted to find out. "And what were you part of?"

"No big deal. Steve just asked me to do him a favor once or twice and bring him some blank invoices from the store. He said it helped him out with the bookkeeping, you know? Like if there was an error or something, because he was expecting more dogs than they actually had, he could easily fix it himself. That way, all the numbers in the books always matched up."

No big deal to Cole maybe, but it was to me. Because that piece of information gave me a pretty good idea how Steve Pine might have gotten himself killed.

25

I left Byram and drove home where I dropped off Faith and picked up Sam and Kevin. Together, the three of us headed over to Davey's camp.

The Field Day had a round-robin format with several games being played at a time, and a call had gone out beforehand for parent volunteers to help out with the busy schedule. Sam and I had both signed up.

He served as referee for a couple of games while I handed out snacks and juice boxes during the breaks. Kevin, whose job was to sit in his stroller and enjoy the spectacle, shuttled back and forth between us like a baby commuter.

Davey and Joey, Alice's son, had been assigned to the same team. Both were playing defense; Davey at center halfback and Joey in the goal. Since Alice was stuck at work, I was also manning the video camera, recording the day's events so that she could enjoy the replays later that night.

Juggling tasks like the experienced mom I was, I also found time to make a quick phone call to Pine Ridge.

"You and I need to talk," I told Candy when she came on the line.

"That sounds serious."

"It is."

"Go ahead."

"Not over the phone," I said. "There are still some details I have to work out. And there's stuff I need your help with. I want to do it in person."

A raucous cheer went up. Somebody's team had scored a goal. All around me, parents were jumping up and down, screaming. Even Kevin was waving his hands in the air. I had to wait for the tumult to die down before I could hear what Candy was saying.

"What's all that yelling?" she asked. "Where are you?"

"Soccer game. It's Field Day at Davey's camp."

"When does it end?"

"Four o'clock, give or take."

"See you then," she said and hung up.

Davey and Joey's team won their first two games, then lost the third. Since the defeat had come at the hands of boys who were two grades ahead of them in school, neither was unduly upset by the loss.

Last game of the day pitted the kids against their parents. Sam played the first half, I went in for the second. If it wasn't for a last minute block by my own son that didn't look strictly legal to me, I would have scored a goal. The game went down to the wire, and the kids beat us in overtime.

When we got back to the house, I grabbed a quick

shower, then explained to Sam that I had to go out again.

"Let me guess," he said, cocking a brow. "Pine Ridge?"

I nodded. "I'm meeting Candy there. I think I've finally figured out what's going on. I just need a few more answers, and then I'll take everything to the police and let them work on it."

"Sounds like a plan," said Sam. "Be careful."

"You know I will."

Candy was waiting for me when I arrived. In fact, she was pacing back and forth in the grassy area between the front office building and the Dog House.

Winston was outside with her. The plump Welsh Corgi had more sense than to stride up and down in the sun, however. Instead, he was flopped down under a nearby tree with his muzzle nestled between his front paws. Only the Corgi's eyes were moving as he kept tabs on her progress from his comfortable spot in the shade.

"I thought you said four o'clock," Candy snapped as I approached.

"That's when the event ended. Then I had to go home and change."

It was closer to five now. But anxious as I was to try to fit together the last pieces of the puzzle, I wasn't about to let Candy bully me. Solving Steve's murder was important to me, but not nearly as important as my family.

"Would you rather we do this tomorrow?" I asked mildly.

"No, of course not. You're here now, let's get on with it. Tell me what you've found out."

"For one thing, I've been told that there are some irregularities in your bookkeeping."

Candy stopped pacing and spun around to face me.

"Bookkeeping?" She sounded incredulous. "That's what you wanted to talk to me about?"

"For starters."

"Who cares about that? I thought you were going to tell me who killed my brother."

"I'm getting there. And the trail starts—or maybe ends— with your books."

"What do you mean?"

"I'm pretty sure that Steve was keeping two sets of records."

"No." The denial was quick and automatic. Candy didn't even stop to think. "That doesn't make any sense. Why would he do that?"

"I was hoping you could tell me."

"Tell you what? I don't even know what you're talking about."

"Maybe I should back up," I said.

"Feel free," Candy muttered.

She walked over and sat down on the bench. Even in repose, she still hummed with nervous energy. Winston watched her take a seat but made no move to join her on the bench.

Taking my cue from the Corgi, I remained standing. "Earlier today, I went over to Byram and had a chat with Cole Demarkian. You know, the guy who makes the deliveries for Byram Pet Supply?"

"I know who Cole is," Candy said shortly. "Why would you want to talk to him?"

"Because for one thing, he's making a lot more deliveries to Pine Ridge now than he used to before Steve died."

"How do you know that?"

"He told me so this morning."

"And I'm supposed to think that matters?"

"Yes," I said emphatically. "I'm pretty sure it does. Remember yesterday when Cole was here and Bailey was complaining that she had so many new grooming supplies that she didn't even have enough room to store them all?"

"Crap," Candy said with a frown. "What are you, omniscient? How do you even know about this stuff?"

"I was here, remember? We'd just been talking in your office and when I was leaving I ran into Bailey and Jason outside."

"Jason? He's just a kid. Summer help. How could he possibly know anything?"

"You'd be surprised," I said.

Candy stared up at me, lifting a hand to shade her eyes from the slanting sun. The look on her face was equal parts frustration and annoyance.

"Let me tell you what I remember from yesterday. I told you I was innocent and you told me you'd help me prove it. And now you're saying that all you've done is discover there's some sort of problem with the books?"

"Not just some sort of problem," I said firmly. "Something potentially big enough to lead to murder."

"How?"

I walked over and joined her on the bench. "Who's been doing the books since Steve died?"

"I have . . . after a fashion. Numbers aren't my strong suit. Anything that resembles actual accounting is a nightmare as far as I'm concerned. Basically all I've been doing is keeping up with the payroll and the purchasing, and then paying the bills when they come in."

"So you haven't made any changes to what Steve set up?"

"Heck no, why would I do that? Just looking at those columns of numbers is confusing enough. It's not like I'm going to jump in and try to improvise. I figure Steve must have had a system that worked, so why mess with it?"

The door to the Dog House opened and a staff member came out leading a matching pair of Bulldogs. While Candy and I had been speaking, there'd been a steady one-way stream of dogs on the walkway between the two buildings. Clients were arriving at the front office to pick up their pets.

Pine Ridge was getting ready to close for the day.

"Eventually I'll have to hire someone who can sort the whole thing out," said Candy. "But in the meantime, I didn't see any reason why we couldn't just muddle along for a month or two."

"So if there was something unusual going on in the accounting—maybe some numbers that didn't add up in purchasing and accounts payable—you probably wouldn't have noticed?"

Candy shook her head. "Trust me, there could be a great big picture of Brad Pitt wearing nothing but a smile sitting in the middle of those files and I wouldn't have noticed. That's how little time I've spent in there. I just get in, find what I need to know, and get out."

Candy's reticence to deal with numbers certainly explained how Steve had been able to get away with what I suspected he'd been up to. As long as he was the sole person with access to the ledger, there'd be no one to complain about figures that didn't always make sense.

"Another question. How do you decide how much stuff you need to order? You know, dog food, grooming supplies, whatever."

"That's easy." Candy looked relieved that I'd finally asked her something she knew the answer to. "That stuff's all in Steve's computer too. I just looked back over the invoices for the last couple of months, saw what he was doing, and kept it up."

Easy for Candy, perhaps. And maybe even logical. But I was pretty sure that that system had had the effect of flooding Pine Ridge with unneeded supplies.

"Would you mind if I went into Steve's computer and had a look for myself?" I asked.

Candy thought for a minute before answering. "You won't erase anything?"

I shook my head.

"Or make any changes to stuff that's in there?"

"Definitely not. I just want to have a look at some of the company accounting and see whether everything adds up the way it's supposed to."

"I guess that's all right," said Candy. "On one condition."

"What's that?"

"When you get finished snooping around my brother's files, will you go back to trying to figure out who killed him?"

I stared at her, perplexed. That was exactly what I *was* doing. How could Candy not see that?

I'd run across people before who had a mental block about math. My sister-in-law, Bertie, was one of them. But the information I needed wasn't so much about the numbers themselves as it was about the internal logic of how money was being distributed within the business. Maybe if I found what I was looking for and then laid everything out in front of Candy in very simple steps, she'd be able to understand.

"Well?" she prompted, and I realized she'd mistaken my silence for hesitation.

"It's a deal," I replied. "Your brother's computer —is it password protected?"

"Of course. Steve was very careful about things like that. I guess I have to give that to you, huh?"

"Either that or come inside and sign me in yourself."

Candy looked down at her watch. "No, I'm already running late. I have a few more things to finish up and then I'm gone for the day. I'm assuming you don't mind if I don't sit and hold your hand while you go on this fishing expedition?"

There it was again, Candy's total disbelief that the files could reveal anything of importance. She must have trusted her brother and the way he was managing their accounts implicitly. Unfortunately, I suspected I was going to be destroying that illusion.

"No, that's fine. In fact, I work better when things are quiet. Password?"

Candy rose from the bench and headed toward the back of the office building. She waggled her fingers at Winston and the Corgi hopped up and scampered along. He and I fell into step beside her.

"It's Nathan," she said.

"Like the dog?" I asked, surprised.

"Yeah." Pulling open the door, she smiled sadly. "Funny choice, huh? Steve had a real soft spot for that old Dachshund. He once said he thought that dog would outlive us all. Too bad he turned out to be half right."

Candy and I walked down the hallway together. The door to her office stood open. The door to Steve's was closed. When I hesitated in front of it, she reached around me, turned the knob, and pushed it open.

"There you go," she said, flipping on a light switch just inside the door. "Computer's on the desk, file cabinet's over by the closet. Knock yourself out."

"Thanks," I said. "I will."

I sat down in Steve's leather chair, rolled it closer to the desk, and got my bearings. The last time I'd seen Steve's office there'd been stacks of paperwork on the desk's surface. In the interim, all that had disappeared. As had the dead plant in the corner of the room. Obviously, Candy had gotten around to hiring a cleaning service to put the room back together.

As the computer powered up, I heard a hum of voices from the reception area, punctuated by the occasional happy bark. Madison was greeting returning clients and checking dogs out for the day. Things were wrapping up out front. Pretty soon the place would be empty. Too bad it hadn't occurred to me to bring Faith along for company.

The opening screen appeared and I typed in Steve's password. That took me to a screen saver whose image was a tranquil river scene. Shortcut icons dotted both sides of the picture.

I'm not a computer whiz by any means. But if I go slowly and take things step by step, more times than not I eventually end up where I want to go.

Now I paused and examined each of the choices. It made sense to me that Steve would have a short-cut leading directly to his business files, and he did. The accounting software was Peachtree. Sam used the same system for his small business.

The first page I came to gave me a number of choices including Business Status, Customers & Sales, Vendors & Purchases, and Employees & Payroll. I was guessing that Business Status most likely held the profit-and-loss statements that I wanted to see, but first I went to Vendors & Purchases.

That screen offered more choices. I typed the name Byram Pet Supply into the search box and watched as a long list of invoice dates, starting in early January and continuing right up until Steve's death, appeared. A tab at the top of the page offered me access to the same records for the two previous years. Now I was getting somewhere.

Starting with the most recent invoices and working my way back, I began to skim through the information. I tried not to get bogged down looking at the individual items, focusing instead on the order patterns and totals, but even so it was slow going.

When Candy stuck her head in the office door to say that she was leaving, I was surprised to see that an hour had already passed. I hadn't even made a dent in the amount of information there was to process.

"I'm the last one out," she said. "And we're all locked up. Feel free to stay as long as you want. Just turn out the lights and lock the back door behind you when you leave."

"I will," I said, blinking as I pulled my eyes away from the screen. "There's a lot of stuff here to go through. I'll stay for a little while now, but I'll probably have to come back tomorrow and finish."

"Whatever."

She pulled her head back and disappeared. I followed the sound of her footsteps, and Winston's, until they reached the end of the hallway and let themselves out. Then I went back to work.

An hour later, I looked up again, realized it was getting late, and called Sam.

"Where are you?" he asked.

"Still at Pine Ridge. What are you up to?"

"Feeding the kids dinner. I thought you'd be home by now."

"So did I . . . sort of." I felt guilty for losing track of time. "But I'm going through Steve's records, and I'm right in the middle of things. I'd hate to have to stop now."

Sam sighed. I heard him, even though I was pretty sure he'd tilted the receiver away to mask the sound.

"Give me another hour," I said. "Ninety minutes,

tops. What I don't have done by then, I'll leave til tomorrow."

"I'm holding you to that," Sam said sternly.

"I love you too," I said, and hung up the phone.

Once again I went back to work. The sun outside began to set. I turned on the lights and kept going. Things were beginning to fall into place now. By the time I neared the end of my self-imposed deadline, I'd found the first half of what I needed.

Steve's buying patterns with regard to the purchases he was making at Byram Pet Supply had changed dramatically from the first year Pine Ridge had been in business to the second, most recent year. Even allowing for the fact that the business was growing and therefore expanding its needs, there was no logical way to account for the fact that—according to the invoices I was reading—the purchases of dog food, grooming equipment, and other dog related supplies had more than tripled. Especially when I factored in a reasonable usage schedule.

Kibble was a resource that would need to be replenished regularly. But dog beds, brushes, clipper blades? I used all those items regularly myself and I knew how long it took to wear them out. Despite what the evidence in front of me seemed to indicate, it didn't happen overnight.

For Pine Ridge to be going through as many supplies as the invoices showed, they would either have to be tending to several hundred dogs a day or else throwing out equipment that had barely been used. Or there was the other option—they were never taking delivery of those supplies in the first place.

I was voting for Plan B myself.

Basically, Steve had figured out a way to steal from himself . . . and his other two partners, of course. He hadn't been satisfied with the profits he'd been drawing from the business through legitimate means, and he'd devised a way to siphon off some extra funds.

Despite what I'd uncovered thus far, however, I was still a long way from proving my hypothesis. A pattern of erratic purchases wasn't enough. Nor was the tracking graph I found on the Business Status page of the software that clearly showed a recent dip in revenue. What I needed now were the bills of lading—the signed receipts showing exactly what had been delivered to Pine Ridge by Byram Pet Supply, and when.

I glanced down at my watch. Time was running out. And yet I hated to stop now when I was so close.

I shoved back the desk chair and strode to the most obvious place to look: the file cabinet near the closet. Of course the receipts weren't there, though I did come across the hard copies of what I suspected were Steve's fraudulent invoices—the ones he'd filled out himself on the blank sheets Cole had so conveniently supplied.

One by one, I slammed the drawers shut. Then I moved onto the desk. Those drawers looked like a tornado had passed through them recently. That explained how the desktop had been cleared—someone had simply swept all the papers inside, out of sight.

But I still didn't find any bills of lading. They weren't on the high shelf in the closet, nor under the cushions of the couch. I looked behind the calendar on the wall and even lifted a section of rug to check beneath it.

Nada.

Now, not only was I late, I was frustrated.

Think! I told myself. I stood in the middle of the room and spun slowly to look in all directions. If you had papers to hide, where would you put them?

When the answer came to me, it was so simple that I wanted to kick myself for not thinking of it sooner.

I stared at the empty dog crate in the back of the room. It was a medium-size Vari-Kennel, so familiar to me, so like those I had at home, that I hadn't even really noticed it. After all, who would pay any attention to one more crate in a facility that was essentially a kennel?

Except that from what I'd heard, Steve hadn't really liked dogs. Winston followed Candy everywhere, but Steve had had no similar companion of his own. Her office was awash with dog hair, his was pristine.

So who, or what, had the crate been intended to hold?

In a flash I was on my knees and leaning down to look inside. The crate had a pile of bedding—towels and a faux sheepskin throw—on top of its pegboard floor. I sniffed experimentally.

Nope. No way. No dog had ever lived in here.

Reaching into the crate, I shoved the rugs to the back of the container, then threaded my fingers around the edges of the floorboard and lifted it up to reveal the small space beneath. And saw a bulky, nine-by-twelve envelope nestled within.

"Finally." I exhaled.

"Indeed," said Roger Cavanaugh.

I whipped around, hit my head on the crate, lost my balance, and ended up sprawled on the rug. But even from that ungainly position, it was hard to miss the glint from the overhead light on the metal object he had in his hand.

Candy and Steve's silent partner was holding a gun.

26

Let me tell you something about guns. Or more specifically about bullets. I've been shot before, and it hurts. Like, *really* hurts.

So when someone holding a weapon tells me to do something, chances are, I'm going to obey.

"Get up," said Cavanaugh.

I scrambled to my feet, then moved over slightly so that I was standing in front of the crate and blocking his view of what lay within. Maybe he hadn't seen the envelope yet. If not, I wasn't about to give him any help.

"Don't be stupid," said Cavanaugh.

So much for that idea.

He gestured to one side with the hand that held the gun. It looked like a move he'd seen in the movies. Why do people always do that? If I was holding a gun, I would want to keep my hand very, very still. Nevertheless, Cavanaugh was using the weapon to indicate that he wanted me to move aside.

So I did.

He took several steps closer and looked inside the crate.

"Hand me the money," he said.

"Money?" I squeaked.

My normal voice seemed to have deserted me. Not that I could blame it. I wouldn't have been there either if I could have avoided it.

"The envelope. Get me the envelope."

I stared to comply, then abruptly stopped. "You think there's *money* in there?"

Cavanaugh looked amused. "You don't?"

"Not really," I admitted.

"Then pull it out and let's see who's right."

I got back down and retrieved the envelope from its hiding place on the floor of the crate. Its contents felt thick and bulky in my hand. Once I had the envelope, I took a minute to replace the crate's pegboard floor and smooth the bedding back into place. Once a mom, always a mom.

"Hurry up," said Cavanaugh. "I don't have all night."

I stood up, turned around, and placed the envelope on the desk between us. Cavanaugh was standing between me and the door. But he couldn't reach the envelope from where he was. In order to pick it up, he'd have to come farther into the room. And maybe that would give me a chance to escape.

It wasn't exactly a great plan but it was the best I could come up with while staring at that gun.

"Speaking of all night," I said. "What are you doing here? And how did you get in? This building was supposed to be locked."

"Candy called me. Since she and I are partners, she felt obliged to tell me that you thought you'd uncovered some irregularities in the company accounting."

Cavanaugh gave a dismissive shrug. As if the turn of events that had landed me in this predicament had been just that unremarkable.

"She told me not to worry. She said you were working late on the problem tonight and that it would all be fixed by tomorrow."

Damn, I thought. That woman was dumb as a brick.

"Candy was just trying to be helpful," Cavanaugh said with a small smile. "And she was."

"To you, maybe."

"Ah, but you see, that's all that matters to me."

"Candy probably gave you a spare key, too, didn't she?" I asked.

"No, that was actually Steve's doing. I've had one from the beginning. And why not? After all, it was my hard-earned dollars that financed this place."

I nodded. Anything to make myself agreeable. "And you expected a reasonable return on your investment."

"Of course. Any businessman would. Otherwise, why invest money in the first place? Steve was the one who came to me, you know. He and Candy had what they thought was a great idea. They were sure they could make it work. But the two of them were just about broke. Without my money, Pine Ridge would never have existed."

"So you must have been really angry when you found out that Steve was skimming off some of the profits for himself."

I trailed my hand aimlessly across the edge of the desk. On the other side of the computer was a paperweight shaped like an old-fashioned dog house, the kind that Snoopy used to sit on, with frame sides and a peaked roof. It didn't look like much of a weapon but you know what they say . . . any port in a storm.

"How'd you figure that out, by the way?" I asked.

"Give me some credit. I'm a businessman. That's what I do. I may not have been keeping tabs on the day-to-day running of this place, but I sure as hell had my eye on the bottom line. Let's just say Steve Pine wasn't as smart as he thought."

"In what way?"

"The business was thriving. Anyone associated with it could see that, and I was here almost every day with Logan. The facility was in good shape and the client roster was growing. So the fact that my share of the profits leveled off, then even began to dip a bit during the second year, came as a bit of a surprise. Funny thing is, if Steve hadn't gotten so greedy, I might never have noticed. That was his first mistake."

No, I thought, Steve's first mistake had been taking Roger Cavanaugh on as a partner. But I wasn't about to mention that.

"I've been going through his records," I said. "From what I could see Steve wasn't taking out a huge amount of money."

"I guess that depends on your perspective. Maybe if the money had belonged to you, it would seem like more. A couple thousand here, a couple thousand there . . . over time those amounts add up."

Cavanaugh eyed the envelope on the desk. As he spoke, he took a step or two toward it. It was as if the mere mention of the money he thought it held was luring him closer.

Me, I was watching the door. Because when it came to shooting someone, I figured a moving target had to be harder to hit than a stationary one. And as soon as Cavanaugh gave me enough of an opening, that was what I planned to be doing—moving as fast as my feet would go.

"Here's what you need to understand," said Cavanaugh. "Steve Pine was stealing from me and it had to stop."

"So you killed him," I said.

"Not on purpose."

He didn't sound contrite. More matter-of-fact. Like he'd merely performed a service that had to be done. Cavanaugh tore his eyes away from the envelope and looked up at my face.

I used the opportunity to quickly palm the paper-weight. Its heft and its sharp edges felt good in my hand.

"I'm not a monster," he said.

"No, just a murderer." My gaze dropped. "And a man who feels comfortable holding a gun on someone else."

"It wasn't like that. You weren't there. You couldn't possibly know what happened."

No, but I was pretty sure he was going to tell me. It seems that confession really must be good for the soul, because most of the criminals I've run across have felt the need to unburden themselves. As if coming up with a good excuse can make every-thing all right.

"I only came here that night to talk to Steve. I intended to threaten him into changing his ways. That's all."

"And yet you brought a gun with you."

Cavanaugh spread his hands. "Call me a realist. It wouldn't have been much of a threat without one, would it?"

I nodded as if conceding the point. The more he was thinking about how to explain what he had done, the less attention he was paying to me.

"Steve Pine was an idiot. Somehow he'd gotten things all turned around in his mind. In the beginning, he couldn't have been happier to take me on as a partner. To help him make his dream come true."

Cavanaugh grimaced at the trite phrase. "But as time went on he began to resent the fact that I was due a bigger share of the profits than he was. Steve convinced himself that the distribution of funds wasn't fair. Especially when he was here every day working his butt off and I wasn't."

"I'm guessing he didn't respond well to your threats," I said.

"He told me to go fuck myself."

"Brave language from a man facing a gun."

"That's what I thought. But Steve just laughed. He said he knew I wouldn't use it. And you know what? He was right. I wouldn't have used the gun. That's not who I am. Jesus, look at me. I drive a Hummer. I wear suits to work every day." His voice rose. "That wasn't how I was going to settle things. I would have sued the bastard. I would have taken him to court."

"So what went wrong?" I asked.

I really wanted to know. Maybe that meant I was buying into Cavanaugh's story, but now I wanted to know how it ended. The man had brought a gun to a business meeting, but he'd intended to walk away when it was over. And yet somehow Steve Pine had ended up dead.

"He jumped me and tried to wrestle the gun away," said Cavanaugh. "Like he'd been watching too many action movies and he thought he was Rambo or something. Of course I fought back. That's just instinct. No way I was going to give up the gun."

"You're saying it was an accident that Steve got shot?"

"Of course it was an accident. How else could it have happened? We both had our hands on the gun when it went off. I don't even know who pulled the trigger. I'm just lucky it was pointing away from me when it fired."

The I'm-just-lucky-it-wasn't-me defense. I wasn't sure it was entirely creditable. Still I was willing to accept it, even if the police most likely wouldn't, because I had a different stake in the outcome.

As long as Cavanaugh believed that he wasn't a killer, that Steve's death had merely been a tragic and unavoidable accident, maybe there was a glimmer of hope that we could both walk out of this room alive.

"You should have called the police," I said.

"I panicked. And then it was too late."

"You'll have to talk to them now."

"I don't think so."

The four short words, spoken so calmly, sent a chill racing up my spine. The hairs on the back of my neck lifted.

"See, the problem is, things have changed. What happened to Steve was an accident. But running made me look guilty. I know that. And the police . . . they're never going to believe me now. And I can't afford to take that chance."

He gazed at me with what looked like genuine regret. "I'm not the kind of guy who would do well in jail. You know what I mean?"

Cavanaugh asked the question as if it were a perfectly reasonable query. And I supposed to him it was. Unfortunately, the answer it led to was going to get me killed.

"So now what?" I asked.

Hand resting lightly behind my back, I squeezed the paperweight between my fingers, then released. Under other circumstances, I could see how that might reduce stress. But right now, what it did was keep me grounded. And offer the slightest possibility that I still had a chance.

"I'm sorry," said Cavanaugh, "but you're going to have to die too."

27

He wasn't half as sorry as I was, I thought.

"Don't worry," Cavanaugh continued calmly. "This time I have a plan. I'll mess up the place so it looks like a robbery, jimmy the lock on the back door, and take a few things with me when I go. Then tomorrow I'll play the concerned partner. Two break-ins in less than a month? That can't be good for business. I'll tell Candy she'd better see about adding a security system."

It couldn't be just that simple, I thought. At least I hoped it couldn't. "Speaking of Candy—she knows she told you I was here. What if she guesses the truth?"

"She won't. Candy's not the type to think things through. Or to go looking for trouble."

Cavanaugh waved a hand dismissively. Again the one holding the gun. I was beginning to suspect he had little more experience with firearms than I did. Certainly he'd never taken a course in gun safety.

"And if Candy does think about stirring things up, I'll threaten to pull my money out of the business. Pine Ridge is all she has left. She'd never let that happen."

Clearly Cavanaugh enjoyed making threats. I could only hope that he possessed more bluster than follow-through. Because holding a paperweight opposite his gun, I felt like David facing Goliath.

"I guess you have it all figured out," I said. "Well . . . except for one thing."

"What's that?"

I nodded toward the envelope. "There's no money in there."

"Sure there is."

I shrugged. Not my problem. Cavanaugh's eyes narrowed.

"What are you talking about? Why else would Steve have bothered to hide it away like that?"

I didn't answer his question. Instead, I moved away from the desk. It probably looked to Cavanaugh like I was granting him access to the envelope. With luck he wouldn't realize that I was also giving myself an easier line to the door.

"See for yourself," I invited.

He reached the desk in three quick strides. Cavanaugh might have been a good businessman, but he wasn't a very good assailant. Probably too much Hummer driving and suit wearing—the man was entirely too civilized to be carrying a gun. And he had no idea how to accord his weapon the respect it was due.

Reaching eagerly for the envelope with his right hand, he switched the gun to his left. If he was ambidextrous, I was dead. But I was betting he was merely arrogant—and flushed with the feeling of importance that the weapon gave him.

He didn't even think about what he was doing, and his carelessness granted me the opening I needed. Lifting my arm, I let fly with the paperweight.

It sailed through the air and hit Cavanaugh square on the side of the head. He lurched sideways with the impact. The blow wasn't hard enough to stun him, but it did knock him to his knees.

In a flash I was past him. By the time he'd regained his feet, shaking his head and swearing loudly, I was already across the office and shooting through the doorway into the darkened hall.

Both directions led quickly to another closed door. The one on the right put me in the reception area. On the left, the door led outside to the walkway that went to the Dog House.

There was no time for conscious thought. All I knew was that I wanted OUT. Left it was.

"Come back here!" Cavanaugh roared.

Like that was happening.

Racing down the hallway, I heard a muffled explosion behind me. A bullet smacked into the wall opposite the open doorway. Cavanaugh swore with frustration.

Panicked, fueled by adrenaline, I was running so hard that I ran right into the door at the end of the hall. The blow hurt, but it was a good pain. It let me know that I was still alive.

My fingers fumbled for the doorknob. I found it, turned it quickly, and yanked hard.

Nothing happened. The lock—the same one that had done nothing to keep Cavanaugh out—was engaged.

Somewhere behind me, I could hear him coming. The sound of his breathing seemed to fill my ears. Or maybe it was my own.

My fingers worked feverishly. The deadbolt slid open. I pulled on the door again and felt cool air on my face.

As I gave one last quick glance back, Cavanaugh appeared in the office doorway. One hand leaned against the frame for support; he used the other to raise the gun and aim. In the dim light, the barrel looked enormous.

I wanted to move. Every instinct told me to flee. But like every bad dream I'd ever had, for a second I was frozen in place.

Cavanaugh fired again. I saw his hand jerk back from the recoil and heard the sound simultaneously. The bullet plowed into the door panel beside my cheek.

Wood splintered and flew, and I shut my eyes reflexively. That was enough to break the immobilizing spell. I slipped through the narrow opening, slammed the door shut behind me, and stumbled down the two steps to the ground.

Immediately, there were more choices.

My car was out in front of the building, but my

keys were in my purse, which was still on the floor in Steve's office. Ditto my cell phone.

It was lighter outside than it had been within the building: dusk rather than dark. I could run, but Cavanaugh would see me. Could I outrun him? Still carting my new-mommy flab, I didn't think so.

Plus, of course, he had the gun.

I heard him on the other side of the door. Three feet away, with only a narrow panel of wood separating us. In another few seconds he'd be right behind me.

Now what? The words screamed in my brain. *Now what?*

The Dog House was at the other end of the walkway. But the building would be locked; it had to be. Then my eyes fastened on the doggie door and I felt a ray of hope.

Strictly decorative, Steve had said, but the opening looked big enough for a small person. Could I wriggle through?

Cavanaugh had had a key to the front building; but there wouldn't have been any reason to give him access to the Dog House, would there? As long as both buildings didn't work off the same lock, this might work.

Choices rapidly dwindling, I turned and ran.

The Dog House could offer a hiding place, and even more important, a phone to call for help. At this point, I'd take whatever I could get.

Reaching the end of the walkway, I dove for the

small, swinging flap. Thankfully, it wasn't barred.

My shoulders were a tight fit. I could feel my skin scrape and tear as I jerked them through the opening. Then I braced my hands on the linoleum floor and pulled. My torso slipped inside, followed by my legs and feet.

Quickly I reached around, grasped the swinging door, and pushed it shut. Pushed it still. And hoped the movement had gone unnoticed in the half-light.

My heart was pounding so hard it was difficult to concentrate on anything else. I drew in one deep, calming breath, then another. They didn't help.

So I swiveled around on the floor, pressed myself up against the inside of the door, and took a minute to just listen.

Cavanaugh was outside now. I could hear his heavy tread on the gravel path. What I couldn't tell was which way he was going.

Then the footsteps stopped.

"Listen Melanie," he called into the gathering dusk. "Maybe we got off on the wrong foot . . ."

I snorted under my breath incredulously. Ya think?

"Look, I'm sorry. Okay? Things just got out of hand in there. I know I made a mistake. Come on out and let's talk. I'm sure we can figure out a solution."

When hell froze over, I thought.

But the offer of amnesty was a good sign. It meant he was unsure. He didn't know where I'd gone.

I inched over to the window beside the door, cautiously raised myself up and had a look. Then quickly ducked back down as the beam from a flashlight played across the front of the building and reflected off the glass.

Damn, where had he gotten that from? Was that why he'd taken an extra half minute in the office? Too bad for me Cavanaugh was turning out to be a pretty resourceful guy.

"Come on, Melanie." His tone was wheedling now. "There's no reason we need to be enemies. Let's try to work together on this."

Work together on what? I wondered. Covering up one murder or committing another one? Was the man even listening to what he was saying?

I needed to get moving. I had to find a phone. I didn't remember seeing one on my earlier visits, but I hadn't been looking either. Surely there had to be one somewhere in the building.

Unwilling to stand up and risk being seen through the windows, I began to slither along the linoleum floor. Dog hair wafted up from the baseboards and tickled my nose. I held my breath so I wouldn't sneeze. Then my hand came down on a sticky spot that bore the distinct odor of old urine. That was just gross.

If I lived long enough to yell at Candy, I was definitely going to throw in a few words about cleanliness.

Cavanaugh had stopped talking now. I didn't hear

him moving around either. I hoped he'd gone looking for me in the other direction, but I wasn't about to count on it.

Then suddenly, unexpectedly, the floor around me lit up. Cavanaugh had pressed the flashlight to the front window; the beam played quickly up and down the hallway. I ducked and rolled to one side, pressing myself into the shadow of the wall. Heart thumping, I hoped I'd been fast enough.

I wasn't.

Because within seconds, I heard the scrape of Cavanaugh's key in the lock. The bolt slid open. Damn, I just couldn't catch a break.

So I stood up and ran again. It was the only thing left to do.

I heard the door open. There was a small click and the overhead lights came on.

"Stop right there!"

I turned to look behind me and raced headlong into something solid. My feet flew out from under me as I somersaulted over the waist-high obstacle. Then I bounced off something soft and landed with a jarring thump on the floor.

Pain seared through my elbow and knees. My ankle bent back at an uncomfortable angle. And although I didn't think I had hit my head I could have sworn I heard bells.

I took a moment to process the pain, then slowly opened my eyes.

A low couch, the kind I'd seen in many of the dog

rooms, had been pushed up against a side wall in the hallway. Probably Larry's doing; no doubt the stupid thing needed maintenance. And I'd managed to run right into it.

Then my gaze lifted. I looked past the couch and saw Cavanaugh standing over me.

And still there were bells. I shook my head slightly. Wait a minute . . . make that sirens.

It wasn't just me, I noted with relief. Cavanaugh heard them too. He stopped and listened.

The door at the front of the building stood open. Cavanaugh hadn't closed it behind him when he'd come in. And from where I lay, I could see a sweep of lights in the night sky.

Headlights, I realized, and they were racing toward us up the driveway.

"It's over," I said.

"No." Cavanaugh shook his head. The look in his eyes was wild.

"Put the gun down."

"I can't."

Car doors slammed outside. I heard the sound of running feet. By lighting up the back building, Cavanaugh had inadvertently shown my rescuers where to go.

I pushed myself up off the floor. Ankle throbbing, I stood and faced him.

"If you shoot me now, the police will hear you. That will be two murders. The first was an accident. This one won't be."

"Let's make a deal." He sounded frantic. "It doesn't have to end like this."

"No deals," I said as the first of the officers appeared, silhouetted, in the open doorway at the end of the hall. His gun was drawn and raised.

"Freeze!" he called out. "Nobody move."

I lifted my hands and stood totally still. Now I had two guns trained on me, which wasn't necessarily an improvement in how my night was going.

I felt rather than saw the motion next to me. There was just the slightest ripple in the air as Cavanaugh shifted the gun he was holding and pulled the trigger.

The explosion, right next to my ear, was deafening. I felt myself scream. I felt the vibration shudder through my body. But I never heard the sound.

Something warm and wet splattered over me and Cavanaugh dropped to the floor.

For a moment, I stared down at him, uncomprehending, then everything went black and I fell too.

28

Overruling my objections, the police officers loaded me into a squad car and took me to the hospital to get checked out. I didn't discover how they'd happened to come to my rescue until we were on our way downtown.

329

When I hadn't come home as promised, and also wasn't answering repeated calls to my cell phone, Sam had gotten worried. Figuring that the police could get to Pine Ridge faster than he could, he'd called nine-one-one and reported suspicious activity taking place at the doggie day care center.

When that had failed to elicit a show of concern equal to his own, Sam had reminded the dispatch officer that the facility had been the site of an unsolved murder a few weeks earlier. Then he posited the theory that perhaps something dire was happening again.

It must have been a slow night in Stamford because three units in the area had responded to the call that went out over the radio. And once they were all on the way, their combined activity ratcheted up the adrenaline. Lights and sirens came on, gas pedals got pushed to the floor.

And luckily for me, they'd arrived just in time.

Smelling salts brought me around pretty quickly. When I opened my eyes, I was relieved to find myself lying on the ground outside the Dog House. I knew that what had transpired in that hallway would stay with me for a long time. What I'd seen and heard was already indelibly etched in my brain; I was glad not to have to revisit it.

Escorted by a solicitous patrolman, I went inside the front building to clean up. Shortly thereafter, I was bundled into a squad car and taken away. I'd managed to retrieve my purse while inside and I called Sam on the way to Saint Joseph's. Both he and Detective Minton met me there.

The detective arrived first. He and I had a long talk while an intern bustled around us, checking my vital signs, which were mostly fine, and taping up my ankle, which had turned out to be sprained.

I explained to Minton about Steve's creative bookkeeping system and the funds he'd been embezzling from his own business over the last year. Then I advised him to check with Candy about Roger Cavanaugh's status as financial backer, and suggested that if he ran a ballistics report on the gun that Cavanaugh had used to kill himself, chances were it would match the one that had murdered Steve.

Minton looked at me sternly. "It didn't occur to you to mention any of this to me sooner?"

"I wasn't sure sooner. I wanted to wait until I had proof."

"Proof nearly got you killed."

He did, however, shake my hand on the way out and instruct the intern to take good care of me. I took that as a good sign.

Sam showed up next. He swept the curtain aside, walked straight to the edge of the bed where I was sitting, and gathered me into his arms. It was a toss-up which one of us clung to the other more tightly.

"Don't do that again," he said.

"I won't," I promised.

Sam finally moved back a step, but his fingers

still grasped my shoulders loosely as if he was loathe to let me go. One hand lifted and his fingers threaded through my hair as he smoothed a strand back off my forehead. His touch, so sure, so easy, was perfect. It was everything I needed.

"I'm sorry it took me so long to get here. Kevin was asleep and Davey wanted to come with me, but I couldn't . . . I didn't . . ." Sam stopped, his voice shifted slightly. "I wasn't sure what I might find, so I had to get someone to stay with them."

I nodded, then leaned into him again, absorbing some of his warmth for myself.

"Alice was terrific. She came right over as soon as I called. She told me to tell you that she's really sorry she got you mixed up in this."

Sam's tone lightened. I gazed upward and saw he was smiling.

"I told her not to worry," he said. "And that none of this was her fault. You find plenty of ways to get into trouble on your own."

"I do have bad luck with that," I admitted.

"Bad luck, hell. You attract other peoples' problems the way a heat-seeking missile finds a target." Fortunately, Sam was still smiling.

I hopped down off the edge of the bed, testing my weight gingerly on my sore ankle. The intern had done a good job of applying support. I wouldn't be running marathons anytime soon, but the leg felt like it would hold if I was careful.

"One more thing," Sam said as we left the cubicle

together. "Alice asked me to give you a message. She said she's finally met James. He's very much alive and thanks you for your solicitude on his behalf. Does that make any sense to you?"

"Oh yeah." I grinned. "I'll pass the news on to Bob."

Sam started to ask, then just shook his head.

That was fine by me. I figured we'd done enough mystery solving for one night.

As planned, Davey went to his first dog show at the end of the month. He started to get excited about competing in his class as soon as the entries were mailed in. We made a trip to Aunt Peg's house the day before the show so that Davey could help with Custer's preparations. No surprise, bathing the big Poodle in the raised bathtub was his favorite part of the job.

Show day turned out to be a family affair. Frank came to watch and brought Maggie with him. The two of them, plus Bertie, stood ringside with us as Davey's junior showmanship class was called and he took his place near the front of a line of eight competitors.

I was holding Kevin in my arms. My son looked around alertly; he seemed to be enjoying the excitement. Sam was beside us, using the video camera to record every moment of the proceedings.

Aunt Peg had walked Davey to the gate, fussing until the very last minute, but once he entered the ring he was on his own and she hurried around to join us on the other side.

"He looks so young compared with the others," I said under my breath.

"He *is* young," said Peg.

At nine, Davey was the minimum age to compete. But even though I was so nervous I could hardly stand still, he didn't seem to lack for confidence. Davey stacked Custer like a pro and stood back to show the Standard Poodle off to advantage as the judge made her first pass down the line.

"Custer looks gorgeous," said Bertie.

"As well he might," said Aunt Peg. She doesn't lack for confidence either.

"Let's hope Davey can keep up when that dog begins to stride out," Sam commented as the judge motioned with her hand to send the class around the ring for the first time. With a much older boy holding a Pointer in front of him, the pace was going to be fast.

We needn't have worried. Davey rose to the occasion beautifully, presenting Custer like the champion he would one day be. There might have been a couple of small errors in Davey's technique, and maybe a bobble or two in concentration, but overall, it was a first performance to be proud of.

The judge placed Davey second in line behind a preteen girl who'd handled her sleek Whippet with aplomb. And when she awarded him the slender strip of red ribbon, we all applauded loudly

enough and enthusiastically enough to paint ourselves as a bunch of tourists who had no idea about
dog show decorum.

Standing beside the second-place marker, Davey
looked over at us and grinned exuberantly, not at
all displeased with the outcome or our reaction to
it.

"He'll do better next time," Aunt Peg said briskly.

I was about to offer a rebuke, but when I glanced
her way I saw that Aunt Peg's eyes were a little
teary. Funny thing, mine were feeling the same way.

She looked at me and smiled fondly. "That's how
I felt the first time I saw you do something worthwhile in the show ring."

I gazed at her with interest. "How?"

"As if I was passing the torch." Aunt Peg reached
over and gave Kevin's head a pat.

"The next generation," she said. "May they go on
and outshine us all."

Center Point Publishing

600 Brooks Road ● PO Box 1
Thorndike ME 04986-0001 USA

(207) 568-3717

US & Canada:
1 800 929-9108
www.centerpointlargeprint.com